D0556287

Also by Frances McNamara

≈

The Emily Cabot Mysteries

Death at the Fair

Death at Hull House

Death at Pullman

DEATH
AT
WOODS HOLE

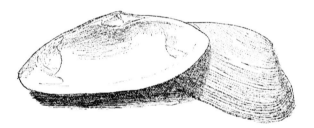

Frances McNamara

WITHDRAWN

 ALLIUM PRESS OF CHICAGO

Allium Press of Chicago
Forest Park, IL
www.alliumpress.com

This is a work of fiction. Descriptions and portrayals of real people, events, organizations, or establishments are intended to provide background for the story and are used fictitiously. Other characters and situations are drawn from the author's imagination and are not intended to be real.

© 2012 by Frances McNamara
All rights reserved

Book/cover design and maps by E. C. Victorson
Front cover images:
(top) Diagram of sea urchin, *Popular Science Monthly*, August 1881
(bottom) Marine Biological Laboratory class collecting specimens, 1895
Photographer: Baldwin Coolidge
courtesy of The Marine Biological Laboratory Archives
Title page image: Clam shell, *Popular Science Monthly*, November 1896

Publisher's Cataloging-In-Publication Data
(Prepared by The Donohue Group, Inc.)

McNamara, Frances.
    Death at Woods Hole / Frances McNamara.

    p. : ill., map ; cm. -- (An Emily Cabot mystery)

    ISBN: 978-0-9831938-3-8 (trade paperback)

    1. Marine Biological Laboratory (Woods Hole, Mass.)--History--19th century--Fiction. 2. Women scientists--Massachusetts--Woods Hole--19th century--Fiction. 3. University of Chicago--Graduate students--19th century--Fiction. 4. Woods Hole (Mass.)--History--19th century--Fiction. 5. Mystery fiction. 6. Historical fiction. I. Title. II. Series: McNamara, Frances. Emily Cabot mysteries.

PS3613.C58583 D438 2012
813/.6   2012938968

*To my writing group, Nancy Braun and Anne Sharfman,
with thanks for all the comments and support over the years*

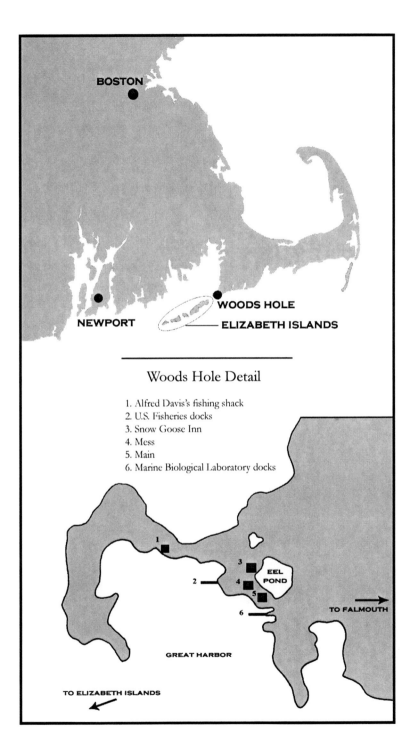

BOSTON

NEWPORT

WOODS HOLE

ELIZABETH ISLANDS

Woods Hole Detail

1. Alfred Davis's fishing shack
2. U.S. Fisheries docks
3. Snow Goose Inn
4. Mess
5. Main
6. Marine Biological Laboratory docks

EEL POND

TO FALMOUTH

GREAT HARBOR

TO ELIZABETH ISLANDS

Death at Woods Hole

≈

ONE

I couldn't leave that man in the stone tank with all those squid—even if it spoiled everything. And it did spoil everything. It was the start of what should have been a beautiful day. The sky over the harbor at Woods Hole was just beginning to lighten. It made me remember the fisherman who glided up to the dock the night before, while Stephen and I sat holding hands and watching a fiery sunset. "Red sky at night, sailor's delight," he told us with a grin as he slid by.

I sighed at the memory. Through the wide open door to the tank room I could see the moored boats floating on the harbor. I could just hear the lapping of the water against stones down the hill from the laboratory. The tangy smell of salt barely tainted the air here. Just enough so that you knew you were at the seashore, not inland. It was not the strong smell of fish you breathed down on the rocks. But it was damp and chilly here among the stone tanks. There were six of them, large tanks, eight by ten feet each. The man was in the first one nearest the door. He was white and bloated, eyes open, bulging even. Small minnows swam by his face without stopping. He was no more than a coral reef to them. The line from Shakespeare, "those are pearls that were his eyes," ran through my mind. There was no question of helping him. He was dead, very dead.

I had to force myself to look again. A squid crawled onto his chest and into the breast pocket of his gray suit. He was dressed in the same gray suit, white shirt, and tie that he always wore. I knew him. He was Lincoln McElroy. Perhaps if he had been a

1

better, more sympathetic person in life I would have felt more for him now, seeing his puffy face and thinning yellow hair floating in the tank. But he hadn't been a good person in life and, in death, he was just as obnoxious and unpleasant as he had been before.

"Emily, what are you doing here?"

I jumped at the voice. "Clara, you scared me."

She was tall, stately, a handsome young woman with dark hair swept up and away from her face. I couldn't help but envy that, as I was smaller and paler with mousy brown hair that frizzled up in the humidity of Cape Cod. Seen beside my best friend and classmate's high cheekbones and delicate nose, my oval face was plain. I thought of that now as I saw my features reflected in the water of the tank. Putting up a hand to button my blouse, I wondered what she was doing here. What were either of us doing here, when we should have still been asleep in the Snow Goose Inn, along with the other women scholars? When I left her there hours before, she was asleep, I thought, in her room on the second floor. Now she was stepping up to the tank. She looked down. I heard a sharp intake of breath. "It's Mr. McElroy. Oh, no."

I shook myself. Pulling away from my reflection in the water, which hovered like glass over the corpse, I hurried to her side. She stared down with horror and I felt her tremble as I put an arm around her. I shivered myself, but there was no time for sentiment. Taking her by the shoulders, I forced her to look at me. "Clara, listen. He's dead. There's nothing we can do for him now, but we need to get someone to help us get him out of there." She looked at me with a troubled expression. I shook her. "Listen to me. You and I just got up…early, and we were going for a walk. We came through here and we found him. All right? Clara, do you hear me? Do you understand?"

She pulled her gaze away from the body and looked at me again. "Yes. I was…I was just…" I realized she wanted to explain where she had been, but there was no time for that.

"Not now. We can discuss it later. It's irrelevant. We should just say we were going for a walk. I need to go and get Professor Whitman or maybe Sinclair Bickford. You stay here." Charles Otis Whitman was the head of the Marine Biological Laboratory. He was an eminent professor from the University of Chicago, which made me hesitant about approaching him. Sinclair Bickford, his graduate assistant, was more of a contemporary. Besides, he was courting our friend Louisa Reynolds back in Chicago, and Clara was working in his laboratory that summer.

I started to move away, but Clara grasped my arm. "No. I'll go. I'll find him." She seemed just a little panicked. It was not like her, but then this was the first time we'd found a corpse together. I thought perhaps she didn't want to be left alone with him.

"All right, I'll stay here. But, Clara, do what I said. Just tell him we were out for a walk. An early walk."

"Yes, yes." She hurried away with one final worried look over her shoulder.

The water of the harbor was serene with just a light early morning wind. I heard sea gulls crying. What a horrible way to die. The large building had been part of a guano factory that produced fertilizer until it went bankrupt. Ships brought cargo to the dock just down the hill and the large stone tanks had been part of the manufacturing process. The harbor was quiet now, with only the tinkling of metal halyards from the masts of several pleasure sloops and the two schooners used for hunting specimens for the laboratory. I remembered there was an outing planned for the afternoon, which I'd been looking forward to. Stephen had promised me that he would leave his laboratory and join me.

The crunch of footsteps on the gravel path told me I would no longer be alone with the poor departed Mr. McElroy.

"Miss Cabot, dear me. Miss Shea found me on the way to the Mess. I cannot believe such an unfortunate thing could occur. Where? Oh, my yes, I see. Doctor, if you would help me, we cannot leave him there. How can this have happened? Luckily we ran into Dr. Chapman as we came up the hill."

There was a messy struggle to get poor Mr. McElroy out of the tank. Stephen carefully felt the man's head and tipped him up. Obviously the body was stiff and did not want to bend. The short Professor Whitman, with his carefully groomed white hair and pointed white beard, attempted to grab the dead man's feet but had trouble getting ahold of them. I rushed to help him. We made a comical group trying to lever up the sodden corpse and barely held on to the slippery body as we transferred him to the canvas sheet Clara had sensibly spread out on the cold cement floor.

"How unfortunate." The professor wheezed a bit, bending over to get his breath. "He is quite dead, Dr. Chapman?"

Stephen knelt by the body, shaking his head with regret. "For quite some time. That's why he's so stiff."

"Most unfortunate." The professor straightened up. "I cannot imagine how it happened." He looked around. The tanks were laid out in regular rows down the length of the large, cool room. They came to just above the knees. How could someone stumble into one? And if he did, why wouldn't he just sit up? There were only a couple of feet of water in the tank. "Did he drown, Doctor?"

Stephen was examining the man's face. "I can't tell without dissection. Emily, come here, just help me turn him." His shirt sleeves were rolled up to his elbows and his shirt unbuttoned at the top. I helped him turn the man onto his side and felt Stephen's hand reassuringly over mine. My heart was beating fast, but that calmed me. He looked up at the professor. "Not as much water coming out of his mouth as I might expect. There are other anomalies…" He contemplated the body, poking it here and there. Then we set McElroy on his back again. I was dripping as Stephen helped me to my feet. He squeezed my shoulder before letting me go and I felt his breath on my cheek, tempting me.

"Doctor, if I might ask you to remain, I will take the ladies to the Mess and telephone for the local authorities. This is most unfortunate." Despite his learning, the eminent scientist was at a loss for adjectives to describe this disturbing event. No one had found a dead body in a specimen tank before and it was at odds with all of the work done here.

The professor squired us down the hill to the wooden structure that housed the common dining room used by all the scholars and staff of the Marine Biological Laboratory. A few early risers were inside and I could smell bacon frying. My stomach was not ready for it, so I dropped down on one of the painted wooden rocking chairs that sat on the deep veranda overlooking the harbor. Clara took the one beside me. The professor hurried inside and I turned to my friend, only to find her trembling, as if overtaken by great emotion. She gripped the arms of her chair and rocked convulsively. Her shoulders shook silently, as if she were fighting to keep back sobs.

"Good lord, Clara," I burst out. "Whatever was Lincoln McElroy to you?"

TWO

The "Mess" and Homestead consisted of gray-shingled buildings huddled together across from the large United States Fisheries building with its wharves set right on the water. The main laboratory buildings were behind us, also along the water. The specimen tanks that held the squid, and various fish and shellfish used in the laboratories, were in a shed appended to one of them. The brick building known as the "Main" was divided into laboratory rooms well stocked with microscopes and glass beakers. A couple of substantial houses between the Mess and the Main were used to house male students. We women slept in the Snow Goose Inn just down Water Street and around the corner on West.

As I sat, patting Clara's shoulders and rocking back and forth, I could watch people spread the alarm, rushing out of the Mess to run to the residences, gathering forces, pulling on jackets as they hurried to the tank building. Eventually, Clara's attack diminished and she sat back, taking deep breaths. Before I could try to find out what was troubling her so much, an old trap pulled by a brown mare came around the corner and stopped in front of us. A chunky older man climbed down, tied up the horse, and looked around from under the brim of a herringbone-checked wool hat. His expression was one of anger and suspicion. I don't think I had ever felt such waves of negative feeling coming from a single human being as I felt when he clumped up the walk to glare at us.

"This the bug hunter place?" he asked. One of the first things I learned when I came to the town was that all people were divided into the "natives," the "dudes," and the "bug hunters."

"This is part of the Marine Biological Laboratory," I told him. "The main buildings are over there." I waved towards the large wooden structures. "Can I help you?"

He eyed us with disgust. "Doubt it. Where's this Whitman fella? Him who called?"

"He called?"

He gave a mighty huff. "Aye, that's what I said. Are you deaf? He called for the local police, like he was in the big city, New York or what have you. I'm the sheriff. Nearest you'll get. Now, if I'm finished reporting to the likes of you, lady, where's this man Whitman?"

From the corner of my eye, I noted that Clara had stopped rocking altogether. She appeared to stop dead, like a cat wound up for a leap away, sensing danger and suddenly becoming still.

"Oh, I see. There's been a terrible accident. It's over in the tank building. They're all over there. Let me take you." I hurried down the steps, suddenly aware that my sleeves were unbuttoned and the neck of my shirtwaist was still open. I struggled with the tiny covered buttons, but their slipperiness defeated me. As the man clomped along behind me in oilskin-covered boots, I was aware how unacceptable my appearance must be. I wore the dark color of mourning as my mother had passed away just that spring. Despite the heat that would descend as the morning mist burned away, it was proper for me to be especially modest and tidy. I was not living up to expectations and I could feel the man's dark little eyes burning into my back as I led him across the lawn to the building housing the tanks.

There was a crowd inside. I led the man to Professor Whitman, who was solemnly standing beside the corpse. "Professor Whitman, this is the sheriff, Mr. ...?"

"Redding. Seth Redding. Sheriff." The rotund little man glared suspiciously and ignored the hand extended by the professor. "What the dickens is this place?"

"This is the tank building, Mr. Redding. The various tanks

contain specimens used in our work," Whitman explained courteously.

"Sheriff to you." The man stepped over to one of the tanks and bent down till his nose was almost touching the water. Something must have swum up to him because he jerked upright a moment later. "Fish, squid, eels. What the devil do you do with 'em?"

"We dissect them, we use them to study embryology, morphology—various studies of great importance. We have scholars here from seven different universities and two overseas institutions. We are busy here all summer long, Sheriff Redding."

The sheriff grunted and stomped over to the corpse. He bent down, balancing on one knee, and attempted to raise McElroy's arm, but it was stiff and stayed stubbornly by his side. He tried again and was again foiled. Annoyed, he huffed and puffed as he straightened up. "So, what happened? Did one of the specimens strike back? Is that it?"

"We don't know. No, certainly not." The professor appeared confused by the man's sarcasm.

"Excuse me, Sheriff." Stephen stepped forward. "I think the dead man may have been ill. There are signs that he was sick as he came through the doorway over there, and on the side of one of the tanks."

The look of distaste on Sheriff Redding's face was so acute I was surprised he didn't hold his nose as he viewed what Stephen had found. He returned to the corpse. "Well, he can't stay here. The medical examiner from Barnstable County, Founce is his name, is on his way over." He looked around, as if accusing all of us gathered in the building. "This is a most unusual death. Drowning we see, yes. Some dumb dude once or twice a year will think he can handle the surf, but we don't go finding dead bodies in stone tanks. It's not something we do here." He glared. "Now, I'll be talking to each and every one of you, and don't you think you can get out of it."

I looked across at Stephen and he shrugged. So much for

an idyllic end to a difficult summer. Another dead body. If I believed in curses, I might think someone had something against me. Then I noticed Edna Thurston. She stood in the doorway like an avenging angel. She was tall and broad and wore a black hat topped with a dead bird, whose beak dipped down on her forehead, while the wings swept up to a point that almost touched the door jamb. Corseted and beribboned with a ruffled parasol, she posed in the doorway. "What have you done with Lincoln? What have you done to him?" she shrieked.

THREE

A spasm of pain shot across Professor Whitman's face. At that point, Sinclair Bickford stepped forward to engage the substantial woman blocking the doorway. "Miss Thurston, you've returned from Boston."

"Yes, that's right. Lincoln McElroy told me what you did. Perfidy, treachery, subterfuge! You thought you could get away with it. After all we've done for this place, you dare to cut us out? Without the Woman's Education Association this town would still be manufacturing fertilizer from bird excrescence." She sailed forward, headed for the comparatively short little Professor Whitman, whose silver-white head was shaking with dismay. The scientific persona, such as his, is more comfortable with cool, intellectual arguments than with the passionate rage shown by Miss Thurston.

Just then Sheriff Redding took one turn, almost like a dance step, and came up directly into the middle of Miss Thurston's course. Stopping short, she loomed above him. He radiated rage in a manner that reflected her own. They glowered at each other as Sinclair Bickford hurried over to part them. "Miss Thurston, there has been a terrible, terrible accident. It's Mr. McElroy. I'm afraid he is dead."

This took the wind from her sails and she balked, attempting a turn but coming up against Bickford. She looked confused. "What do you mean? He telegraphed me last night to come by the early train. He said, 'Meeting held in your absence. Betrayal. Come at once.' I have it here." She fumbled in the crocheted bag that hung from her lace-gloved hand. The bird perched on her forehead trembled. "It can't be. He should have met me at the station." She held out a telegram, waving it like a flag. Suddenly she became aware of the body lying on the floor. They had covered it with a sheet. Her big, plain face turned white. "Dead? Lincoln? Surely not? How could it be?"

Sinclair Bickford was a personable young man behind his gold-rimmed eyeglasses. He quickly took the woman's arm and tucked it in his own. "There, there, let me take you back to the Homestead where you can sit down. We'll get you a drink of water, this is a shock."

"*Stop!*" Sheriff Seth Redding stamped one of his booted feet. "You people are a pain in the butt. Now listen up. Here come my reinforcements." He pointed to a group of men who were climbing down from two wagons and a black canvas-topped trap stopped on the harbor road. "That's the medical examiner and my men. Now you," he said, pointing to Stephen, "you stay here. The rest of you clear out, but make yourselves available, you hear? 'Cause I'm going to want to talk to you bug hunters, you hear?"

The group nodded and murmured, then wandered meekly through the door as the officials began to arrive. Professor Whitman looked uncertain, but Stephen nodded to indicate that he would be all right and he winked at me after the older man turned away. I headed back to the Mess with the others.

There was no getting around it now. They were going to hear all about the secret meeting that had been held the night before. All the childish maneuvering and plotting would have to come out. And this group of eminent academics was going to be made to look like a foolish gaggle of adolescents pulling one over on their nanny. I did not look forward to the outcome.

When we got back to the Mess I returned to the rocking chair on the porch. Most of the others went in to partake of the big breakfast that was always served at that time of day. Soon after, the sheriff appeared. Following the aromas, he established himself at a table with a full plate, while he questioned witnesses and sent minions on various missions.

I still felt sick; I could not face food. Clara rocked beside me, staring out at the calm water. I thought she was not nearly so calm inside, but I still had no understanding of what was troubling her. We could both hear the sheriff, since he'd established himself at a table just inside the door. He must have known we were there. He'd stopped and questioned us briefly on his way in, but luckily he was more interested in following his nose inside. So he was satisfied by the tale from both of us that we had risen early and come through the tank shed on our way to breakfast, stumbling on the corpse in the water.

Once Redding started questioning people we could overhear the retelling of the whole story that had led up to the evening before. We did not speak as we strained to hear what was said. I was torn between wanting to ask Clara what was bothering her, and wanting to hear what people were telling the sheriff.

≈

I had arrived only the week before after a difficult summer in Chicago, dealing with the Pullman strike and its repercussions. When all of that came to an end, I heeded Clara's plea to join her in Woods Hole. She had been so excited to be accepted as a student in the new summer study plan that drew scholars from many of the most prestigious universities in the country. Although I lacked the funds to vacation in the pretty town, or in nearby Newport where our friend Louisa Reynolds spent her time, Clara assured me I could pay my board by collecting specimens for the laboratory.

I am no scientist, but I had spent childhood summers at the sea shore, so I was able to take instruction and go out walking and wading in the marshes to bring back pails of creatures that Captain Veeder, a local man who maintained the boats for the laboratory, paid for. He was in charge of the collection and breeding of specimens. Apparently there was quite a demand for the little creatures. The work in the laboratories depended on a plentiful supply of such "beasties." It was a pleasant enough way for me to spend the last days of summer. I had settled in easily, yet I was always aware of the undercurrent of strain in the little community. Now I heard all the details.

"So, now what's this all about, this treachery and iniquity you all were up to last night, according to this big lady from Boston?" I could hear Redding slurp his coffee as Professor Whitman prepared a measured response.

"It is all just a matter of administrative and organizational concerns, I assure you, Sheriff Redding. You see, Miss Thurston and Mr. McElroy are representatives of the Woman's Education Association and the Boston Society of Natural History, both based in Boston. As such, they have been extremely active and helpful in the work that preceded formation of the Marine Biological Laboratory here at Woods Hole. As you probably know, there was a guano fertilizer factory on this property until it went bankrupt in the 1880s."

I heard the sheriff sniff and swallow. From the aroma wafting out the window, he had a full plate of bacon and eggs in front of him. "Mmph. Well, I'll say that for you, Professor, at least the place smells better."

"Yes, that is true. Well, there were several previous attempts to run summer zoological educational courses, which were quite successful in their ways and benefited greatly from the support of those Boston organizations, you see. But then the laboratory itself was established with the object of developing and supporting the work of serious scientific investigators. The intent is to support a national marine biological station similar to what is done in several European countries."

"Teach summer courses, do you?"

"Certainly instruction is one of the aims, but the real goal is to forward the work of scientific investigation. To that end the researchers are members of the corporation and research projects are supported by various universities who contribute to the fund in order to support the work. We are attached to no single institution, but rather we seek to serve all on the same terms. In this way the laboratory is becoming a great success."

"So why does Miss Thurston have her britches in a twist?"

"Well, the changes have made it a bit different from the earlier organization and, as the membership grows, I fear some of the early members feel they're losing control, if you understand my meaning."

I heard the sheriff put down his fork and slurp his coffee. "Eh, jealous are they? The little misses from Boston don't get a say in everything. Is that it? What did they do? Close tight the purse strings?"

"Not exactly. They did raise objections. We usually have been able to just about cover expenses with the fees for each year but, of course, not all of the money comes in at the same time, though by the end of the summer we should be straight. Miss Thurston and the others from Boston wanted to sell the laboratory, the boats, and all the assets to Clark University."

"That wouldn't suit you, eh?"

"We truly believe that it would be best for the laboratory to remain independent. We have a number of members who are very willing and able to tide us over should we need funds. In any case, the investigators here have formed the Biological Association with the idea of keeping the laboratory independent."

"So last night?"

"Last night there was a vote to reject the offer from Clark. First there were preliminaries, and Miss Thurston may have thought her group had carried the day, but after she left for her Boston train, the vote was put formally to the test and it was rejected. There was more than a quorum present, you understand. So it was all above board."

"Only you waited till she was on the train, eh? Whose idea was that, then?"

"We all thought it would be…less disruptive. It was inevitable, you know. But my assistant, Sinclair Bickford, suggested the tactic."

"Wasn't he the one led the lady away?"

"Yes."

"Got a way with the ladies, doesn't he?"

"He was only trying to be helpful."

"Yes, well, send him in next, would you? I'd like to talk to this helpful fella. And by the way, do you think they'd have a couple more slices of this bacon? Good stuff, that."

I had been listening intently but, when I heard Sinclair Bickford's name mentioned, I saw a movement from the corner of my eye. It was Clara. Her eyes were closed, and a tear squeezed out and rolled down her face.

"Oh, Clara. Is there something you need to tell me?"

FOUR

Clara shook herself and gripped the arms of the wooden rocker as if she would pull them off. "No, no, no. It's all wrong. That man was evil, Emily, evil," she hissed. "He was a nasty, small-minded, mean little man."

"I came as soon as I heard." Jane Topham bustled up the stairs of the veranda before I could answer Clara. I was shocked by the vehemence and vitriol of her response, but we were both distracted by Jane. She was a round and jolly nurse from Boston who spent her summers renting a room from the Davis family. They were our landlords at the Snow Goose Inn. Now she puffed a little from her exertions and plopped down on a wicker chair across from us. "Truly, is there anything I can do? I'm happy to offer my services."

"Too late, I'm afraid. The man is past all help."

"Oh, really. How awful. Tell me all about it." Her face sported a few drops of perspiration. She was dressed in checked muslin with white flounces. A corset strained against her plump middle and she wore a small straw hat tipped over her forehead, with a broad swath of ribbon tied in a sharply pointed bow under her chin. It looked uncomfortable in the growing warmth of the morning. The sun had burned off the mist and was shining down beyond the deep shadows of the veranda. It reflected off the water of the harbor and the shiny boats swinging on moorings. Miss Topham removed a lacy handkerchief from a capacious pocket and drew it across her brow.

I glanced at Clara, who appeared to grit her teeth. Miss

Topham was a very nice, friendly person, but she felt no compunction about finding out everybody else's business and then telling it to anyone she met. Apparently she was a very well respected nurse in Boston. I supposed such gossip must help to while away the time spent with seriously ill patients. So I relented and told her about what had happened.

"Mr. Lincoln McElroy, no, really? I must say I thought he did look a little green last night." She sat back, fanning herself with her handkerchief. "Oh, yes, I snuck into the meeting. So dramatic. I was talking to Miss Clapp on the porch after dinner, don't you know, so when she started down I just trailed along. People were very het up, weren't they? Oh, you didn't go? Neither of you? It was mostly the men, of course, but Cornelia is not to be left behind. She spoke up. She's with them, wanting the investigators to have the last say, don't you know. And with Miss Thurston gone to her train, Mr. McElroy was practically alone. He didn't really want to stand up against them all by his lonesome, I could tell. He kept trying to get them to put off the vote. He kept saying he needed to contact the Woman's Education Association. Oh, he was in a tither, but those scientists, they just carried on. And finally I saw Mr. McElroy rushing out the door. He looked a little sick, he did, like the shellfish didn't sit well or something. That is so often the case. You'd be surprised how many people suffer from a reaction. I was almost going to follow him but then one of Minnie's boys, Jamie, came to get me to help them with his aunt Genevieve."

I must have looked at her blankly.

"Oh, I forgot, Miss Cabot. You only just got here, you may not know about the tragedy the Davises have had this year. I say the Davises but really, Minnie is a Gibbs now. She married a ship captain, don't you know. But he's away and after what happened to her mother, she shut down her house in Plymouth and came over to keep house for her father, what with all the summer guests."

I was only vaguely acquainted with the sallow woman Mrs. Gibbs, who ran the Snow Goose Inn. I looked across at Clara, but she had a hand up to her forehead as if fending off a headache. I could see how Jane Topham's chatter could bring it on, but I didn't want to be rude. Besides, it seemed a good idea to think about something other than the man in the water tank this morning. "I had no idea. What happened to her mother?"

She bent forward confidentially, still fanning herself with her handkerchief. "Mrs. Davis—that's Minnie Gibbs's mother—went up to Boston. It was the very last week of June. She was stricken down and went into a coma. Five days later she was dead. So quick. It was diabetes, the doctor said, and I can believe it. I've seen it before. It was so awful for them. She had gone up to meet her other daughter, Genevieve, Mrs. Harry Gordon, who comes in from Chicago every year. Perhaps you know her?" I shook my head in the negative. "You're from Chicago, too, aren't you though? Well, she comes every year at this time and I guess her mother had gone up to meet her. The father is a little off, you know. It's something that happened a long time ago. The natives know all about it.

"So, Mrs. Davis went up on the train, got sick and passed before she ever came out of a coma. I didn't know till she was gone, but they invited me down for the funeral. I told them they should have contacted me. For heaven's sakes, they know I'm a nurse. I work with all the best medical men in Boston. I've been staying here summers the past…oh, it's five years now so they know my reputation. I really cannot understand why they never contacted me when she fell ill. It's too bad. You never know, I might have been able to find a specialist who could have helped her. I don't like to bring it up but I do regret it. It's what I've always said, they are a queer family. No wonder, really, with their past. Anyway, when they finally did contact me, I came down on the train with Mrs. Gordon, to help her. She decided to come be with her sister, Minnie. Poor woman, she's been poorly ever since. So depressed. I suppose she must blame herself, although I'm sure there's nothing she could have done."

"So that's why you were called away from the meeting last night?" I asked, trying to get her back to the point.

"That's right. Minnie, Mrs. Gibbs, sent one of her boys down to ask me to take a look at Genevieve, Mrs. Gordon, don't you know. I gave her a sleeping draught, but I have to tell you," she looked around and lowered her voice. "She's not in a good way. Not in a good way at all. She told me she'd had enough, like to do away with herself. Well, I just tried to soothe her down. I'm hoping she doesn't do anything extreme. It's so sad, her mother passing like that, but what can you do?" She sat back to fan herself vigorously.

At that moment Stephen came pounding up the steps of the veranda. He looked tousled and hot, which only made me want to take him someplace cool and shady where we could be together and discuss what was going on. It was so hard being discreet, but we had agreed to it. "I must see Sheriff Redding."

"He's inside. Stephen, what's happened? Did you assist the medical examiner? What did you find?"

He had eyes only for me. He was shaking his head. "I'm afraid it will be very unpleasant. We are quite sure Mr. McElroy didn't drown. Whatever killed him, he was dead before he went into the water."

FIVE

"Oh, dear, how terrible," Miss Topham piped up. Stephen seemed a bit alarmed to realize she was there. Even Clara stopped rocking and staring into the distance long enough to shake her head at him.

Something occurred to me. "Miss Topham was just telling us that she thought Mr. McElroy looked ill when he left the meeting last night."

"That's right. He looked a bit green. I thought he must have eaten something that didn't agree with him. I was going to go after him, but they came to get me to go back to the inn. Oh dear, if only I'd followed the poor man."

"There were traces of his being sick in the tank shed," I reminded Stephen. "Perhaps he became ill and fell in. They're only hip deep."

"I doubt he would have fallen on his back like that. No, we're pretty certain he was dead before he was put in the water."

"Put! You mean someone did this to him? Why?" I asked.

"I'm afraid that's a question for the sheriff."

As if in answer to a call, the man himself appeared in the doorway. "Here, you, doctor, what's your name?"

"Chapman."

"Chapman, what are you doing out here? If you've got news, give it to me. Don't be gossiping with these snoops."

"Really, Sheriff Redding, you've no call to be insulting," Miss Topham said.

"Oh, it's you, is it? Why don't you go stay put in your inn you pay so much rent for? Eh? What're you doing snooping over here? Looking to lodge another complaint?"

"I have every right to go wherever I choose in this town, *Sheriff* Redding. I hear you're up for reelection and there's a younger man going to beat you. Don't take it out on the summer visitors. I know your tricks."

There seemed to be some long-running feud between these two. I looked across at Stephen, whose eyebrows were raised in amazement.

Redding turned to him. "Never mind that old harpy, just tell me what Founce says."

Stephen told him their conclusions.

"Hah, knocked on the head and dumped in the tank, is that it? One of these bug hunters run amok, is that it?"

I felt obliged to question this outrageous assumption. "Sheriff, you have no evidence that someone from the laboratory was involved with this. You really cannot assume any such thing."

"Don't tell me what I can or cannot do, missy. I'll thank you to mind your own business. There was a big to-do here last night and this McElroy person went running to the telegraph office to alert that amazon from Boston. Somebody might have wanted to stop him."

"Well, they weren't very successful, were they? Miss Thurston did get a telegram and, in any case, her presence won't change anything, will it?"

"Damned if I know. You, in there." He waved at someone inside the dining room. "Come out here." Sinclair Bickford responded to the command.

Clara stopped rocking and seemed to hold her breath.

He was a slim young man with wire-rimmed glasses and wavy dark hair. His face was handsome, with a cleft chin. Even the spectacles could not disguise the clear blue of his eyes. I knew him slightly from Chicago where he'd become engaged to Louisa Reynolds. Her brother, Robert Reynolds, was a student of chemistry with Clara and Sinclair. Robert was not in any way up to their standard, as both were stellar students, but he was one of the wealthy advocates of the laboratory who could be counted on to help with the finances. Without the backing of Robert Reynolds, and others like him, there was no hope that Professor Whitman would be able to keep Woods Hole independent. In addition to being engaged to his sister, Sinclair was Robert's best friend.

"Here, you. What happens now?"

"Sir?" Sinclair was puzzled. "I'm not sure what you mean."

"About the laboratory thing and selling it to Clark University—what happens to that?"

The young man's eyebrows shot up above his glasses. He had a soft voice. You had to lean in to hear him. "What happens? Nothing, as far as I know. The vote was taken last night and the plan was rejected. I suppose Miss Thurston may object or try to bring it up again, I don't know."

"So, with this McElroy gone, does she lose because he's dead and can't vote?"

Sinclair adjusted his spectacles. "Oh, dear, no. Nothing like that. We had more than enough votes to reject the proposal. If we voted again someone else would surely take Mr. McElroy's place, but the measure would still be rejected."

The sheriff glared at him. "Then how come you went to such pains to have the vote after you got rid of the amazon, huh?"

The younger man looked uncomfortable. "We simply thought there would be less unpleasantness if Miss Thurston was not present." He cleared his throat. "The lady has a very powerful personality, as you may have observed. Some of the researchers find it very disturbing to have to face her…well, her emotional arguments. She shouts. We don't shout. We engage in vigorous debates here all the time and we disagree about scientific theories constantly, but we don't shout at each other. It was very disconcerting for some of the scholars, that's all."

Redding frowned, but I could understand how the intellectual researchers would not know how to handle the vituperative Miss Thurston. It didn't surprise me at all. The sheriff was not convinced, however. He seemed to believe that McElroy's death was somehow connected to the rancorous arguing over the vote the previous night.

Sinclair Bickford cleared his throat again and raised an issue with the sheriff. "Sir, we are all most anxious to help in any way that we can. And we are grieved at the untimely death of Mr. McElroy. However, we had planned an outing on one of our boats today. We gather most of the researchers and Mr. Elliott—"

"Elliott? E.C. Elliott?"

"Yes."

"I know him."

"He runs the trip for us. Captain Veeder skippers the boat. They'll take the group over to one of the Elizabeth Islands where we'll collect specimens. We'll also dig clams and finish with a clambake. This was to be the final outing of the season and everything is prepared. But I wanted to let you know our plans. I hope you will have no objections to our going ahead with it. We are all very sorry for Mr. McElroy, but he was not known personally to any of us. May we proceed?"

I thought it spoke well of Sinclair Bickford's political skills that he was asking permission of the cantankerous sheriff. I didn't suppose Redding had any real authority to stop the outing, and I, myself, had been looking forward to it so much. It was the first good thing I'd heard all day. But Sheriff Redding's face was turning a deep shade of ruddy. I suspected he was a candidate for apoplexy.

"What in heaven's name are you all thinking? A man's been found dead in one of your tanks, under the most suspicious circumstances you could ever imagine, and you want to run a clambake? Now, listen here. There are only the natives, the dudes, and the bug hunters here and somebody helped that man to his death in that stone tank. He had no connection to the natives, and the dudes have mostly packed up for the summer and gone home to the city. That leaves you bug hunters, so it's one of you who must've done him in. And until I find out who, you're not going anywhere, you hear? There's not a single other person as could have done it. There's no strangers around could have done it or I'd have heard of it. So it's one of you."

"You're all wrong there," Jane Topham interrupted, looking smug with her hands folded on her tummy.

"You!" He turned to face her, furious at the interruption. "Who asked you?"

"You said there were no strangers. But you're wrong. There was a fellow dripping wet and carrying a carpet bag came to try to book a room at the inn just this morning. Who's to say he didn't do it?"

So there, her attitude said, even if she didn't voice it.

SIX

Jane Topham's announcement infuriated the little sheriff, but it also sent him scurrying off to the Snow Goose Inn, trailed by Sinclair Bickford. The younger man was still trying to get permission for the afternoon outing.

Meanwhile, Jane told those of us who stayed behind that the sopping wet stranger had been turned away. It did seem like a relief. Whoever this person was, no doubt he'd followed McElroy from Boston and was the one who'd caused his death. Whatever the reasons, they must have been unconnected to the Marine Biological Laboratory.

That sense of relief was compounded a few minutes later when Sinclair Bickford came bounding up the steps to report that he had gotten the sheriff to agree that the sail and clambake could go ahead as planned. He urged us to meet at the dock within the hour, all the while looking over his shoulder as if he feared the sheriff would change his mind.

We jumped up and I was amazed at the change in Clara. She patted her face with a handkerchief and actually smiled. Her eyes followed Sinclair Bickford as he spread the news among other people in the Mess. Both of us needed to return to the inn to change our shoes and skirts but, before I could follow her, Stephen pulled me away from the chattering crowd.

"Emily, I can't go. I have to return to assist the medical examiner."

"Oh, Stephen." I was so disappointed. I'd been looking forward to this outing all week. I'd been patiently collecting specimens by myself while he worked long hours in his laboratory. I knew how much it meant to him and how excited he was to be doing his research, but I longed for his company. I only had him to myself when we would slip into the night after the big communal dinners. Sometimes there were even evening lectures to be endured. At any other time I would have reveled in the academic atmosphere but, since we had finally declared our love for each other, I wanted him with me every minute. We had a secret I had not yet shared with Clara or anyone else at the laboratory. Of course, in reality, the time spent apart, or in the company of others, only made our time together more wonderful. But I could not appreciate that, in the state I was in. It was not a rational state of mind.

I could see that Stephen was exhilarated by the work. His mentor, Professor Jamieson, had introduced him to Jacques Loeb back in Chicago. Loeb was a German, married to an American woman, whose research was in physiochemistry. He had gotten Stephen funding to attend the summer session at Woods Hole. When we arrived Stephen found himself sharing a laboratory with Thomas Hunt Morgan, a man he knew from his time at Johns Hopkins years before. Loeb had encouraged Morgan to study regeneration. It was easy to understand how Stephen had quickly become engrossed in that phenomenon. Worms, sea urchins, and hermit crabs were creatures that grew back damaged limbs and organs. Of course, Stephen and the other men would never have imagined a connection between his injured arm and his fascination with the topic. Yet to any woman, especially me, it was obviously the reason for his interest. I never commented on it to him. It was enough that his eyes lit up when he described their experiments. His deep enthusiasm made me realize what he had sacrificed to remain in Chicago with me for most of the summer and I was grateful for the time he had to at least finish out the session. And he was happy to see me recovering my equilibrium under the soothing influence of the sunshine and sea breezes that I loved.

"I know. You're disappointed." He surreptitiously squeezed my waist and I felt a whisper of kisses on my neck. We stood in a shaded corner behind the steps. It was not the sort of thing to do in full view of our colleagues, but they were busy gossiping about the events of the day and hurrying away to prepare for the trip. "I've agreed to set up a place so Founce can do the autopsy here. You know, the sooner they determine what really happened, the better it will be for all of us."

"Of course, you're right." At the back of my mind there was a nagging doubt. I was disturbed by the reaction I'd seen in Clara. I had yet to find the opportunity to ask her what her relationship to the dead man was. I didn't like to mention it to Stephen until I knew what was bothering her. "I'll stay, too," I announced.

He smiled at me fondly. "No, Emily. Go. I know how much you want to dig clams."

I'd been boring him with stories about how my brother and I had learned to dig clams from our grandfather. "But you'll miss it. I don't want to go without you."

"Go. I'll be with Founce. Even if you stayed, we wouldn't be together. I'll meet you when you come back. Besides," he said, leaning away from me to see my face, "I'm not sure I'd eat them anyhow."

I tapped on his chest. "Coward. You would. I'd make you."

"Make me?" He was skeptical and I had to admit to myself there were few things I could make him do, no matter how much he loved me. It would be a challenge to try, however.

"Never mind. I'll go and eat them myself. I'll miss you."

He smiled broadly at that, which made me think perhaps he would have little trouble to make *me* do what *he* wanted. We parted with promises that he would meet the boat when we returned.

I caught up to Clara and we hurried off to the Snow Goose Inn. Like the Mess, it was a gray clapboard building with a wraparound porch. Cottage roses and beach plums thrived in the salt air, while the grass was sparse in the sandy soil and the paths were paved white with crushed seashells. When you stepped inside, the low ceilings gave a sense that they were sheltering you from the light outside, which was magnified by the reflections off the harbor. Like the cottages I had visited in the summers of my childhood, it had a feeling of peace and repose. The Davis family had decorated it with white wicker furniture and bright chintz cushions. There were rag rugs on the wide plank floors and the bead board of the walls was painted white as well. It was a style that made me think of my grandfather's cottage in Chatham where I had spent so many summer vacations.

As Clara and I hurried in to change for the boat trip and clam-digging expedition, our path to the narrow staircase that led up to our rooms was blocked. Sheriff Redding stood facing off across the counter from Minnie Gibbs. I nearly ran into Clara, who had stopped short at the unwelcome sight of the lawman. She looked warily from him to the staircase.

Minnie was a thin woman in a high-necked blue serge dress with a plain white apron. Her brow was knotted in a frown. "That's what I said. I turned him away. He was dripping all over the rug. We cater to a nice class of visitor here, people from the laboratory. We won't be having any that will disappear without settling their accounts. We can't afford that." There were dry little lines around her mouth from pursing her lips as she did now. She must have been around forty years old.

"But what did he look like?" Redding demanded. "Did you know him? Was he from here?"

Minnie was becoming impatient. "What? Of course not. Why would he need a room if he was from here? Of course I didn't know him. If I'd known him I'd have told you his name, wouldn't I?"

I hesitated for a moment, seeing our landlady in a new light. Until Jane Topham had told us, I had not known that the real lady of the house had passed away in June and that this was her daughter. That must explain the curious figure who sat in the parlor all day long and into the evening. I glanced over to that room now, while Redding continued to badger the poor woman for a description of the unknown man. Minnie's father, Alfred Davis, sat beside the empty fireplace—the only place I'd ever seen him. He was clothed in his fine wool suit, reading from a small Bible bound in soft leather. His lips moved as he murmured to himself. I'd greeted him politely on one of my first days at the inn but he was so absorbed in his contemplations, and so wild-eyed when he looked up at my greeting, that I avoided further encounters. We were all so busy out at the laboratory, between the lectures and combing the shore for specimens, it was easy to ignore the man who made me a bit uncomfortable. Now, I felt some pity for him, bereft and confused. No doubt the recent loss of his wife had left him like this. Having lost my own mother the previous spring, I ought to feel sympathy.

Minnie was dismissing the volatile sheriff in her dry way. "I've naught else to tell you. Now, I've bed linens to attend to and my sister is ailing upstairs. I've no more time for wet strangers and nothing more to say about it."

Redding growled. "Well, you just send for me if you see this man again, you hear? I've plenty of things to do myself, you know, and it's not for the pleasure of your company or your smiling face that I'm here now." With that, he stomped past us and we raced up the stairs.

I'd been put in a small attic room with sloping eaves on the third floor. It was only by luck that I had the room which had been let for most of the summer to a pair of sisters who had left their laboratory work in late August to join their family in Bar Harbor, Maine. If they hadn't departed, I would have had to find a room with a family in town. That would have created difficulties, not the least of which would have been my frequent evening absences. As it was, with the room to myself there was no one to look askance at my failure to return during the night, as I had failed to return the previous night.

I quickly pulled out the old brown skirt I wore when I foraged for specimens. It was already stiff with salt water stains along the hem. I changed my soft leather boots for an old pair swollen and cracked from wading in the surf. They would do for clamming. Satisfied with my preparations, I knocked on Clara's door on the second floor. She flung it open and hurried out. She, too, had changed to an already worn out skirt although, unlike mine, it had been fashionable that spring. My Kentucky friend had learned the hard way that the seashore can be ruinous to the wardrobe. She took it in stride, though, and she brandished a plunger as she led the way down the steep and narrow staircase.

"Clara, what is that for?"

She grinned. "You'll see. Come on, they'll have the *Vigilant* at the dock and, if the tide is turning, Captain Veeder won't wait for strays."

I picked up my bucket, rake, and small shovel from the porch and followed Clara down to the dock. I was glad to see my friend recovered from the upset of the morning. It would be good for all of us to get away from the scene of the tragedy. The death of the man in the tank was a burden, but we hadn't known him, certainly I hadn't, and I longed to escape the horrid scene we'd witnessed.

At the dock the swordfish schooner, *Vigilant*, was already filling up with passengers. It was a beamy wooden boat with two masts and a very long bowsprit on which two men and a woman were already balancing over the water. The boat had been neatly drawn up to the dock and some three dozen people were in the process of stowing themselves along the deck, perching on the cabin top and bulkheads. At the stern, beside a very long wooden rudder, Captain Veeder sat in suspenders and a straw hat. Everyone knew to keep clear of the steering device.

We were handed aboard by a broad-shouldered, middle-aged man wearing a checked wool jacket with many pockets of various sizes and a cloth cap. He had a large moustache and sucked on a sweet-smelling pipe. Blue eyes glinted under hairy eyebrows and he seemed to take a special pleasure in gallantly assisting the ladies, while the younger men carried on their conversations or moved away to claim good seats with a view.

"Thank you, Mr. Elliott." Clara jumped aboard lightly. She'd grabbed a pail from a pile on the dock. "This is my friend, Miss Emily Cabot, lately come to join us."

He doffed his cap while firmly guiding me aboard. "Pleased to make your acquaintance, Miss Cabot." He held on till I was safely on the firm deck, although it swayed a bit as boats do. I kept my balance, though. I was intent on proving my seamanship as a girl who'd spent her summers on boats. "And as we say, Miss Cabot, 'What is your beastie?'" He smiled down at me.

"Any that is needed, Mr. Elliott. I'm not a scientist, I'm afraid, but I'm very willing to wade through the water and gather any beasties on the list for Captain Veeder and Mr. Grey."

Mr. Elliott laughed at that. "Good for you, Miss Cabot. I'm sure science will benefit. Glad you could come along for the picnic. You'll have to gather some specimens if you want to eat, however."

"So I've been told, Mr. Elliott." I held up my pail. "There's nothing I like so much as a clambake and I'm ready."

He laughed again. "Indeed you are. You'll show up this academic crew, I'll wager."

Clara and I edged our way across to the opposite side of the boat. I asked about Elliott.

"He's an independent scholar," she told me. "Like Robert Reynolds, he contributes money to the laboratory. He's not attached to a university, but he does serious work on regeneration in earthworms, among other things. He writes and presents papers here in the summer. Not sure what he does in the winter months. But he helps with the administration and getting a store of specimens for the work. He's older than most of the students here, but he gets along with everyone and Sinclair says his financial support is crucial to the effort to have the laboratory remain independent."

I was about to ask her about Sinclair Bickford when we were

interrupted. She was looking over my head when I was suddenly aware of the clop, clop of horse's hooves on the dock. There was an intake of breath and a quieting of conversation. I turned around to see what had caught everyone's attention.

A small buggy had driven right down the dock from the road. The poor horse did not look happy about that and his eyes were rolling back in his head. The driver half stood in his effort to restrain the beast, so he was not able to help his passenger descend. Mr. Elliott realized the dilemma and, in two strides, he was off the boat and helping a woman from the buggy. Dressed in delicate white muslin, trimmed with Belgian lace, it was Louisa Reynolds, our friend from Chicago who was betrothed to Sinclair Bickford.

SEVEN

Tut, tut, I don't think the lady is dressed for this expedition." The comment came from a woman who was firmly planted on the cabin top with a straw hat on her head and an old skirt and boots like mine. I recognized her as Cornelia Clapp, a professor from Mount Holyoke College, who also roomed at the Snow Goose Inn. She was small, sturdy, and at least a dozen years older than the rest of us. I knew she was a researcher in her own right and one of the founding members of the laboratory. She gave me a sharp look. "Miss Cabot, do you know that young woman?"

"Why, yes. She's a friend of ours from Chicago, Louisa Reynolds. She's engaged to Mr. Bickford, but I thought she was spending the summer in Newport."

Miss Clapp snorted. Newport, Rhode Island was a much more formal place to visit. It was where the fashionable people went. "A friend? A friend of Miss Shea's as well, then?" Clara had stepped away towards the side of the boat where Louisa was boarding.

"Yes, certainly. Her brother studies at the University of Chicago with us. Miss Reynolds is attending some classes, too, although she's not enrolled in a degree program."

"Ah, her brother. That would be Robert Reynolds?"

"That's right."

"I see. He is a generous benefactor to the laboratory. I suppose we must welcome the sister of such a good friend. I think she had better get aboard, however, or Captain Veeder will take off without her."

There was some yelling going on and several of the men

were loosening the dock lines as Mr. Elliott gently persuaded a hesitant Louisa Reynolds to board. She had barely stepped over the coaming when we began to glide away. The large sail at the back of the boat had been raised in preparation and it was used to power us through the harbor. A great flurry of activity, with the ducking of heads and yelling, was followed by the raising of the big sail on the forward mast and then the foresail out on the bowsprit. Soon we were gliding along at a brisk pace, heeling slightly despite the weight of so many people. As I felt the cool breeze I looked back and saw that we were trailing two dinghies off the stern of the boat.

We settled into our course and I leaned against the railing, enjoying the salt breeze and the occasional spray. There is nothing so peaceful as a glide across the water on a pleasant day. It was for this that I had escaped the dirt and hunger of the city of Chicago to return to the place where I had spent so many happy summer days in my girlhood. After the dark days of a smallpox epidemic in the winter, and then the grim specter of hunger and rebellion that was the Pullman strike, it felt like a huge weight had been lifted from my chest. Stephen had been right to insist we come and I was truly grateful.

I looked around to share my joy with Clara. She had moved towards the bow and I saw a look of pain on her face for just a moment as Sinclair Bickford elbowed his way from her side towards me. He fumbled past and stopped in front of Louisa. Mr. Elliott had perched her on the cabin top a few feet from me and he had wedged himself in front of her, pointing out the scenery while he made sure she stayed secure with any movement of the boat. Sinclair brushed past him to confront his fiancée.

"Louisa, darling, whatever are you doing here?"

She shrank away, looking a little guilty. "I wanted to surprise you."

"But, my dear, you're meant to be at Newport with your parents."

"Not any more. I've come away. You never came to join us and Robert kept telling us what a wonderful time you were all having."

"But, darling, I asked him to report to you. I didn't want to neglect you, but we're so very busy with the research. It would bore you, you know."

She blushed. "Of course it won't bore me, Sinclair. I'm as excited as anyone else. I want to help you. I want to be part of it. I know how important your work is to you."

"Yes, but you've no notion how dirty it can be."

"I'm not afraid."

"No, of course not. It's only that I need to spend time with my specimens."

"I know and I can help." She looked around, clutching the cabin top as the boat bounced on a wave. "Is that what this trip is for? Collecting specimens?"

Sinclair looked a little shocked.

"I'm sorry," she said. "I called for you at the laboratory and they said you were at the dock so I came straight away."

"It's a picnic, dear. It's a clambake, actually. But we have to dig for the clams, then they're steamed in seaweed on a fire of coals, layered on hot rocks. It takes some work, you see." He eyed her with some dismay. "I'm afraid it will ruin your dress."

She looked down, embarrassed, and I couldn't help but sigh. It was a beautiful dress. The delicate white muslin was layered over silk and the large puffy sleeves were gathered at the elbow to allow a fall of lace that matched the flounce on the front of the bodice. It was gathered into a trim waist with tiny pleats flowing down the skirt in more layers and more lace. Not quite the outfit for digging clams, however.

"It's all right," Mr. Elliott laughed. "Miss Reynolds can stay with me and Captain Veeder while you all go digging. We need to get the coals going and dig the trench. You're welcome to sit by and watch, Miss Reynolds."

Louisa looked a little crestfallen and I couldn't help but

sympathize. However, if you are going to descend on a marine laboratory, you should know better than to wear the latest Newport fashion. Still, she was a nice girl who meant well, so I moved over to greet her and proclaim myself another newcomer. I thought she looked a little less uncomfortable when she heard me asking ignorant questions about where we were and where we were going and what was happening. Then, suddenly, we all had to snap to and keep our heads down for a tack.

Soon enough the men pointed out that we were approaching our destination, Kettle Cove on Naushon Island. Mr. Elliott explained that this island was owned by a family named Forbes, but that they allowed people to picnic on the beaches. It was one of the largest in the chain of Elizabeth Islands just off the coast. There was more yelling and moving of bodies and then the anchor was let loose with a clanking of chains and the sail was dropped with a whoosh, gathered in, and flaked across the boom. I was assiduous in staying out of the way of those who knew what they were doing during all of that. For the most part it was the men who performed these operations, although I noticed a few women, including Cornelia Clapp, who stepped up quietly to make some crucial corrections or disentangle lines before they caused problems. Truth was, I did know what was happening, due to my experience sailing with my grandfather. But I also knew it was more important to stay out of the way of people doing their known series of steps to safely sail or stop a boat. My help might prove my own mastery, but would likely throw off someone else and cause a problem. So I hung back with the landlubbers and let the others do their work. Soon enough we were swinging at anchor and they brought the dinghies forward to ferry people and supplies ashore.

At that point I abandoned Louisa to the gallant Mr. Elliott. I wasn't going to miss the opportunity to paddle around digging an inordinate number of clams. I was ready to compete with anyone in that activity, so Clara and I were among the first to lower ourselves into one of the dinghies. I did so very carefully, so as not to rock the tippy little boat and, as I slipped onto a seat in the bow, I found myself facing Sinclair Bickford, who was to row. Clara was by no means so squeamish. She leapt down and bounded into the boat. I crouched, clinging to the gunwales with both hands, trying to keep us from capsizing. She landed behind Sinclair's back, but unceremoniously climbed across to sit with me. I scolded her, "Clara, be careful. You'll put us all in the water."

Mr. Elliott handed down our pails and utensils and other people filled the stern. Clara laughed. "Never fear, Em. Mr. Bickford would save us. Did you know he's a very good swimmer?"

"I'd just as soon not find out," I snapped. Meanwhile, Sinclair had turned to look at the people arranging themselves in the stern. His neck was red, though whether from sunburn or embarrassment I couldn't tell.

As soon as we were pushed away from the *Vigilant*, Sinclair put the oars in the oarlocks and began to row us to shore. He could not avoid us, although his exertion was such that it was unreasonable to expect him to keep up a conversation. His shirt sleeves were rolled up and his shirt open at the neck in the warmth. His dark hair fell across his brow with exertion and sweat gleamed on his moustache. His spectacles glinted with sun reflecting off the water. It was a beautiful day with a few puffy clouds in a blue sky and an occasional whitecap in the choppy seas. He rowed well and soon we were beached on a sandy strip with a few black rocks reaching out to sea to make this a sheltered cove. I sat primly as the men in the back pulled the boat up a bit. Then we carefully stepped to the stern and were handed ashore in a few inches of water. It was great to be on land.

Clara helped Sinclair haul out a tarp and some bags, while I went to help guide the second dinghy in. When I looked back, Clara had grabbed Sinclair Bickford by the arm. He looked down into her eyes and I thought he blushed. But he quickly shook off her grip and went back to the dinghy. He leapt in, pushed the boat off, turned the boat with a few strokes, and then began to row in earnest back to the *Vigilant*.

"The west side, near the rocks," Clara yelled as I reached her. But Sinclair ignored her.

"Clara, what is it?"

She continued to stare at the retreating boat for a moment, her hand shading her eyes. Then she turned to me. "Come on. I know where the best clams are. Are you coming?" She sprinted over to where her pail and plunger lay and grabbed them, hurrying off through some beach grass.

"Wait, I'm coming." I gathered up my own utensils and started after her, stopping for a moment at the top of a hill to turn and see the tableau behind me. The boat was still full of figures, some loading the dinghy for the return. A few of the men had started to dig a ditch in an area with wooden tables and benches and a stone circle for a bonfire. Obviously, there was a set organization for these adventures and everyone had their role. I knew ours was to dig the clams as quickly as possible so that when the fire burned down to coals they were ready to be cooked. It was a perfect setting. The blue of the sky, and the darker green-blue of the water, the movement of the figures, and the graceful shape of the schooner, made a lovely picture. Where it had been hot and still on the mainland, there was a pleasant breeze that swept across the island, with a tang of salt in the air and a slight fishy smell. The bright sunlight reflected off the choppy water, making it dance. I couldn't think of anywhere I would rather be. I only wished I could share it with Stephen.

I heard a yell. "Come on!" It was Clara, waving for me in the distance. I turned my back to the campsite and followed her. She had found another cove on the other side of the island. As promised, the clams were abundant. I was amazed to see Clara strip off her boots and stockings, hitch up her skirt and petticoats, and wade in knee deep where she began shoving her plunger up and down.

"Clara, what do you think you're doing?"

But she was grinning as she stuck the plunger in the bucket and stooped till her chin was level with the water, rising again with hands full of clams. "See, it works!"

I shook my head and began to walk along the beach just where the water came up and receded, looking for the little air holes my grandfather had taught me would indicate that clams were below. Soon I was happily digging them out, rinsing them in the gurgling water that continued to wash in and out, and tossing them in my bucket. It was glorious listening to the waves break, scooping out the clams, and smelling the salt in the air. When we had both filled our buckets, Clara came back to shore and we sat, while she attempted to brush the damp sand from her toes to put on her stockings and boots.

"Clara, I saw Alden in Boston before I came. Have you seen him since you've been down here?"

The previous spring I'd thought there was something between my friend and my brother. He had escaped an accusation of murder only after being shot and Clara had been the one to nurse him back to health. The attachment had shocked me then, but now I was equally confused by the way they seemed to have suddenly parted.

Clara paid close attention to the sand between her toes as if to avoid my question. Finally she responded. "No, I haven't seen him. I did feel something for him, you know, after that time in Chicago, but it seems that my fortune was too much of a burden for him. He insisted on the need to bring a fortune of at least an equal amount to any attachment." Her cheeks were crimson but she kept her gaze firmly away from me. I tut-tutted. "Alas, Emily, I find either men are much too enamored of my money, like poor Leon, or they are not enamored of it at all, like your brother. I cannot win."

I knew that, before she came to study at the university, Clara had suffered a broken engagement to a young man from her home town in Kentucky who had made the offer on the presumption that she would inherit from her wealthy grandmother. When her grandmother disabused them of this expectation he married someone else and Clara followed her grandmother's wishes by enrolling at the university. Her grandmother had since made her the heir to the fortune, so presumably that was what had offended the male pride of my younger brother. He was ever a problem to me. This did explain why my brother had avoided my suggestions that he contact Clara.

"Clara, I cannot believe my brother could be so stupid. But I must congratulate you for an escape from his foolishness." Still, there was a subject I wanted to broach carefully. "It was a surprise to see Louisa Reynolds join us today, wasn't it?" I tried to see her reaction, but she became busy with gathering her things for the trek back.

"We'd better be going. They've probably gotten the fire going by now."

EIGHT

I scrambled to catch up with her as she trudged up the sand dune. The pail of clams was heavy and my rake and shovel were awkward to carry. Nonetheless, I caught up with her at the top. We could see a brisk bonfire crackling and spitting sparks over the top of another sand dune ahead. She ignored my comment about Louisa Reynolds and explained how the clambake worked. "They have cords of wood stored over here and piles of stones—they build up the fire to heat the stones. It takes a couple of hours to get it all hot enough. Meanwhile, we gather the clams. We'll need to get them cleaned and ready for when they rake it all back." With that, she began to lope back to the campsite and I had to scurry to keep up with her long strides.

Sure enough, there were people busy with preparations. Mr. Elliott stoked the fire that climbed into the air from a pit that had been dug in the sand and stacked with kindling, wood, and stones. Meanwhile, Captain Veeder directed some men filleting fish bought from fishermen at the harbor. We joined a group that had lined up two rows of pails and were washing the clams, and checking for dead ones which were discarded. Another group was wading near the rocks, filling baskets with rockweed. Soon we were bent over the pails, cleaning our clams so they could be put in the burlap bags that would be used in the bake. There was an animated discussion going on about the events of the morning.

"So, just when we thought the sheriff would be arresting Professor Whitman or Sinclair here, that Miss Topham comes up with the information that there was a stranger who came in soaking wet and tried to book a room at the Snow Goose Inn," one of the men was telling Mr. Elliott. "So, it must have been a stranger after all. Someone who knew McElroy from Boston, perhaps."

Mr. Elliott grunted. He was more concerned with his preparations. "I'd say it's about time, what do you say, Veeder?" The captain rose and came over to glare down into the pit. Flames rose in a dramatic arc and the smell of wood smoke tinged the air, even though we were positioned upwind of the fire.

"Aye, looks ready," was his pronouncement.

With that, Mr. Elliott and his helpers took long rakes and began to rake the coals and hot stones. I noticed Louisa Reynolds was sitting on one of the benches helping to shuck corn. My group began to hurry to finish filling the bags with clams. Pretty soon the flames were gone, and Mr. Elliott yelled to the people gathering rockweed to come while others brought baskets of onions and potatoes to the edge of the pit. I stood and moved to where Louisa was sitting to hear Mr. Elliott explain the process to her.

"All right, here we go now, down in with you." Sinclair Bickford and two other men jumped down beside the rocks and coals while others began handing down the layers. Elliott oversaw the whole process. "First a layer of seaweed, rockweed actually, you see the little bubbles." He held up a strand for us to look at. "Those have seawater that helps to steam in the bake. Now the clams." The burlap bags were handed down and placed over the hissing layer of seaweed. "More weed, now, then the fish and the sausage." These were wrapped in brown paper and quickly added on as a layer. Then more seaweed, and the baskets of potatoes, corn, and onions were handed down to make another layer. From above, seaweed was draped over it all, and a group of eight men brought a huge dripping tarp that was soaked in seawater and quickly laid it over the whole pit and weighed it down with stones. There was a definite sizzling noise as they completed the process. "And there you have it."

Mr. Elliott gestured with his pipe. "And naught for us to do but wait for it all to cook."

There was further practiced movement as people unpacked tin plates and utensils from one hamper, while bottles of beer and cups of cider were handed around. Some of us cleaned up the remaining clamshells and pails. Mr. Elliott sat down opposite Louisa Reynolds and Captain Veeder joined them.

"Did you see the *Sterling*?" Veeder asked.

Elliott nodded his head. "Aye. There's no good to come from that. And, from what they were saying, it may have something to do with the man they found in the tanks, then."

"What are you talking about?" Sinclair Bickford asked, wiping his spectacles with a handkerchief.

"The *Sterling*. It's a sloop we saw in the harbor as we came out. It's the boat captained by Henry Pittman," Mr. Elliott told him.

"Say, wasn't he arrested in Boston?" somebody asked.

"That's right. Him and Samuel Dixey. Dixey was captain of the *Missouri*. It was scuttled off of Gloucester last month and Pittman came in with the *Sterling* and plundered it. They're accused of a conspiracy. There was a storm, but it was not so bad as to abandon the boat. They were carrying gold and silver, it's said."

"So what's the *Sterling* doing in Falmouth?" Sinclair asked.

"An interesting question. It seems the *Sterling* was underway before they could stop it, even though they arrested the captain. They must have got word and they upped anchor and got out of there. So having them turn up here will cause a stir all right."

"What do you mean?"

Captain Veeder grunted. "Treasure hunters."

"That's right." Mr. Elliott gestured with his pipe. "You can bet the authorities will be all over that boat as soon as they know it's here. They'll be looking for the gold and silver that was plundered. They claimed it for salvage, but with a conspiracy it'll be taken away. They must have brought it here to hide it. You can bet it won't be on that ship anymore."

Sinclair Bickford looked stunned. "Wait, the man who was seen at the inn, dripping wet. He must have come from that ship. We'll have to tell the sheriff about this."

"Oh, Redding will know all about it," Mr. Elliott told us. "There's no flies on him. Everybody knows about that trial and everybody will know what it means that the *Sterling* turned up here. The trouble is, like Veeder says, there'll be no end to the number of treasure hunters trying to lay their hands on the loot before the authorities find it. After all, it's gold and silver, and who's to say where it came from."

There was a lot of excitement about this news and plans to take part in the hunt when we returned. That lasted through another round of drinks and then the bake was ready and the unveiling took place. It was obvious they had been doing this all summer, as there was a smooth organization to it. Mr. Elliott had to make the weighty decision that all was ready. He bore the responsibility cheerfully and, once he had lifted a corner of the tarp and smelled the escaping steam, he signaled the start. The tarp was quickly rolled back and spread out over some beach grass to dry. Sinclair and the others jumped down and began to fill baskets with the vegetables, and to use forks and shovels to move the layers of seaweed until they could deliver up the packages of fish and sausage, and finally the bags of clams. All were emptied onto platters. We each managed to make up a plate of steaming food for ourselves and soon there was relative quiet as we sat at the wooden tables or on the ground, breaking open the hot shells to spear the juicy clams.

Clara showed her expertise in getting the clams out of their shells and skimming the membrane off the neck to be able to get to the body, and I showed my familiarity with the process as well. It had been years since I had dug and eaten clams like this, but it brought back memories of family picnics by the seaside much like this outing. I had learned to relish the slightly salty taste of the silky clams and I found the Portuguese sausage that had been cooked with them a poignant flavor in contrast. The fresh fish had taken on the clam and wood flavor as well, and the corn was sweet.

Most of the others had developed a taste for the feast over the summer, even if they had originally found it strange. But Louisa Reynolds seemed unsure. I could see it was considered a rite of passage amongst the others to take the strange flavors in stride and Sinclair Bickford looked a little put out by his fiancée's reticence. Mr. Elliott was more understanding. He showed her how to open a clam shell, remove the membrane, and swallow the clam. When she looked like she had swallowed castor oil, he laughed and took the rest of her clams, replacing them with fish and sausage. She was happiest with the corn and potatoes. I felt sorry for her, as she seemed to feel out of place, but it did nothing to spoil my own pleasure in the feast. I only wished Stephen had come so I could have made him try the clams and then forced him to admit that he liked them. Of course, if he hadn't, I might have been as disappointed as Mr. Bickford.

The sun was starting to go down when we were sated and began to clean up. While we rinsed and packed the plates and utensils, some of the men built up the fire a bit more so there was a blaze again to chase off the cool of the evening which was just beginning to descend. A few hearty souls began ferrying Captain Veeder and some of the supplies back to the *Vigilant*. Most of us were content to sit and stare at the blaze or watch the shadows lengthen. I thought it was a splendid ending to the day.

Someone was asking Mr. Elliott about ghosts of Cape Cod and whether there were any in the town.

"Only of dead birds from the guano factory," somebody joked.

"I suppose there's not enough going on in such an out-of-the-way place, anyhow," someone else said. "Not like in the city where terrible things are more likely to happen."

"Well, now, terrible things can happen anywhere. Like the death of Mr. McElroy," Mr. Elliott commented, sucking on his pipe as he relit it. I sniffed appreciatively at the smoke as it wafted over to me. My father had smoked a pipe like that.

"There's the Freeman baby," someone murmured. "Not much worse than that."

"Oh, that's a horrid thing to bring up. Not worth remembering," Mr. Elliott bemoaned. He sounded truly upset. He did not want to pursue the story, but a number of the listeners insisted.

"It's a terrible thing. I'll tell you about it, but you must not mention it to the Davises. You must promise."

"At the Snow Goose?"

"That's right. The Davis family. They had only a peripheral connection, it's not their tragedy, but you must not let on that you know. Especially the ladies who are staying there." We were all made to swear we would not repeat the story, but now everyone wanted to hear it.

He sighed. "It was twenty or twenty-five years ago now. There was a man named Charles Freeman. He fancied himself a preacher. But he wasn't satisfied with the local Lutheran church so he broke away. He was a fine speaker to be sure. He moved people, and he had followers that were wildly loyal to him. They thought he knew the way. He had visions and he'd describe them so vividly he had people believing he had a direct link to the Almighty. He read the Bible and then he came up with visions and predictions that sounded like they came right out of it, but they were different. The Davises—Alfred Davis, the father who you see sitting reading his Bible in the chair there all day long, and Mary Davis, his wife, who was tragically taken ill in Boston this spring and passed away there—they were followers. Loyal followers. So one day, Charles Freeman announced that the Lord had instructed him to take the life of his daughter Edith. Now she was a little four-year old girl. It was a sin, but those who followed him were so worked up by him they didn't see it. He told them he had this vision, described it in great detail. And he loved his little daughter, they all knew it. It wasn't like he was cruel or anything.

He just said he had this vision and sure enough one night he went up to her and kissed her good night and he took a knife and slit her throat. Just like that. Praying all the time."

There were groans of horror. It was still light, but the shadows were growing long. I shivered. So did Louisa Reynolds. I saw Sinclair Bickford put a protective arm around her.

"Well, the local authorities came to hear of it, but it was too late for poor little Edith. They put Charles Freeman on trial, but it was decided that he was out of his mind and they put him in the asylum down here. Then, Alfred Davis proclaimed to all the world that Freeman was right to kill the little girl, he believed the man was told to do it by the Deity. And so he was sent to the same asylum."

"How awful," I said. "How long did he stay there? Is that why he is the way he is now?"

"That's right. He was never quite right after that. He only stayed a few months. Then his family was able to get him released and they sold the farm they had before and bought the inn. It was really Mary who made it a going thing. Now, Charles Freeman, he was there in the asylum for some years—eight or ten—but there were always people, including the Davises, trying to get him out and finally they proclaimed him cured and released him."

"No. Never. They let him go?" We were all shocked.

"Sure as anything. They let him go and he lived out the rest of his life and died in bed."

"What a horrible story," Louisa Reynolds proclaimed.

"That it is. But now you know. Just don't go letting on you heard it from me. Here, what do you say we put out this fire and get home before the stars are out?"

With that, we all stirred and packed up what was left. I turned to comment on the awful story to Clara, but found she was following Sinclair Bickford down to the dinghies where Elliott was helping Louisa Reynolds into one of the boats. Clara grabbed his arm before he reached them. They argued, although I could not hear what they were saying. Then he pulled away and went to the boat, where he took the place of the rower. They were pushed off and headed towards the *Vigilant*. I stepped up to Clara, thinking to get aboard the second dinghy, but she grabbed my arm.

"Let's wait. Sinclair will be right back."

I saw the other boat was full, so we both dropped to the sand to wait. I wanted to ask Clara about Sinclair Bickford, but I hesitated. She couldn't keep from watching him as if drinking him in. When he was rowing back, she jumped up to meet him and I joined her. We helped to land the boat, then got aboard in the bow. Clara was waiting anxiously, but she was disappointed when Sinclair whispered to one of the other men, who jumped into the rowing seat. Then Sinclair pushed us off. The last dinghy was just landing to pick up the remaining people. I could see Clara was unhappy as she strained to watch his figure on shore all the way back to the *Vigilant*. It made me very uncomfortable to realize there must be something between them. I thought when we returned to the inn it would be time for us to have a talk.

NINE

By the time we entered the harbor, the sun had gone down. Purple painted the horizon and the wind had died down so much that the water looked smooth as glass. There was still enough breeze for us to glide along at a good pace, but all was quiet. Even the sound of voices was reduced to murmurs. Captain Veeder put out green and red lanterns to mark port and starboard, but we saw no other boats. It was only when we swept up close to the docks that we were aware of a stir of activity. At first I thought someone had hung out lanterns for our return, but as we got closer I saw there was a crowd of about a dozen people hurrying down the dock.

"Treasure hunters," Mr. Elliott commented.

Meanwhile, the captain did a sudden turn and expertly slid up to the dock. He had taken down some of the sails when we reached the harbor, and now the large sail that remained was allowed to flap softly. Lines were thrown to waiting hands on shore. I recognized the figure who took the bow line.

"Alden, what are you doing here?" I called out as he walked along the dock with the rope in his hand.

"Hi, Em. I'm here for a story. Wait a minute." He wrapped the line around a large bollard and waited for one of the men to jump off and take it from him. Others followed spoken orders to take down the remaining sail, while still more set up the ramp to let us debark. Mr. Elliott fended off shouted questions from the other reporters on the dock, telling them we had no news of the missing treasure that was supposed to be aboard the *Sterling*. He tried in vain to make them understand that we were a scientific expedition that had nothing to do with the investigation or the search for the treasure.

Pretty soon, Clara and I climbed onto the dock. I felt a bit unsteady after all that time on the boat. Lithe as a cat, Alden took my arm. "Emily, Miss Shea, here's Miss Bly. You've met my sister before, Miss Bly. And this is Miss Clara Shea, who is also a student at the university. And oh, Em, I saw Dr. Chapman. He said to tell you he couldn't come down and will see you tomorrow."

"Oh, no. Well, never mind." I was disappointed. I had expected Stephen to be at the dock waiting for me. Things were taking a strange turn. The fact that Alden was addressing Clara so formally, as "Miss Shea," did not bode well for their attachment, and she appeared to stiffen at the introduction. Clara had said that attachment was broken off, but I had assumed they remained friends. There was an odd tension between them. "Clara, Alden and I met Miss Nellie Bly when she came to Chicago to report on the Pullman Strike," I told her.

"Pleased to meet you," Nellie said. "Now, what can you tell us about the man who showed up dripping wet at the Snow Goose Inn? You're staying there, aren't you?" She had her notebook out. "And what is this about a body being found at the Marine Biological Laboratory? Is it true that you found it? It was a man from Boston, wasn't it? Do you have any knowledge of a connection between the dead man and the men who are accused of gutting the *Missouri* and taking the gold and silver that was being transported?"

The other reporters, who had been trying to get similar information from the debarking passengers, surrounded us, trying to break in with their own questions. I took a step back and felt Clara's hand at the small of my back. Glancing over my shoulder, I suddenly realized how close to the edge I was. She took a step forward. "Well, I do declare," she began in her best Kentucky drawl, "it is so nice of y'all to come to meet us, Mr. Cabot. How very civilized of you to want to escort us back to the inn after our busy day. And that you should bring your lady friend to meet us. I'm sure your sister is very flattered, I know I am. But if you do not clear the path and move away so we can reach the shore I am very afraid your sister here may just faint from exhaustion. It's been a very long day, don't you see, and Miss Cabot here is feeling the strain. Mr. Brinkley, Mr. Craven," she called to two of the scientists from the boat. They rushed to her side. "If you would each just take one of Miss Cabot's arms."

"Clara, I'm fine, I—" but I felt a kick to the back of my legs that made me stagger. "Wait," I said, and fell into the arms of the two young men. Each took an elbow and began to escort me through the crowd and towards the shore.

Meanwhile, Clara kept Alden and Nellie from following. "Please, please, don't let us keep you from your reporting duties. We quite understand. It's been so very interesting to meet you, Miss Bly. Do get on with your trip. We just need to rest after our activities. Now here are Miss Clapp and Mr. Lewis, who will be more than happy to fill you in on what happens at the laboratory, won't you, Miss Clapp? Thank you." I couldn't see behind me, but I could imagine that Clara had managed to blockade the dock with disembarking scientists and people unloading all the things from the picnic. It took me a few minutes to persuade my saviors that I was quite all right, and to disentangle myself from their supporting arms. I was red-faced with embarrassment by the time Clara reached us.

"Really, I am quite all right, thank you. Clara, whatever were you thinking?"

"Yes, thank you, Mr. Brinkley, Mr. Craven. Miss Cabot is quite recovered. I don't know what we'd do without your help, but I think they do need someone over there to help unload the pots and pans, if you wouldn't mind, thank you." They fawned over her, while I collected myself. I started to scold her, but she was paying no attention. Instead, she was watching Sinclair help Louisa Reynolds up into a buggy at the end of the dock. Clara stepped forward as if to speak, but I grabbed her arm.

"Oh, no you don't. Don't you dare try to tell them I'm ill and need a ride." They drove away before she could respond. "Clara, what is this all about?"

She shook her head and handed me my pail and utensils. I saw she had retrieved her own as well. "Very well, if you insist on walking back, do let us proceed."

"But, Clara, don't you want to see Alden? To talk to him, at least?" I found I was talking to her back. She had already stalked up the hill, which made the answer to my question quite clear—she did not want to see Alden. I looked back. Knowing my brother, he would have time only for his story. Perhaps that was the real cause of the break between the two of them. In any case, I was tired out by the long day, so I ran a little to catch up to her. She refused to speak even after we crossed the threshold into the inn. Before we could reach the staircase, Minnie Gibbs stepped in front of us. I could hear men grunting above us, as if they were carrying something up the narrow stairs. Then there was a thud as if they'd dropped it on the wooden floor. "Ladies, I've had to move Miss Shea in with you, Miss Cabot."

"I beg your pardon," Clara said in her most regal Southern belle manner.

"I'm sorry, but I had no choice. They brought the things for Miss Reynolds while you were all out on the boat. I'm full up. The room Miss Cabot has is a double and knowing you two were friends, I thought you wouldn't mind. Mr. Whitman said it would be the best thing. I don't know for how long this Miss Reynolds will be here, but it's the best I could do."

Clara looked dumbfounded. No regal response was forthcoming. "Of course," I said. "We can share a room, can't we, Clara?"

Without replying, she stomped up the stairs. Minnie Gibbs frowned. "I'm sorry if it's not convenient, but I really had no other choice."

"I'm sure it will be all right," I told her. "We're all a little tired from the trip. We were surprised by Miss Reynolds's arrival. She came just as the boat was leaving. I suppose she'll return to Newport tomorrow."

"Not from what Mr. Whitman said. The lady will stay." She looked harassed. "You'll have to discuss it with Mr. Whitman if it won't work out. I have no other rooms. And you would not believe all these reporters. They got here about an hour after you left and they've been underfoot the whole time. They're all looking for rooms as well. I told them they'd have to go into Falmouth. There's no more room here, not a square foot. And my sister is still very ill. She needs quiet."

"Yes, yes. I'm very sorry to hear that. It must be very troubling for you. I'll just go up to my room now."

Upstairs I found Clara brushing her long dark hair in front of the mirror. She attacked it so vigorously with her monogrammed silver brush that I thought she would pull it out by the roots. They had piled her boxes in the far corner and hung several dresses on the hooks along the wall. Poor Clara did not appear to be at all content with the situation.

I sat on my own bed, pulled off my boots, and curled my legs beneath me. It felt good to sit down. Although I considered Clara one of my dearest friends, we had not been together much during the previous year. In our first year at the University of Chicago we spent nearly every day together and became very close, but then I was dismissed and went to live at Hull House. I was surprised when it seemed that Alden and Clara had also become close. But now it seemed that attachment was over. And what was the relationship between Clara and Sinclair Bickford? It made me very uneasy to see that my friend appeared to be closer than she should be to a man who was engaged to somebody else. She bristled as she stared at herself in the mirror, her back to me. I tried to catch her eye in the reflection, but she looked away.

"Clara, I hope it isn't too much of an inconvenience for you to share a room. I certainly don't mind. In fact, I haven't had time to talk to you nearly as much as I'd hoped. I have things to tell you. But first there is something I want to ask you."

The brush slowed a little and her back stiffened. She looked at me in the mirror. "Yes, what?"

"It's about Alden. You said you did have feelings for him, but he was too stubborn about the difference in fortune. Do you still care for him?" There was something so unsettling about her relations with Sinclair Bickford, and something so startling about Alden's sudden presence in Woods Hole, that I found myself regretting that the attachment to my brother had been broken off. And that was despite the fact that I had never approved of what I thought was his pursuit of my best friend.

She brushed more vigorously.

"I'm sorry. It was presumptuous of me."

"No." She stopped and stared at her reflection in the mirror. "Alden gave me up because I was too rich, and he was too poor. At least that was his excuse. Presumably, he went to make his fortune and found Miss Bly."

"I wouldn't assume that," I hurried to reassure her.

"Well, if he has made his fortune, why doesn't he come looking for me instead of looking for a story about a treasure?"

"Ah, I wouldn't say he made his fortune. He came back to Chicago where he got a job as a reporter."

"Exactly suited to his talents, I should think."

"And even more to his insatiable curiosity. Alden writes well, Clara. He described the fate of the strikers in Pullman and how unfair it was. At first, they printed his stories, but then later the newspapers supported the railroads. After that, he wrote his stories, but they didn't print them or, when they did, they put them on the back pages. It wasn't right. Finally he quit and came back to Boston to work in our uncle's bank. That's what he was doing when I saw him there just before we came here. I could tell he wasn't happy. Perhaps he returned to the bank to try to make a fortune and to offer himself to you, but he is not made to work in a bank. You know that as well as I do. He must have left the bank to be a reporter again. He has no fortune to offer you, Clara. I know that's the truth."

She heaved a sigh and continued to brush. "Fine, that's fine. So here we are and Mr. Alden Cabot is merrily chasing robbers who have stolen treasure from a sunken ship. And he is in the company of a lady reporter as penniless as he is, which is fine because, of all things, he cannot abide a woman who has more money than he has. And, meanwhile, Miss Louisa Reynolds has come to join us to check up on her fiancé. And oh, dear me, in her silk and laces and her dainty feelings, she must have a room to herself—my room. And she must have dear Sinclair to call her 'my darling,' and 'dearest,' and 'poor girl.' Why didn't she stay in Newport where she belongs? And then the onerous Mr. McElroy must be found drowned in a tank, while they all squabble about who'll run the laboratory. It's enough to drive one mad." She dropped the brush on the bureau and grasped her head in her hands. "And you and I, Emily, must become serious spinsters dedicated to our books and microscopes like Miss Clapp. That's all there is to it. Goodbye to men, Emily. Goodbye to Alden, and Sinclair, and the awful, horrible, despicable Mr. McElroy." She moved to her bed and fell back on it, lying flat on her back. She seemed considerably moved and disturbed by all that was going on, but I had to tell her the truth.

"Clara, there's something I have to tell you. I've been wanting to tell you, ever since I arrived here, but I couldn't find the right time. I have to tell you. I'm not a spinster anymore. In fact, I'm married."

TEN

It was after the strike was over. I haven't told you quite how awful all of that was, Clara. You would never believe it. But I realized that I love Dr. Chapman, and I very nearly lost him. He'd proposed to me before…I never told you. It was when my mother died. But I told him I couldn't accept, because it would mean giving up my lectureship at the university. Really, though, I didn't believe he loved me. I thought he only asked me out of pity. But, when I realized he *did* love me, I knew how awful it would be to lose him. So, he took me away to Boston and he insisted we have a quiet wedding. He thinks we can keep them from finding out and taking away my appointment, but I don't know if it'll work. He says that once I start teaching I'll be so good they won't be able to dismiss me when they learn the truth. They don't allow married women to teach or even do research. But Stephen says that he's sure Dean Talbot will help fight for me."

Clara sat up straight and stared at me with her mouth open.

"I wanted to tell you. We were married in Boston in a small ceremony. I thought Alden would bring you from Woods Hole. But he kept procrastinating and finally he showed up without you. We came here because Stephen knew how much I missed being at the seashore. We used to come to my grandfather's place in Chatham when I was young. He wanted to get me away from the city to recover, after Pullman. He thought it would be perfect, and it was, at first. But now, what with finding a dead body, I don't know if that's true anymore."

"Oh dear, oh my." She came to sit by my side, and put an

arm around me. "Dear Emily, of course that's wonderful news. You and Dr. Chapman. I should have guessed. Of course you're married and of course you must keep your lectureship. I can keep your secret. I'm so glad for you."

"But what of you, Clara? I couldn't help noticing something between you and Sinclair. But he's engaged to Louisa, isn't he? Is there something wrong?" I myself had very nearly become attached to a man who was not what I thought he was and had nearly lost Stephen in my foolishness. I didn't know how to tell my friend that. I didn't know if she wanted to hear it.

She sighed. "Something wrong?" She got up and began to remove her stockings and prepare for bed. "Oh, there are so many things wrong, Emily, I couldn't count them all. But at least now that odious man is gone and it may all go away." With a start I realized she meant the dead man, Mr. McElroy. "I'm fine, Emily. I *will be* fine. We'll all be fine. The laboratory will remain under the control of the researchers, and we'll all complete our research this summer and return next summer, and the next summer, and forever into the future, piling up scores of reports and findings. And Louisa will marry dear Sinclair and support his work and that of the laboratory and so will her brother. They have quite a fortune between them, you know. And Sinclair will be so successful, he'll succeed Professor Whitman and become director and every summer he'll be here and Louisa will be in Newport and we'll all work and work until we go back to Chicago for the dreary winter. It'll all be just fine. There is nothing wrong at all, not at all."

"Clara."

"No. It's time to sleep. Put on your nightgown and we'll put out the light." She refused to discuss it further, so I followed her suggestion and fell into a troubled sleep.

≈

Clara was gone by the time I awoke. It was raining heavily. At the Mess there was no sign of my friend, but I was joined at one of the round tables by Miss Cornelia Clapp. We had plates loaded with eggs and sausages, and mugs of coffee. Stephen was nowhere to be seen. When I bemoaned the fact that the weather would prevent me from going out hunting specimens and thus leave me with nothing to do, Cornelia invited me to visit her laboratory. I'd not spent much time in the building, so I hoped that, with her help, I might find my way to Stephen or Clara in an inconspicuous manner. It was becoming tedious to have to hide my relationship to Stephen, especially when I had so much to ask him about the death of Mr. McElroy. But I'd agreed to the subterfuge when we made our plans to spend time at Woods Hole, and I had to keep it up for his sake.

There was a Chinese ceramic jar full of large umbrellas at the doorway of the Mess. As it was still raining, we armed ourselves with two of them and rushed across the muddy road to the main building. It was covered with gray shingles, weathered to different shades as a new section had been built each year. It faced away from the harbor towards Eel Pond, but I didn't stop to look at the view, as I wanted to get in out of the wet. We hurried up the wooden stairs and ducked into the chilly shadows of the corridor.

Stopping to shake out wet drops and scrape mud from our boots, we deposited the umbrellas in a canister set out for that purpose. Then I followed Miss Clapp through the hallways to the newest addition. When we arrived I was very impressed to find that she had been allotted her own private room. True, it was not so large as some of the spaces we had passed—where men like Professor Whitman, Frank Lillie, and even Sinclair Bickford had tables and cabinets for students and assistants, as well as themselves—but it was a fair-sized room nonetheless. I knew Stephen worked on the second floor of the new wing. As soon as possible I would find some excuse to go looking for him.

Meanwhile, I followed Miss Clapp into a high-ceilinged room of new wood, with exposed pipes and a large window facing Eel

Pond, against which the main table had been pushed for the best light. In the place of honor on the wide top was a microscope with a high stool beside it. I guessed that Cornelia spent most of her time there. The rest of the table was covered with glass bottles of various shapes and sizes, having cork tops or glass appendages. Against the right wall was a large stone sink with faucets and in the corner I was attracted to a large box made entirely of glass. It was filled with murky water in which a rather ugly-looking fish was slowly swimming around.

Cornelia stopped by the door to retrieve a white apron she used to cover her white blouse and brown skirt. As she tied it behind her back she noticed that the fish had captured my attention. "Meet Kenneth. *Batrachus tau*, commonly known as the toadfish. Ugly, isn't he?" She grinned.

Indeed he was. He was a sort of dirty yellow with brown markings, about ten inches long. He seemed to stick out his hoary chin in a frown, with bulging black eyes and a ripple of black and yellow fins down his back. I suddenly realized that the reason I was so drawn to the tank when I walked in the room was that he was making a noise. It almost sounded like a foghorn. "What is that?"

"Ah, poor Kenneth, randy as always. We named him after a particularly unattractive suitor the family of one of my students was pressing on her." She laughed a guttural laugh. "It seemed to be appropriate and it cheered her up no end. But, actually, Kenneth here is a devoted father, if not a faithful spouse. Toadfish are unusual in that. The noise you hear is a mating call. You see the driftwood in the back of the tank? He's got a nest there. The call attracts the females, more than one, you know. They lay the eggs and promptly leave. Not exactly an example of maternal instinct. He fertilizes the eggs, and then stays around to protect them. Even after they hatch. Rather unusual in the animal world, really."

"My goodness, who would have known? Is that why you study them?"

She laughed again, going over to her table. "I'm afraid that behavior—good or bad, moral or immoral—is not, in itself, of interest to us. No, the main quality of the toadfish, which makes it useful to study, is the size of the eggs. They are unusually large for fish eggs—makes them easier to examine. And another thing, they're adhesive. That may not be significant to the world at large, but it offers a great opportunity to study the effects of gravity and other forces on cell cleavage in the embryo."

I must have looked as blank as I felt because she laughed her guttural laugh again. She turned to her microscope and prepared a shallow glass dish to look at. When she had it placed to her satisfaction, she waved me over. I perched myself on the stool and struggled to keep both eyes open and not to squint, as she instructed. Finally, I saw a tiny world become huge. I spotted several circular forms with a smaller circle inside each. I pulled my head back and blinked. "What am I looking at?"

"Life! The very beginning of life itself. Those are fertilized eggs and if you watch long enough you'll see them split and become two, four, eight, until there's a new little toadfish swimming around." She beamed, as if it were her own accomplishment she was describing. Her enthusiasm was certainly infectious, she was so excited by it all.

Just as I opened my mouth to comment, Edna Thurston whirled into the room, her skirts swirling like a hurricane.

ELEVEN

Cornelia Maria Clapp, you have betrayed us!" Edna Thurston was dressed in black and her dangling jet earrings quivered with the emotion behind her accusation. Cornelia clucked. "Edna, please."

"No, it's true, you can't deny it. We started it all. We followed Louis Agassiz. We raised the money to go and stay at Penikese Island. We arranged to move the school here to Woods Hole so it would be near the fishery. Then they came; they took it all." She was a tall woman, and when she waved her hands she looked like a flailing windmill in the small room.

Cornelia Clapp folded her arms. "That's right, Edna, but now it's time to move on. This is science and this is progress. We did good work with our field trips and our drawings, but now we need to go further." She gestured to the microscope and glass bottles standing on her work table. "We're doing good work here, Edna. This is important research. You don't want to bring that to an end. Not really."

Edna Thurston looked at the instruments with suspicion. Watching as she wrinkled her nose in disgust, I realized she must be very confounded by the newfangled scientific equipment. But she was not ready to concede. She turned on Cornelia. "They're men. They are all men. You're going over to the men. They're taking over. We started it all, but the men are taking over. What about the women?"

"Edna, I know you're worried, but you cannot bring back the past, and the Woman's Education Association of Boston cannot support the research of the laboratory. We need to have men like Professor Whitman. Don't you know how much we're learning? It's terribly exciting and terribly important. We don't want to drive the men out, we need to welcome them. We need to join *with* them. We don't need to fight them off from invading our laboratories, we need to go out there and invade theirs. We need to participate and do investigations and publish our research. That's the only way to prove that we can do it. Don't you see?"

The larger woman stood there, stumped for the moment. Finally, she shook her head, a black feather jiggling atop her elaborately arranged hair. "How can you say that, Cornelia? They'll never recognize your abilities. *You* should have been the director, not Whitman."

"Edna, that is not true."

"It is. And when Whitman chooses his own replacement, he won't choose you. He would never choose a woman. You know that *is* true and it is not fair. He'll choose that Bickford man or Frank Lillie to succeed him. Lincoln McElroy had leverage. He told me he could make Whitman choose you. He knew something that would bring them down."

"Oh, Edna, I don't think that's true."

"It is. And I told Sheriff Redding."

"You told Sheriff Redding?"

"That's right. I told him Lincoln knew something they didn't want exposed. They killed him...one of them killed him. I told Redding." She stumbled a bit, unsteady on her legs, and gulped back a sob. "He must find out what happened. How can I ever tell her?"

"Tell who, Edna?" Cornelia asked.

"His mother. Lincoln's mother." She began to sob. "They won't even let me see the body."

Suddenly I realized what she must have been suffering, as she faced the prospect of telling Mr. McElroy's mother that he had died. Not only that he had died, but that the authorities had his body and that she had no idea when they would release it.

"Oh, Edna." Cornelia rushed to her side. She put an arm around the woman's shoulder and gestured towards a chair in the corner. I brought it over just in time to catch Miss Thurston before she fell. She was weeping. Cornelia knelt down in front of her, patting her shoulder in an attempt to comfort her. "Edna, I know you and Lincoln were close."

Edna wept loudly, then took a breath and said, "They won't tell me, so how can I tell Mrs. McElroy? How can I tell her she can't even have the body?" Her face scrunched up and she began to blubber. It was extremely unattractive, but it made me feel terribly sorry for her, much more so than when she was yelling. Sincere grief is not pretty but it is very strong and very sharp.

"You are staying with the Loomis sisters," Cornelia told her. "They have a telephone. You must call Lincoln's mother and tell her."

"But what can I say?" she wailed.

"It'll be all right. You need to tell her there's been a terrible accident, Lincoln was hurt, and he passed away, there was no way to save him. You can tell her we'll find out about the body and make the arrangements to return him to her in Boston. Don't worry, Edna, we'll find out for you."

I interrupted. "Dr. Chapman will know, or he'll be able to find out. He was helping the medical examiner with the autopsy."

Edna wailed at the word "autopsy" and I realized my mistake. "Oh, how can I tell her they plan to cut him up?"

"No, no, you won't tell her that," Cornelia replied. "You'll just say that everyone is terribly upset and sorry, and they all want to find out the cause of the accident. We have no reason to believe it was anything but an accident, Edna. Do you understand? Do you want me to come back with you? You must tell her as soon as possible."

Miss Thurston sniffed like a child and rubbed her red eyes, but looked relieved. "No. But if you *could* find out when, and how, we can get the body, I mean Mr. McElroy…" she gulped down a sob, "…and get him back to his mother in Boston, that would be such a relief." We promised her we would do that.

When she was gone, Cornelia removed her apron. "We must go see Dr. Chapman." I followed her out to the hallway and up a flight of stairs to the second floor, where we found Stephen wearing a white coat over his shirtsleeves.

It was another high-ceilinged room, larger than Cornelia's, with room for four or five investigators, although none of them were present. Stephen had a table with a microscope near a glass tank full of squid. He worked slowly because his right arm had been badly damaged by a shotgun blast the previous spring. He was intently dissecting a hermit crab and didn't notice our presence for several moments. When he looked up, his face flooded with pleasure at the sight of me, and I felt my heart race. I had to restrain myself from rushing to him, and once again I regretted our decision to keep our marriage secret. But now was not the time to make a sudden announcement. It would only confuse people.

Cornelia seemed not to notice the tension. She was pre-occupied with other concerns. When she told Stephen about the need to contact the dead man's mother, he immediately wrote down the names of the medical examiner and the local funeral home where the body had been taken. "Samples from the organs have been sent to a pathologist at Harvard. Dr. Founce is waiting for the results."

"But surely it was an accident?" Cornelia asked.

"It's not entirely clear. He seems to have been sick. He may have been dead before he went into the tank."

"He was ill?"

"That's what they hope to determine by the analysis. Unfortunately, Founce was not able to call it an accident and, since Miss Thurston burst in on the sheriff with her accusations about rivalries in the laboratory, he is obliged to investigate. Apparently, she claimed that Mr. McElroy had damaging information about one of the researchers. She implied he was a threat to someone, so he might have been killed on purpose. I believe the sheriff would rather be pursuing the men who stole gold from the ship that was scuttled, but he's forced to investigate McElroy's death. When I last saw him, he'd set himself up in Professor Whitman's office and he's demanded that every single researcher present themselves to answer his questions. That's why there's no one else here." He gestured towards the empty tables. "He's not in a very good mood, I'm afraid. I've already been interviewed. He must not have notified the female investigators or you, too, would be sitting waiting to talk to him, Miss Clapp."

"Oh dear, what a terrible waste of time for all of them. And we only have a few weeks left to complete our work." She shook her head. "Poor Frank Lillie. This is the last thing he needs."

When I looked puzzled they explained that, a few weeks before, Frank Lillie lost all of his work for the entire season when a pipe burst and flooded his laboratory. "He's been working night and day to reproduce his results," Cornelia said, shaking her head.

"But surely he had copies of the results written down?" Stephen asked.

"Yes, but the final results are cumulative, and while it would be perfectly reasonable to infer his conclusions, that would not be good enough for Professor Whitman. He has very rigid standards about academic honesty. No, Frank will have lost the whole summer's work if he cannot reproduce it all before the end of the session. He must be climbing the walls sitting around waiting for an interview."

Just then Clara joined us, looking around at the empty tables. "Hullo. At least you're here. Where is everyone? I've been working in our lab since early morning. I can't believe no one's turned up. Have you seen Sinclair? I have questions about some work I'm doing for him, but he hasn't been in all morning."

Stephen explained that they were all being interviewed by Sheriff Redding. When he mentioned that Miss Thurston had insisted the dead man claimed to have threatened one of the scientists, Clara looked stunned. "Oh no! Sinclair…I must talk to the sheriff." She turned very pale.

"Clara, what is it?" I grabbed her arm, afraid she would faint.

"Miss Shea, are you all right?" Stephen came to her, but she brushed him away.

"I'm perfectly fine. I must speak to the sheriff. He's in Professor Whitman's office?"

She hurried away and the three of us followed. When we reached the corridor on the first floor, we crossed over to the oldest part of the main building. Outside the professor's office there was a crowd of scientists milling around, waiting to be questioned.

"I must speak to Frank, see if I can help him," Cornelia said, and headed for a tall young man with a moustache who was striding back and forth in front of a window.

Meanwhile, Clara was asking after Sinclair Bickford and listening to bitter complaints from the others about how he had been in the office with the sheriff for an inordinate amount of time already. They were all anxious to get back to their work, so they resented having to remain there.

"Oh dear," Clara said. She stood for a moment, then pulled herself tall and strode to the door of the office.

"Clara, what are you doing?" I hurried after her and Stephen followed me. She had already opened the door to find Sinclair Bickford sitting in a straight-backed chair facing Sheriff Redding, who sat behind the professor's massive desk, head bent over a notebook. He looked up at our intrusion with an annoyed expression on his face.

"What do you think you're doing? Wait your turn. Out there." He pointed.

"I must speak to you," Clara said. "It's about Mr. McElroy."

The sheriff frowned, looking very put out. Stephen closed the door to the corridor. "Sorry, Redding," he said. "This is Miss Clara Shea."

"I don't care if she's the Queen of Sheba. I'll hear what she has to say after I finish with Mr. Bickford here. Whatever she has to say can't be nearly as interesting. It seems that three separate persons heard Mr. Bickford here arguing with the dead man the day of his death. And Mr. Bickford has yet to give me a satisfactory explanation. So—"

"That's what I have to tell you," Clara interrupted. "He's protecting me, my reputation. He'll never tell you. I know what they were arguing about. I know what Mr. McElroy wanted him to do and why he thought he could make him. Sinclair might argue with him, and despise him, but he would never hurt him. He's not capable of it. McElroy didn't just try to blackmail Sinclair, he tried to blackmail me as well. He was a despicable man."

"Clara." Sinclair Bickford started to rise from his chair, but the sheriff stopped him with a firm hand.

"You sit down. Now!" he snapped. Then he turned back to Clara. "Exactly what is it you say the dead man knew, that he wanted to blackmail you about?" He glared at Clara with narrowed eyes.

I saw her gulp. She'd grown pale again. "Mr. McElroy came upon us." Her face flushed now. I looked over and saw Sinclair was red-faced as well. "He came upon us in a shed, on the dock. He saw us together...in a compromising situation."

TWELVE

Silence fell on the room for a moment. The weight of Clara's admission was enormous. She had just destroyed her own reputation and I was afraid for her. The sheriff's eyebrows rose nearly up to his hairline.

"Compromising?" I had a sneaking suspicion he was enjoying her humiliation. He obviously did not appreciate the "bug hunters" who took up summer residence in his town, and this was confirming his suspicions of the whole class of people.

"Yes, compromising. Surely you can imagine, Sheriff. We were together, alone, and we should not have been," Clara snapped.

With a huge sigh, Stephen moved two straight-backed chairs behind Clara and me, allowing us to sit. I reached out to hold one of Clara's hands and saw Stephen place a reassuring hand on her shoulder. This would not be easy.

"I see." The sheriff smirked. "Exactly what happened when McElroy surprised you *in flagrante* as it were? Do go on. And you be quiet," he snapped at Sinclair Bickford, before he could interrupt. "Miss Shea, go on."

I squeezed her hand. "Nothing happened then. We were all quite embarrassed. He left, and we followed once he was gone," Clara told him. I hated to think what it must have been like for her to have McElroy come upon them like that. It must have been so embarrassing. "It was later, several days later, when he caught me alone and lectured me on morals." She made a face as if she smelled something disgusting. "Morals. He made it clear that he would not go to Professor Whitman and tell him what he had seen, but only if Sinclair fully supported him when the time came. It was a threat."

"I see. And did you tell Mr. Bickford of this threat?"

"I warned him, of course. But he would not succumb to such a threat."

"Surely, if McElroy had reported what he saw to Professor Whitman, you would both suffer, wouldn't you?"

Clara blanched and gripped my hand. "We would have suffered great embarrassment, but certainly not enough to warrant harming that despicable little man. It was a mistake." I could see her jaw muscles strain. "Sinclair and I worked very closely together this summer. We became close, we were tempted. But he is engaged to Miss Reynolds. It was not important. It was a mistake for both of us. We know that. We have already ended it."

I thought of how hard she had tried to get his attention at the clambake. If they had agreed to end it, she was having a hard time abiding by that agreement.

The sheriff was writing in his notebook and he let the silence fall heavily. Clara gripped my hand so hard it hurt. Finally, Redding looked up. "So, you were seduced by Bickford here, but he had no plans to break off his engagement to Miss Reynolds for you. And if McElroy exposed the two of you, you would both be embarrassed. But, in that case, isn't it true that he could still marry Miss Reynolds, while you would be ruined? Isn't that the truth?"

Clara gritted her teeth and glared back at him. Sinclair Bickford looked appalled. He was staring at Clara. It was obvious that he could not deny the truth of what she had said, but to admit it would be ungallant in the extreme. He was stumped. I had to say something.

"Sheriff, you can't believe either of them killed Mr. McElroy. They certainly had reason to dislike him, but they did not succumb to his pressure. Neither of them supported him when it came to the vote…" Suddenly I realized my mistake.

"Exactly. So, McElroy would have taken his revenge by

exposing them, so one or both of them could have kept him quiet by pushing him into that tank." He gave me a self-satisfied smirk.

"But you don't even know that's what killed him."

"She's right," Stephen spoke up. "He almost certainly did *not* drown."

"Almost certainly," Redding grunted. "These doctors. So what happened? You sent the organs to be tested. So, if we find out he was poisoned, why wouldn't we think one of them did that?" he asked, gesturing towards Clara and Bickford. "You work with all sorts of chemicals, don't you, Miss Shea? They say poison is a woman's weapon. Did you poison McElroy to stop him from ruining you? Is that what you did?"

Clara gasped and released her grip on my hand completely. I was afraid she would faint. But Clara was stronger than that. Instead, she took a deep breath and stood up. "I most certainly did nothing of the sort, Sheriff Redding. I've told you all that I intend to. If you have additional questions, I will be available to answer them. My purpose was to tell you the truth, which I knew Mr. Bickford would be too much of a gentleman to admit to you. I am embarrassed and humiliated. But I hope you believe me when I say that Mr. McElroy's threats, while embarrassing and hurtful, would never cause either Mr. Bickford or me to do the man any harm. Now, if you will excuse me, I am done."

The men rose as she swept out. I stayed behind for a moment. "Sheriff Redding, please. I'm certain Miss Shea and Mr. Bickford had nothing to do with the death of Mr. McElroy. Surely what we have just heard does not need to be repeated outside this room?"

He glared at me. "I'm not nearly as sure as you are, Miss Cabot, that they had nothing to do with his death. Time will tell. But if we do find some unrelated cause of the man's death, I would have no need to make the story public. If I were you, though, I wouldn't count on it."

Stephen and I caught up with Clara. She was weak-kneed from the confrontation and we each took one of her arms, to help support her without looking too obvious. I glanced over my shoulder, hoping to see Sinclair Bickford. Surely he would follow us to talk to her after such a horrendous scene. But he was nowhere in sight. Clara said nothing, so we took our time strolling back to the inn, arm in arm. I didn't want to press her with Stephen there.

"You should rest," Stephen told her when we reached the inn. She nodded and headed for the stairs. She looked exhausted, but waved away my offer of help. I was sure she needed privacy, so I stayed behind with Stephen on the veranda. The rain had stopped, but everything was wet, too wet for us to be together in one of the places where we had been meeting secretly. At least we were alone, although we could easily be interrupted, so we needed to be discreet, especially after what we had just heard.

"Poor Clara," I said. We sat on a wicker sofa, and he surreptitiously held my hand, hidden under the fold of my skirt.

"Yes. And Redding is right, it will ruin her if it gets out, but Bickford will barely suffer. I don't know what his fiancée will think, but even she may well forgive him."

"And if it doesn't get out, he'll marry her and she'll never even know it happened. I don't think much of Sinclair Bickford," I said.

"No. But he was already engaged to Miss Reynolds before the summer. These things happen, Emily. He and Clara were together, passionate about the same things, here at the beautiful seaside. It's easy to see how they could give in to their natural impulses."

I knew he was right. I knew I had nearly done something similar. But I felt the warmth of Stephen beside me, knowing we had each other forever, even if we were pretending otherwise. It made me pity my friend. I would never think Sinclair Bickford deserved her, even if she wanted him. And Alden. I sighed for my brother. How much had he lost by letting Clara go? I thought that now they would never be together and I was sad.

"Oh dear, I hope I'm not disturbing you. I've been cooped up inside all day and I thought, since the rain let up, I'd just come out here and get a little air." It was Jane Topham, carrying a basket holding balls of yarn and knitting needles. "Don't get up. I'll just take this rocking chair. It's one of my favorites. I just love rocking here, looking out at the sea. It's one of the things that brings me back year after year."

I introduced her to Stephen, first carefully disengaging my hand from his. As a nurse she was interested to quiz him about his past medical practice. After patiently answering a few of her questions he excused himself to return to his laboratory.

"My, my, he was very nice. Do you know him well?" she asked as he retreated. I told her we were acquaintances from Chicago. I wasn't at all sure she believed me. "How is your friend Miss Shea? I saw her come in just now. She looked quite peaked." She bent forward to pull some slack on her yarn, then began to click away at the piece she was knitting. Whatever it was intended to be, it was a pale yellow color. "Now, Miss Shea has been working with Mr. Bickford this summer, hasn't she? I'm not really involved with the laboratory, but I keep track of what's going on, don't you know. Did you know that he's in the running to succeed Professor Whitman as director? No? You hadn't heard? Of course, you and Dr. Chapman came late, didn't you? But you come from Chicago, same as Professor Whitman and Frank Lillie and Sinclair Bickford, isn't that so?" She looked up with bright inquisitive eyes, as she reached forward again to get more slack from her ball of yarn. "Now, Cornelia Clapp is from a women's school, Mount Holyoke. So, which of the three do you think it will be?"

I didn't know what she meant.

"Well, everybody knows it was between the three of them. One of them will be groomed to take over whenever Professor Whitman decides to step back. He's gotten very involved with his pigeons, you know."

"Pigeons?"

"Oh, yes. Instead of the fish, don't you know. He had crates and crates of them shipped from Chicago this year so he could continue whatever it is he's doing with them. They say he'll get the laboratory set up as an independent institution, not part of any particular university, and then he'll hand over the reins. Of course, Cornelia is the oldest and has the longest connections to the laboratory, but then, being a woman, she's a dark horse. Most people thought it would be Frank Lillie, but I heard his research got ruined this year, and that could be a real setback for him. So now, some say it's bound to be Sinclair. I guess he's been getting really good results. And that Miss Reynolds is his fiancée, I hear. And her brother is a big, big contributor to the laboratory, so that can't hurt. So what do you think? Which one?" She was rocking and knitting contentedly as she spoke.

"I have no idea," I said. I could see how important to Sinclair Bickford's career this summer must be. "I suppose it must be important to maintain a good reputation if they're trying to impress Professor Whitman."

"Oh dear me, yes. He's a real stickler for propriety, you know. He's got quite a reputation for being unbendable. He doesn't mind if they disagree, you know, or argue about their theories, he encourages it. You should hear them argue sometimes at those Friday night lectures, you'd be amazed. But if there's ever a hint of slackness in technique, or fudging results on experiments, they say he's implacable. And once you lose his respect you're dead to him. So I'm sure they're very concerned to make a good impression."

And if Whitman was so rigid about laboratory results I wondered how he would react to a moral lapse like the one Clara had admitted to. Perhaps it was not true that Sinclair Bickford could have survived exposure of their illicit affair after all. Perhaps it *would* have ruined his career.

When I finally followed Clara up to our room, I found she was pacing back and forth in an agitated manner.

"I've been so stupid. He's been stupid. I know you think I've betrayed Louisa Reynolds, Emily, but his obligation to her is based on a false feeling. Listen, when I came, I thought I would just while away the summer. You'd told me how much you loved the seashore when you and your brother were children. Of course I knew it was an honor to be asked to come. I did good work last year in the laboratory. Very good work. That's why I was asked.

"But it was a lark for me. And a way to get over Alden. Yes, I thought we would be together, Alden and me, but he had other ideas. I suppose I even thought at first it was a way to reconnect with him. I stopped in Boston before coming down here. I let him know I would be there. Do you know what he did? He left town and fled back to Chicago to be a reporter. Or to escape me.

"I was chastened by that. So I came here, prepared to lick my wounds and start on my career in earnest. Professor Whitman assigned me to Sinclair's laboratory. I had met him, of course. I knew him from classes and I knew he was Louisa's fiancé. Working for him was as good as anyone else as far as I was concerned.

"But then I saw how desperate he was to succeed—how much it meant to him. I suppose he didn't feel worthy of Louisa...he has no money. It even reminded me of Alden." She gulped.

"Since I didn't care, I had nothing to lose and nothing at stake, so of course I was the one who found it. It was a mistake, really. I spilled some saline water into one of the jars. I saw the difference. I showed him. It took him a while to realize the implications. It's just the kind of thing Jacques Loeb is suggesting. It's not just a case of observing, it's a way to actively make an experiment that will cause a change.

"We were so excited. We had to plan and calculate and set up all the measurements with painstaking precision. It was a case of getting the concentration right. You see, it was a combination of salt and magnesium chloride. My work in chemistry came in handy. It took a lot of experimentation, but when we started to see results we were thrilled. The unfertilized eggs actually developed to the blastula stage when they were returned to the normal concentration of sea water. But we wanted to go beyond that to the next stage. We couldn't tell anyone else until we were sure it would work. It was such a bold thing to do." She stopped and put her face in her hands for a moment. When she looked up she was biting her lip. "It was at one of the clambakes that we decided it was going to work. It wasn't planned. We just fell into each other's arms, we were so happy. Of course, we were shocked by what we'd done."

I was shaking my head now. Her tale was painful to listen to. Clara rushed on before I could protest that they were betraying Louisa. Sinclair was engaged, after all.

She knew what I was thinking. "We said we'd never do it again, but how could we not, Emily? Once we'd felt such passion, we couldn't help it. We were very careful—until that man came upon us in the boat shed. That was like a bucket of cold water. Sinclair was afraid that Louisa and her brother would find out. He wanted to stop it.

"But I didn't see why he should feel forever attached to her. Engagements can be broken."

"Clara."

"No, wouldn't it be better for her in the long run to break it off? Sinclair and I would be working together. She has no interest in such things. They are nothing to her. But he couldn't see it. He refused to break it off with her. I think he's afraid of what Professor Whitman would think." She ran her hands through her hair. "It's too late for that now. That awful man McElroy... he ruined everything."

"Clara, how could you hurt Louisa like that? She's our friend. You knew he was engaged to her."

"It just happened, Emily. Can't you see that she's wrong for him?"

"And you're right?"

"We share the same interests. We could pursue our studies together."

"It's not fair to her, Clara."

"I can't help that. I won't give him up for mere propriety."

"What about Alden?" It slipped out before I could stop myself. I hadn't meant to say that.

"Emily, Alden doesn't want me. Don't you understand?" She turned her back on me and I had to leave the room. I went for a walk along the shore to relieve my feelings.

I frittered away the rest of the day, checking on Clara occasionally. She feigned sleep and refused food. I ate dinner at the Mess with Stephen and afterwards we were able to slip away for a while in the quiet of the evening. He said Redding had continued his interrogations, but nothing new had turned up. Neither of us felt good about Clara's position. It seemed that she remained a suspect, although they still were not sure how McElroy had died.

I returned to the inn before midnight and was careful not to wake Clara as I undressed. I fell into a fitful sleep in which I found myself walking through water, pursued by the glassy-eyed corpse of Mr. McElroy. I could see Miss Thurston and Cornelia Clapp trying to reach into the water to pull me out, but they couldn't reach me, and I just wanted to escape the dead man. I looked over my shoulder and suddenly right in my face someone yelled, "Fire! Get out! Fire! Wake up! Fire!"

THIRTEEN

I coughed. It was dark in the room, but a flickering light came from the doorway. I sat up in my nightgown. I looked across, but Clara was not in her bed. I heard people running and yelling, smelled the smoke, and coughed again. I had to get out.

I grabbed a robe and ran barefoot out to the hallway. Smoke came up the narrow staircase, but I needed to go down. At least it was not terribly thick. I hurried down, following other figures. The smoke was thickest on the second floor and I heard crackling and saw flames at the doorway of the room that had originally been Clara's but was later given to Louisa Reynolds. I didn't stop. Everyone was rushing out and I couldn't breathe.

I found myself outside. The crushed seashells of the walkway hurt my bare feet, so I jumped onto the sandy grass of the front yard. Looking up at the flames that licked a second floor window, I almost stumbled into Jane Topham. She looked unexpectedly neat in a flowered nightdress covered by a red flannel robe. Her belt was tied and there was even a ribbon in her dark hair. She was the composed and collected nurse as always, only she was uncharacteristically speechless. The light of the fire was reflected in her eyes as she stared, open-mouthed and fascinated.

"Did everyone get out?" I asked.

She looked mesmerized.

"Jane, did everyone get out? Where is Clara? Did Louisa Reynolds get out? That's her room."

She blinked and smiled at me. "They're over there."

I looked where she pointed. Louisa Reynolds and Clara

Shea stood together, with ash streaks on their faces and clothes, barefoot, with hair hanging down in front of their eyes. At least they were safe.

"Your friend, Clara Shea, was very courageous. When I came out of my room, I saw her kick open the door and jump over the flames to wake Miss Reynolds and get her out. It looked like the fire started right in front of that room."

Suddenly, I felt myself swept up and embraced. It was Stephen. "Thank God, you're all right," he said. I buried my face in his chest and felt him kiss my hair. "You're all right." He pulled away to look at me as if to reassure himself. "Stay here, I'll help them."

I could see over his shoulder that a bucket brigade was forming to pass water buckets from a pump in the yard into the house. Stephen ran to them. I saw Mr. Alfred Davis, incongruous in a suit and tie, passing a bucket to Cornelia Clapp, who wore a nightgown with an afghan around her shoulders and an untidy braid flapping on her back.

I was about to join them when Jane Topham grabbed my arm. "Here they are. It's Genevieve Gordon. She's ill. I told them to get her out."

I could see figures struggling to carry a woman on a mattress out the door and down the steps. "Over here, bring her over here," Jane called to them.

"Do you want me to get Dr. Chapman?" I asked.

"No, no, I can see to her. I have her medicine right here." She raised a flask in her hand while she directed them to place the mattress in a spot away from the path. The blanket fell away and I retrieved it. "Poor thing," Jane murmured, as she brushed the woman's hair away from her eyes and gave her a sip from the flask. "I'm afraid there's not much anyone can do for her," she whispered to me.

Nonetheless, I peered into the darkness looking for Stephen. He should see the woman. With his crippled arm surely he would be of more help here. I saw Minnie Gibbs desperately running to the pumps with more containers for the water and I heard bells in the distance. Perhaps it would be the local fire brigade. It looked like the fire had not spread to other floors—the flames were only visible in the room Louisa Reynolds had occupied on the second floor.

Suddenly a small figure flew towards us. "You leave her alone. You get away from her." It was Billy Gordon. "You get away from my mother." He hurled himself at the mattress, but I grabbed him before he could reach it. "Ma, Ma," he called.

"Your mother is sick," I told him, as he struggled. I looked across at Jane Topham. "Maybe I should get Dr. Chapman."

She was staring at the flames with a dreamy look in her eyes as she gently patted the sick woman's head. "It's too late, I'm afraid. She's been quite sick, you know."

Billy let loose a howl and I let him go, so that he could fling himself on his mother's body. Minnie Gibbs heard him and, dropping the pail she was carrying, came running. I saw Stephen and yelled for him just as a horse-drawn fire truck arrived with its bell ringing wildly.

As people rushed to the truck to help unroll hoses, Stephen pulled the boy off his mother to check her heart and breath. He had a low-pitched conversation with Jane Topham. She shook her head and stood up while he continued his examination. "I'm sorry," he told Billy and Minnie. They both wept.

Meanwhile, the fire brigade brought lanterns and, when I looked across, I saw my brother Alden's face in the crowd. He saw me, too, and hurried over. Behind him I recognized Nellie Bly.

"Em, are you all right? We're staying in Falmouth. We heard the fire bells and managed to jump aboard." He looked at the flames on the second floor. "You weren't in there, were you?"

But obviously I was, otherwise why would I be standing there in my nightclothes? "I was, but we got out."

"Who was hurt?" Nellie asked, notebook in hand. She was looking at Billy and Minnie Gibbs.

"Mrs. Gordon. She'd been ill. They got her out, but she passed away," I told her.

Meanwhile, Alden was staring at me. Suddenly he hugged me. "Emily, Emily. Are you sure you're all right? Who else is here? Stephen?" He saw Stephen still kneeling over the dead woman.

"He wasn't inside, he came to help. I was sharing a room with Clara."

Even in the dim light I could see him blanch. "Clara? Where is she? Has anything happened to her?"

After all that Clara had gone through that day, I doubted she would welcome the sight of Alden with Nellie Bly hanging on his arm. Before I could answer, Alden spotted her a few feet away, huddled together with Louisa Reynolds. They both looked bedraggled and dirty.

"Clara," Alden yelled.

She turned to look at him and I saw her eyes roll up in her head as she started to faint. I hurried to help her, reaching her in time to catch her and lower her down to the ground. A moment later, Stephen was by my side, followed by Alden. "Clara! Is she all right?" My brother reached out, but I brushed his hand away.

"Leave her alone," I told him.

"We need to get her inside," Stephen said, gathering her into his arms awkwardly. Despite his injured right arm, he managed to lift her. "Emily, come with me. The two of you can stay in my room. Sinclair, take care of Miss Reynolds and get the rest of the men to help the women to shelter."

Sinclair Bickford appeared, taking Louisa's arm. He and several other men had come at the sound of the fire bells. "Yes. We can put the men in the Mess for the night and give up our rooms to the ladies. Don't worry, I'll handle it." He began waving and giving directions.

"Follow me, Emily," Stephen told me. "No, Alden, not tonight. Just stay out of the way. Come, Emily, the fire brigade can handle it. I need to get both of you indoors."

I followed him and others came with us to the rooming house where he and some of the other men had been staying. They cleared out and I found myself in Stephen's room, sharing the bed with Clara.

"She'll be all right, she just needs rest," Stephen told me. Then he kissed me. "You'll be all right, too. I need to go back and make sure no one needs medical attention. I'll spend the night in the Mess with the others. I'll see you tomorrow." He gave me another kiss and left.

I felt secure, despite the scare of the fire. It felt safe to be in Stephen's room, among his things, with his scent in the air. I was so tired I quickly fell into a deep sleep, uninterrupted with thoughts of all that had happened since Clara and I found the dead man in the tank.

FOURTEEN

I woke late the next morning. The sun was streaming in and quickly heated up the room. I could hear the cry of sea gulls. There was even a faint sound of surf, which had provided a reassuring recurring melody all night. Clara was still in a heavy sleep, snoring lightly, with her back to me. My face and mouth felt gritty from the ash of the fire the night before. The sudden vivid memory of the flames shooting from the second floor windows made me want to jump out of bed and into the sunshine.

Suddenly I realized I had no clothes, only my nightgown. How could I go anywhere without putting on proper clothing? I heard a few noises from downstairs, but I knew the men had moved to the Mess for the night and they all took their meals there in any case. Whoever it was, it was not laboratory people; perhaps it was the family who owned the place. I supposed they would not want to disturb our rest. It seemed unlikely to me that the men would think of the clothing dilemma. To remain in bed would only leave me prey to memories of the night before. I wanted to get cleaned up and changed into day clothes. But I didn't want to waken Clara. I looked around Stephen's room, which was plain and bare. His overcoat hung from a peg by the door, and his work boots stood in the corner. Being as quiet as I could, I got out of the bed and put them on over my night clothes and bare feet. They were too big, but my plan was to avoid being seen as I sneaked back to the Snow Goose Inn to retrieve clothes for both of us.

I was careful to close the door quietly and listened for a moment. When I was sure there was no one around, I clumped down the stairs of the men's rooming house. From the sounds and smells, the family who owned the house might still be eating on a lower floor or in a back room, but there was no one in the parlor as I hurried past and out the front door. It was a bright, hot morning. The street was empty. I hurried along, using the trunks of trees to provide some cover as I peered ahead. I did not want to be seen clad in Stephen's coat and boots if I could avoid it. If only I could get to the inn unseen, I could change to my own clothes. It was only a few houses away.

But, as I approached, I saw Sheriff Redding's horse and buggy on the street in front. I peered around a tree trunk and spotted him sitting on the porch talking to Minnie Gibbs. Alfred Davis sat nearby, rocking with his Bible in his lap, and little Billy sat on the floor, way back in the corner, his knees pulled up to his chin. Poor boy, he had lost his mother.

Wanting to avoid the sheriff above all, I doubled back to the last house and carefully moved to the rear. Laundry waved from a line, but there was no one to see me. I crossed to where I could see the back door of the Snow Goose. It looked empty, so I hurried in. Stopping just inside the doorway, I heard noises from the kitchen and smelled coffee and bacon. Pausing, I considered sneaking up the back stairs, which were against a wall on the right, but whoever was in the kitchen was probably female and would understand my plight. On the other hand, if they heard me and called out, that could bring Sheriff Redding from the front porch, so I peeked in through the kitchen door. It was Jane Topham, wearing a massive, blue-figured apron with her hands in a pan of water up to her elbows, humming as she cleaned. I cleared my throat so as not to startle her too much.

She looked around. "Ah, Miss Cabot. Do come in. There's coffee and bread." She got a look at me as I stepped into the room. "Oh...of course...you had nothing to change into this morning." She pulled her hands from the water and wiped them on a dish towel. "I understand. I was in the same position earlier.

Miss Clapp and Miss Reynolds and I were at the Standish home last night. I, too, had to sneak in to get something proper to wear. Luckily, I had closed the door to my room when I left, don't you know, so it wasn't so bad. I'm afraid you'll have dirt from the smoke all over your things." She shook her head. "It's a pity. But don't let me stop you, do run up and get changed before that nosy Sheriff Redding realizes you're here. I already fed the man bacon and eggs for heaven's sakes. You'd think he was a paying customer and I was the help." As usual with Miss Topham, it was unnecessary to add to the conversation. She was fully capable of carrying it off single-handed. When she waved me away, I was grateful. I just wanted to change into my own clothes before anyone saw me.

I had to hold my breath passing by the second floor, where most of the damage was. The air was still tainted with smoke and ash. On the third floor I saw that we had imprudently left our door open and the gray ash covered everything. But who would have the presence of mind to close the door when awakened in the middle of the night by yells of "Fire!"? Only a trained nurse, apparently. I certainly did not have Jane Topham's ability to respond so quickly and rationally to such an emergency.

So, I looked at our filthy room with distaste. I stepped to the window to throw it fully open, sticking my head out for a taste of fresh air. Then I quickly dressed myself in my oldest skirt and blouse, after shaking each out the window as well as I could to remove some of the dirt. That they were the black of mourning might be a benefit today, as they didn't show the ash as much as the white petticoat and shirtwaist of Clara's that hung from a peg. I pulled out my carpet bag and filled it with underclothes and other garments for the both of us. There were some things from the bureau drawers and Clara's trunk that were much cleaner than the pieces hanging from the pegs, so I chose those, and I wiped off brushes and toiletries as well as I could, wrapping them in other pieces of clothing as I put them in. Feeling more prepared to face the day, even if I was still dirty, I headed downstairs. Clara would need her things when she awoke.

I couldn't help stopping on the second floor despite the ash in the air. There was an angry-looking black scar on the wall just outside the front room that Clara had been in until Louisa Reynolds arrived. Putting down the carpet bag, I went to the open doorway. Inside was a mess. There was a thick layer of black sodden ash all over everything. The lace curtains had been consumed and the window frames charred. The four-poster bed was water-logged and rested uneasily on a wooden floor that had been eaten away by the flames. Some of Louisa Reynolds's dainty frocks, trimmed with beautiful lace, had been destroyed, leaving rags on the floor and pieces stuck to the scorched walls. The smell was nauseating and I stepped back into the hallway.

"So this is the room that was under dispute, is it?" I jumped at the voice. It was Sheriff Redding, standing in the hallway examining the charcoal-black hole in the wall. "And this is where the fire started, I would say, wouldn't you?"

"I guess so." I looked at him uneasily. Somehow he seemed antagonistic to me.

"But you do know this is the room your friend Miss Shea had occupied and that she was forced to give it up to make room for Miss Reynolds. Isn't that right? I suppose Miss Shea was not happy about that, now, was she? Don't try to hide it. Mrs. Gibbs told me all about it."

"I don't know what you mean. Yes, when we returned from the picnic we found they had moved Miss Shea's things into the room where I was, upstairs. But that was because Miss Reynolds had appeared unexpectedly, and Mrs. Gibbs assumed, since we were friends and it was a double room I had, that it would be acceptable."

"But it wasn't acceptable, was it?" He pushed past me into the bedroom, looking around. "Minnie Gibbs says your Miss Shea was not pleased. Said she seemed very upset by it. Yes, I can see this must be the best room in the place, with the bay windows and all. So Miss Shea had been in here all summer, but as soon as Miss Reynolds, the very Miss Reynolds who is engaged to the charming Mr. Bickford, comes to town, Miss Shea is kicked out of her room." What was he suggesting? His eyes narrowed and he had a look of smug satisfaction. "It must have been galling to Miss Shea, after her encounters with Mr. Bickford in the boat shed, to find out his fiancée had arrived. No wonder she was upset."

I was worried by his insinuations. "I wouldn't say she was upset. It just caught her by surprise. In any case, it was Clara who woke Louisa Reynolds and got her out of the room last night. She might have been injured. Clara saved her. Ask Miss Topham. She saw it all." As I looked over his shoulder at the devastation in the room, it struck me that Louisa Reynolds could have died in that fire. The ugly streaks left by the flames looked angry and very dangerous.

Sheriff Redding grunted. "That busybody. Perhaps Miss Shea set the fire in a moment of jealous rage but, when she realized the object of her jealousy might actually be killed, she changed her mind."

"You cannot mean that. You cannot be accusing Clara of setting the fire!" But I could tell from his face that was exactly what he was thinking.

There were voices and the sound of feet climbing the stairs.

"Let's take a look and see how bad it is." It was Mr. E.C. Elliott's voice, but the first person to appear was Louisa Reynolds. She looked petite, in a plain cotton dress she must have borrowed from a local woman. There was a kerchief tied around her head, which made her look like an aristocrat disguised as a peasant. She was followed by the broad-shouldered figure of Mr. Elliott in his tweeds. His presence filled the room, but then he was followed by what seemed to be a crowd of people. Despite the fact there were only three others, it suddenly felt like we were surrounded.

A small man wearing a belt hung with tools began to examine the hole burned into the wall, while a second man, who was a younger replica of him, hung back to let through the figure of

Cornelia Clapp. She wore an old skirt and a shirtwaist streaked with ash. She had hastily pinned up the braid that had flapped down her back the previous night.

"How bad is it?" Elliott's voice thundered and they all gathered round like the family of a patient waiting for a diagnosis. The small man refused to be rushed. Meanwhile, Sheriff Redding stepped forward. "Redding, there you are," Elliott greeted him. "Miss Reynolds and Miss Clapp here were staying at the house where I'm rooming last night, due to the fire. Bickford and some of the others gave up their rooms. So this morning, when the men went off to the laboratory, I told the ladies I knew just the man to take a look at the damage. We rode into Falmouth and brought back Dunbar, here, and his son, Jeb." He turned to me. "Mr. Dunbar's really a local boat builder, but he's the one to look and see what it will take to get the place ship-shape again."

The little boat builder paid no attention as he finished his examination of the damage in the room and pushed past the sheriff into the hallway. His son scurried after him and they talked in low murmurs as the rest of us stayed in the doorway. "Poor Mrs. Gibbs," Cornelia said. "If it wasn't bad enough to have this happen, to have her sister pass away at the same time..." She shook her head.

Louisa Reynolds took up the story. "We weren't certain how she would be. She'll have to take care of the funeral, and everything. We were talking to Mr. Elliott and he thought we should go ahead and try to help, didn't you, Mr. Elliott?"

"That's right. How is she anyhow, Redding? You've seen her, I imagine."

"She went to telegraph her brother-in-law in Chicago, about his wife."

"Poor Minnie. And to have it happen so soon after her mother passed away. It's a real shame. And then to have the fire at the same time! We really need to help her. What do you say, Dunbar, is it fixable?"

Mr. Dunbar came back into the room. I heard his son sneeze

explosively behind him. I sympathized with the boy as my nose was still tingling from the ash floating in the air. But the father seemed unperturbed, despite the black streaks on his face and forearms from his examination. He told us in a few words that the room was salvageable. They would need to move all the detritus out, then repair the floor boards, the baseboard, and the window casings. He seemed to believe that the two of them could get it done in a day, provided Jeb went back and got his wagon full of tools and some wood.

"What about the rest of the house?" Cornelia Clapp asked. "Is it safe?"

"Safe enough. Need to clean it is all. Some fresh paint, maybe. Leastways she'll have to take it all out and scrub it down."

Cornelia Clapp looked around at us. "Poor Minnie is in no shape to do that. Not while she's seeing to her sister's funeral, and keeping an eye on her father. He hasn't been right since his wife passed away, if he was then. We'll need to see if we can get her some help."

I looked around and took stock of what I knew about the kitchen, the pump in the back yard, and the laundry room I had peeked into one day. "Shouldn't we volunteer?" I asked. "We could do it. We'll need to move everything out to the yard, but it's a clear day. Then we'll wash all the linens, clean off the furniture, beat the rugs and take down the curtains, wipe down the walls. If we gathered enough people, we could get it done before she has to have the funeral, poor woman. I certainly can take time off from hunting specimens. I suppose some of you may need to get back to the laboratory…"
Personally, I was glad of the opportunity to do something useful.

"I can help," Louisa Reynolds said. I could see she was sincere, although I doubted she had done the type of heavy housework we would be engaged in. She had servants for that. To be honest, I had expected her to retreat to Newport. Especially with all her lovely clothes spoiled. But she appeared to be game. Only Mr. Elliott didn't seem surprised by her offer.

"Oh dear, this is much more important than the laboratory at this point," Cornelia Clapp said. "We're near the end anyhow. I'm sure most of the other women would be willing to help and we'll get it all done sooner with more of us. I'll go round them up."

Mr. Dunbar turned to his son. "Jeb, when you go back, tell your ma about Minnie Gibbs and how her sister passed away on top of the fire. She'll get some of the church ladies to come out and help. They know Minnie and they were all sad to see her mother pass away. Tell her to bring mops and pails."

"Now, wait one minute," Sheriff Redding interrupted. "We need to find out who it was set this fire, so's to keep it from happening again."

"But we must clean the place up in any case, Sheriff," Cornelia argued reasonably. "I don't know who would do such a thing, but there have been a couple of other fires this summer. In no case was anyone harmed and the damage was much less, but it has happened before."

"Minnie Gibbs told me that. There was a bonfire on the beach, spread to the beach grass."

"That was put out handily by some of the men coming home from a Friday lecture," Mr. Elliott told him. "They thought it might have been set by children."

Redding grunted. "And then the tool shed out back. There was a fire in there in early August, she told me."

"That's right," Cornelia said. "We assumed it was an accident but, after this incident, one has to wonder."

Redding was looking across at me, glaring. "Seems like there's more than mischief at work here. I'm thinking you folks need to take care. Especially you, Miss Reynolds."

"Me?"

"Well, yes. The fire was started right in front of your room here, wasn't it?" He gestured to the blackened hole in the wall.

"Do you mean to say you think the fire was set purposely to harm Miss Reynolds?" Elliott asked. "That's a very serious accusation."

"I'm just saying you want to be careful. Seems like someone

who's around here is doing this and, until we know who it is, it might not be safe for the lady. Weren't no other outsiders, now were there? So who do you think might want to do you harm, young lady?"

I wanted to moan. Louisa had no idea about Clara and Sinclair. I was sure of that. The sheriff was about to hint at something that had never even entered her imagination. And what would the result be if she came to understand what he was suggesting? How would her engagement to Sinclair Bickford, or her friendship with Clara, survive? We'd all been friends in Chicago. Not as close as Clara and I had become, but Louisa and her brother had been part of our group. We were all young and terribly enthusiastic about the new endeavors we'd taken up when the university opened. Even though Louisa enrolled in only a few classes, she'd been part of our group and had shared our enthusiasm.

I bit my lip but, to my relief, the discussion was interrupted by the arrival of Jane Topham. We heard the clump of feet on the narrow stairs, and people shifted to make room for her as she came through the door. When she reached the middle of the room, she stopped to wipe her hands on her apron.

"That's where you're wrong again, Sheriff. I thought you were talking to Minnie on the porch. Didn't you even ask her about strangers and whether she recognized any?" She shook her head in disappointment while the sheriff glared at her.

"What are you going on about now?"

"The man you were looking for. The stranger who was dripping on her doorstep, who she turned away. Didn't she tell you? She saw him again last night. He was helping to put out the fire. It was the man you are looking for from the boat *Sterling*. The one they think got away with the plunder from the boat that was wrecked."

FIFTEEN

Cursing under his breath, the sheriff pounded off down the stairs to follow up on this new information. Jane Topham folded her arms with a satisfied expression. I wondered about the ongoing antagonism between those two. They seemed to know each other's flaws and the exact right spot to press to get a reaction. Jane had been coming to the town as a summer visitor for a number of years. Perhaps they had a past together.

When Jane disappeared down the stairs there was a smug smile on her face. Meanwhile, Mr. Dunbar and Mr. Elliott were discussing what to do. They decided more help was needed to shift the heavier furniture, especially from the second floor, so Mr. Elliott went off to recruit Captain Veeder and some of his men.

I went downstairs to find cleaning supplies. I was outside lining up pails and other containers by the pump when Stephen found me. After a furtive embrace, I told him how we planned to repair the damage from the fire for Minnie Gibbs. He wanted to help. I was grateful, knowing how much he must want to return to his research, but with his injured arm he would be of little use moving furniture. I knew it would only frustrate him so, when I saw Mr. Elliott returning with Veeder and half a dozen men, I asked Stephen to take the carpetbag of clothes to Clara and to check on her, to be sure she was recovering from the previous night's adventures. I also told him that the sheriff had gone in search of the dripping wet stranger who was seen during the fire. He promised to try to find out if the man had been found, then he hurried off to see Clara, carrying the carpetbag in his good hand.

Veeder and his men began to carry down smoke-damaged furniture from the second floor and I directed them to place it outside near the pump. Poor Minnie. It would be a shock for her to see her whole house turned inside out like this, and the streaks of soot on the white wicker furniture were particularly disheartening. The sooner they were wiped off the better. With luck we could finish much of it before she returned.

Soon Cornelia arrived with seven of the laboratory women, who quickly joined Louisa in gathering up the bedding and taking down the soiled curtains from all over the house. They brought them down and threw them in piles in the laundry room and outside near some large wash basins, while Jane helped to heat water, and some of us began to wash and rinse the soiled linens. I got them started on that but soon left Louisa up to her elbows in soap bubbles, and was moving on to organize the next set of tasks, when Jeb Dunbar pulled up with a wagon load of lumber and tools. Perched on the building materials were his mother and four of the church ladies. They brought their own mops and pails. After consultation they took over work on the inside where they would mop and wash down the walls while the laboratory women and Veeder's men did the laundry and washed down the furniture outside. Soon we could hear the sawing and hammering from the carpentry work of the Dunbar men and Mr. Elliott on the second floor.

Cornelia and I searched for extra line. When we found it, we recruited a couple of the men to help string it between the house and a tree to dry the sheets and curtains. We strung some heavier line between two trees and they helped us hoist up the braided rag rugs for beating. Just at that moment Clara arrived, looking haggard but calm. I sensed it would be a relief for her to be able to beat away at something, so I enlisted her help and, sure enough, the color returned to her face as I left her to the task a short while later.

By early afternoon we had accomplished more than I had

hoped for. There was time for a welcome break as we waited for things to dry. Even the hammering from the second floor came to an end, as Jeb and his father and Mr. Elliott came out to the porch and settled in the rocking chairs.

Jane and Louisa appeared with trays containing bowls of steaming fish chowder and platters of buttered bread.

Some of us spread out one of the recently beaten rugs on the sparse beach grass by the side of the house and sat on it to sip spoons of the rich white chowder. Cornelia and Louisa were there, and Clara sat at the edge quietly savoring the hot soup. We were tired and hungry and the salt air made the chowder taste even better. I was grateful for the break and joined them after I'd walked around to make sure everyone was served.

A buggy passed on the road, headed towards the Mess, and Sheriff Redding leaned out, glaring at our group. I thought it was Clara he was looking at. She colored slightly. Another horse-drawn buggy stopped at the inn and Nellie Bly climbed down, looking fashionable in a trim suit with a perky hat perched on the side of her head. She held a notebook and pencil and came right up to me, asking if she could join us for an interview. Alden waved from the buggy before driving off after the sheriff. I introduced Nellie to the others and we offered her a bowl of chowder. Soon, she was sitting among us putting aside the soup to ask her questions.

"We came to find out about the gold and silver that was looted from the boat that sank and that they believe was transported here in the sloop *Sterling*. My colleague, Mr. Cabot, has gone after the sheriff to see if there's anything new on that. Meanwhile, as long as we're here, I'd like to tell the readers of our paper, *The World*, about the Marine Biological Laboratory and the women who do research here." She turned towards Cornelia Clapp. "I understand you're a long-time researcher at the laboratory, is that true, Miss Clapp?"

Cornelia smiled at her. "Yes. I'm glad to say I've been attending the summer sessions since the laboratory began in 1888."

"Now you teach at a women's college, is that right?"

"That's right, Mount Holyoke College. A number of my students are able to attend as well. It's a wonderful opportunity for them."

"Right. So tell me, what is this controversy with the Woman's Education Association? Aren't they upset that the men have moved in and taken over what they began? How do you feel about that?"

I couldn't help glancing across the yard to where Edna Thurston was sitting with some of the local women. I wondered if Nellie Bly had talked to her. Had Edna told her about McElroy's death? Did Nellie and my brother know about that and the sheriff's suspicions about Clara? I looked at Clara, but she was attending to her chowder, not seeming to notice the dangerous trend of the conversation. Meanwhile, Cornelia's expression had become grim. She attempted to set the reporter right, telling her about the history of the laboratory and her belief that the participation of scholars from many different universities contributed to the work and the opportunities for everyone involved. She made it clear that she supported Professor Whitman and the other men who came to do research.

"I see. So you don't object to that. But what is the status of the women here? Can you tell me about that? Can the women do real work, or are they relegated to the job of handmaids to the men?"

"There is certainly ample opportunity to do good work," Cornelia told her. "I, along with other women here, am able to contribute to the research by giving lectures and publishing in the annual set of papers."

"But how does that compare to the men's contributions? Now, you've been a scholar for a long time, haven't you? What is your age? Over forty, perhaps? How about all these young men in their twenties? How does it feel to have them get ahead of you? Isn't it true that women don't get faculty appointments unless it is at a women's college like the one you come from? How do you feel about that?"

"We've made a lot of progress, but there is more to be done," Cornelia told her. "We are working to break through these prejudices and to demonstrate that women can contribute to scientific research. I believe the opportunity to attend the summer sessions here with men from so many of the important universities can only help demonstrate the competence of women scholars."

"I see, well, thank you for talking with me. Now you, you're Miss Reynolds, is that right?" Nellie moved on to Louisa. "What are you doing to contribute to the work here?"

"I only came the other day. I haven't been here all summer, like the others."

"Oh, and where did you come from, then?"

Louisa looked embarrassed. "I was in Newport with my family. But I'm engaged to Mr. Sinclair Bickford, who's been attending the summer session. We hoped he might spend some time with us in Newport, but he's been very busy, so I thought I would come and join him here since he had so little time to enjoy the seaside with us. He's been extremely busy with his work and he really is Professor Whitman's right hand man."

"Ah, Newport." Nellie was writing that down. "And Mr. Bickford. That's right, I've heard him mentioned. Is it true that he's expected to succeed Whitman as head of the laboratory? Is he being groomed for that?"

Louisa looked confused. She obviously had no idea what Nellie was getting at, so the reporter turned back to Cornelia. "What about that, Miss Clapp? Is that true? And how do you feel about having a man so much younger than you being groomed for that post? He's in his twenties, isn't he? Do you find that discouraging at all?"

Cornelia looked surprised by the sudden attack. "Of course not. I think you're wrong in any case. I believe Mr. Frank Lillie is most likely to succeed Professor Whitman as director, when it comes to that. But Professor Whitman is very much engaged in making sure the laboratory is established in a way that will ensure the work can continue far into the future."

"But what of your own ambitions? Don't you want to be director?"

"That is not something I am ambitious for. My ambition is to continue to contribute to the work here and to help more and more of my students to further their careers by giving them the opportunity to do research here."

Nellie looked askance at that. "You mean you would sacrifice your own ambitions for the sake of your future students? That's certainly admirable of you, Miss Clapp, but perhaps those members of the younger generation will have less modest ambitions. What about you, Miss Shea? How do you feel about your work here? Will it help you to get ahead in your academic career?"

Clara looked her over, taking in the pert little hat and the stylish walking suit. She must have been aware of her own less than stylish shirtwaist and drab skirt. We were all dirty from the work as well. But I don't suppose my friend had any idea of how much more striking her natural beauty was compared to the rest of us. She never saw that. When she spoke, her Kentucky accent was more pronounced than usual. That was always a dangerous sign. "I am happy to be assisting Mr. Bickford—Miss Reynolds's Mr. Bickford—in his study of parthenogenesis in the sea urchin. I have been here since the beginning of June, bent over my microscope and working with dyes and chemicals. I can only say it has been most satisfying, as we have discovered and proved, at least to our own satisfaction, that unfertilized eggs may be brought not only to the blastula stage but even to the pluteus stage. I cannot tell you what a thrill it is to know for certain that submersion in a particular concentration of chemicals can achieve parthenogenesis."

She declared all this in the most serious manner and her complexion was pale enough to make her seem quite sincere, but I detected a very slight note of sarcasm. I didn't know if Nellie Bly heard it, but it made me wary. Louisa Reynolds had no inkling of the attachment Clara and Sinclair had formed and it made me cold to think what would happen if that were revealed to the reporter.

"Sounds like you've spent the summer furthering Mr. Bickford's career rather than your own, Miss Shea. But then, not all of us have the resources to spend the time at Newport, like Miss Reynolds here."

"Oh, but Clara could have been at Newport if she wanted," Louisa hurried to correct her. "In fact, I met her grandmother there. She was staying with the Vanderbilts. Clara is a real scholar, not like me," she confessed. I looked across at Clara, but her head was bent over her soup bowl. "We both come from the University of Chicago, but Clara and Sinclair and my brother are all enrolled in a degree program. I'm just attending some classes. Clara is a real scholar."

Nellie Bly smiled at her. "How very lucky your Mr. Bickford is to have the both of you helping him. And what about you, Miss Cabot? Are you also furthering some man's career by your work here?" She looked down at her notebook with a sly smile, after asking her question, and I suspected Alden had told her about my marriage to Stephen, as well as the fact that it was secret. I blushed, unable to stop myself, and silently cursed my feckless brother. The last thing I needed was an announcement or even a hint at that secret in a New York paper.

"I've only been here for a little over a week," I told her. "As you can imagine, I was quite exhausted after my experience at Pullman...where we last met. I'm here visiting my friend, Clara, and recuperating." I hoped that recalling our meeting would distract her.

"Oh, yes. That was very dramatic. Those poor folks. You certainly did good work there. What made you abandon it?"

"I never abandoned it. I plan to return to my studies in the fall. In fact, I have a lectureship, but before that, I decided to take the opportunity to visit the seashore. I don't know if my brother told you, but, as children, we often came to Cape Cod in the summer to visit our grandfather. Those are some of my happiest memories."

"Of course, I'm sure it's a relief after Pullman. Say, who is that now?"

We looked across and saw Minnie Gibbs and her father Alfred Davis descending from a horse-drawn trap. She was helped down by Mr. Elliott. After she was quickly swept up by the church ladies, Mr. Elliott came towards us. We explained to Nellie that this was our landlady and her father. She looked interested, but was interrupted by Mr. Elliott.

"Excuse me. Are you by any chance Miss Nellie Bly?"

"Indeed I am."

"Mr. Alden Cabot asked me to give you a message. He says you might want to come along to the Mess. Sheriff Redding found the men from the *Sterling*. He's interrogating them now about the missing treasure. Mr. Cabot thought you'd want to be present, as the sheriff seems to be doing the interrogation in public."

SIXTEEN

Nellie needed us to show her the way to the Mess and in any case I was very curious to hear what the unknown men had to say. Perhaps they had caused Mr. McElroy's death. It certainly seemed possible. Louisa Reynolds stayed behind with Mr. Elliott. They assured us that the remaining work on cleaning up the inn could continue without us and under the direction of Minnie Gibbs, now that she had returned. All of the women from the laboratory were anxious to hear what was going on, so we set off together.

At the Mess, the main room had filled up with researchers and also some of the local men, but Alden waved us over to where he'd found a perch on the veranda. From there, we could see and hear through a wide open window. Sheriff Redding sat at a table in the middle of the room with a plate full of steaming roast beef and mashed potatoes in front of him. Opposite sat two bare-headed men in rough garb.

"Why is he doing this in public?" I whispered to Alden. Nellie had crowded in front of him and I had the laboratory women, including Clara and Cornelia, behind me.

"There's a method to his madness," Alden told me. "He *wants* everyone to hear. Shh."

"Says here, William Pittman and Clifford Dunham. Are those your names?" Redding was reading from a paper in one hand while he took bites of the meat and potatoes with the other. "Hey, answer me." There was a mumbling from the men, whose heads were hanging down. "Speak up, speak up."

Just inside the window, I could see the thatch of white hair belonging to Professor Whitman, and beside him the straw-colored hair of Frank Lillie. I looked all the way across the room and spotted Sinclair Bickford. He saw us, too, and after a brief glance he worked his way through the crowd and out the door opposite us. I thought he must be taking the opportunity to go and talk to Louisa while we were away from her. I wondered how much he would tell her about his summer with Clara. As the sheriff held the crowd's attention with some badgering questions to his prisoners, I looked around and noticed Clara was gone. I hoped she wasn't following Sinclair. What kind of a scene would there be if she confronted him when he was with Louisa? I sighed. There was nothing I could do. I hoped the sheriff was going to prove these men were responsible for Mr. McElroy's death. Then, at least, the story of Clara and Sinclair's attachment might not have to be made public.

"It's a simple question." The sheriff was waving his fork at one of the men. "Are you or are you not related to Captain Henry Pittman who was arrested in Boston on suspicion of plundering the ship *Missouri*? Huh?" There was a murmur. "Oh, so you admit he's your brother. And exactly what are you doing with his ship, the *Sterling*? Didn't you bring it down here from Boston and anchor in Falmouth? You admit that, do you? So what did you do with the swag? Don't lie to me." He held up a paper. "It says here that Captain Pittman is accused of conspiring with the captain of the *Missouri*, a certain Samuel Dixey, to scuttle the *Missouri* but not before they removed fourteen bags containing gold and silver coins to the amount of sixteen thousand dollars. That money was on the *Sterling* when you sailed it down from Boston, wasn't it? But it's not there now. What did you do? Sneak it off the ship? So where did you put it? It was too heavy for you, wasn't it? Your dinghy went aground on the sandbar, didn't it? Captain Veeder here and his men found the dinghy. So what did you do with the bags of coins? Did you hide them? Where?"

The two men sat with their heads still hanging down. Meanwhile, Sheriff Redding looked up and addressed the crowd of people.

"Now, you all listen, and listen good. These men stole that money and they tried to bring it ashore. The weight of it made them go aground, so they unloaded the cargo and sunk the dinghy. We don't know where they hid the bags of coins. You can all go out looking all over the shoreline for it. But let me make one thing clear, that money belongs to the owners of the *Missouri*. Now there'll be a reward for whoever finds it, but if you find it and you don't turn it in, let me tell you, you'll regret it. Just like these here men will regret it. Because that money is nothing but bad luck to all of ya." He turned his attention back to his prisoners. "So, what happened? Did Lincoln McElroy see you dragging that loot ashore? Did he challenge you? And did you hit him over the head and dump him in one of those tanks? You killed that man because he saw you with the money, didn't you?"

Suddenly we could hear one of the men. "Killed? What do you mean killed? We ain't killed nobody. We ain't," he wailed.

"Sure you did. Mr. Lincoln McElroy was down from Boston and the very night your boat got to town is the night he was killed. He was found the next morning in a tank of water by the laboratory. Yup, I see you boys as the ones who done it and you'll hang for it."

"No! No!" The men began to argue and accuse each other of blundering and stupidity. They yelled at each other, the sheriff looking on with satisfaction as he chewed on his meal.

"How did they find them?" I asked Alden.

He shook his head. "Not the brightest lights. They were camping in the woods, but when they saw the commotion about the fire last night, they came out to see and got pulled into the line of people passing buckets to put it out. The innkeeper lady recognized one of them, but when her sister died, she didn't mention it until the sheriff asked her. He took men and fanned out and found them in the woods. They were too dumb to run away after the fire. They salvaged some blankets and food during the confusion." He turned back towards the drama inside the room as the sheriff finally intervened.

"Yep, I'm telling you, you're gonna hang and it serves you right."

"No, no. OK. We brought the *Sterling* down with the bags on board, we did that. We took them ashore, but they were too heavy, like you said. The boat got stuck and started sinking. We had to wade ashore and then go back again and again for the bags. Finally we got them, or most of them, but we had to hide them, so we buried them. But that took all night. We didn't see nobody. We for sure didn't kill nobody. It wasn't us. I swear it. He swears it too, don't you, you dumb schmuck?"

The sheriff pounced on their admission. "Where? Where'd you bury it?"

Both men looked sheepish "That's it. We lost track like. It was dark. We marked it, but we spent yesterday and today trying to find it and we lost it."

"You *lost* it?" The sheriff was incredulous. "Sixteen thousand dollars' worth of coin and you lost it?"

The men were squabbling again. They claimed they had marked the spot with a kerchief, but when they tried to return to it they couldn't find it.

"Exactly when did you bury this?" Captain Veeder stood up and asked the question. "Was it past midnight the night before last?" When they confirmed the time, he shook his head. "Well, that's the problem, then. It was low tide. If they didn't bury it far enough up from the surf, when the tide came in, most likely it took away their marker."

This caused another spate of curse-laden argument between the two men, but Sheriff Redding pounded a fist on his table to get their attention. "So you two geniuses buried the treasure too close to the water, and then you did in McElroy and that made you forget where you left it, is that it?"

They started shouting at this, protesting their innocence and claiming they never met McElroy and knew nothing about his death. Meanwhile, I saw Stephen making his way through the crowd to the sheriff with a telegram in his hand and, after a brief exchange, the man read it. He frowned and pounded on the table again for attention. "Well, you two geniuses are going to jail. We'll keep you here till they come get you and take you up to Boston to go on trial with your brother and his conniving captain friend, and a good riddance to the lot of you. For the rest of you," he addressed the crowd, "it seems their claim that they didn't kill McElroy is something we have to take seriously." My heart dropped at this announcement. "It seems he wasn't hit over the head, he was poisoned. They found arsenic in his organs." He flapped the telegram at them. "So you bug hunters still have something to explain about that man's death. So don't none of you leave town until we've got this straightened out." He pushed his plate away and stood up, directing two of his men to take the prisoners to jail. Then he shoved his way through the crowd to the door near us.

I looked around and saw that Cornelia had also left at some point during the interrogation. People were hurrying away and I realized the sheriff had purposely recruited an army of treasure hunters while at the same time delivering a strict warning about what would happen if anyone found the bags of coins but tried to hide the fact from him. The sheriff reached the doorway just as Sinclair Bickford bounded up the steps, returning from seeing Louisa. They were suddenly face to face.

"You," the sheriff addressed him. "You! Where is your fi-an-cee? You better pack her up and send her back to Newport. It's not safe for her here, you understand?"

Sinclair looked pained. "She's helping to clean up the Snow Goose Inn for Mrs. Gibbs. I don't believe she plans to return to Newport."

"Well, make her." He spotted me on the veranda. "And you,

Miss Cabot, where is your friend Miss Shea?"

"I believe she's also helping at the inn," I told him reluctantly.

"You tell her not to go anywhere, you hear me?" He grunted and turned away. I saw Nellie Bly dash to follow him.

Meanwhile, Alden was staring at me. "What was that about? Why is he asking about Clara?"

"Oh, Alden, don't you know what this means?" He always had the ability to exasperate me. "Because he thinks Clara killed Lincoln McElroy. I hoped when they found these men, that would change his opinion, but it hasn't."

"What do you mean? Why would he accuse Clara? Why would she want to kill the McElroy man?"

Suddenly, I realized that Alden had no knowledge of Clara's summer attachment to Sinclair Bickford or of how Lincoln McElroy had found them together and threatened to make their alliance public. Alden had once had feelings for Clara himself. I couldn't be the one to tell him. How could I have been so foolish as to mention it? Furious with myself, I looked around, desperately hoping to see Stephen. He must have gone back to the Main. Ignoring Alden's questions, I hurried to find my husband. How could I have revealed Clara's secret to my brother? I was so angry with myself, and so flustered, that I could only run away.

SEVENTEEN

I strode along towards the laboratory building, Alden scrambling to keep up with me. He fired questions at me, which I ignored. He finally took a breath, just as I rounded the corner of the building and saw Clara.

She stood in the doorway, her hands gripping the railing of the low stairs. Her jaw was stiff, her eyes closed and her face lifted to the sun as if for relief. She heard us and stiffened even more as she looked around.

"Clara, I thought you'd gone back to the inn." I'd been sure she was following Sinclair, so I was surprised to find her here.

Alden was in a stubborn mood. "Clara, what's all this about the sheriff accusing you of murdering the man they found in the tank? What's going on here?"

Clara looked like a fog had descended on her. I told her about the public interrogation of the men from the *Sterling*. "Stephen came in with a telegram that said Mr. McElroy died of arsenic poisoning, so now the sheriff doesn't believe those men did it. He said we shouldn't leave. Oh, Clara, he said that you especially shouldn't leave until they find the killer."

She wiped a hand across her brow as if to brush away the fog. It was as if she were returning from some dream. She came down the steps and started to walk away. Alden followed.

"Wait, Clara. What's happening? Why would he accuse you? Tell me," he insisted.

She spun towards him and he backed away at her sudden movement. I groaned. Why did he have to insist so much? He would not like it when he learned what this was all about. I didn't know if he still had feelings for Clara, but I knew I still felt sick about the way she'd described her relationship with Sinclair Bickford. I didn't want them to have this conversation, and I felt as if I was watching them on the brink of a precipice from which they were about to knock each other over without intending it.

She glared at him. "Because of Sinclair. Sinclair Bickford. That man…that desperate pitiful little man found me and Sinclair…in a boat house. And he threatened to expose us if Sinclair did not vote his way against the plans for the laboratory. Sinclair did not vote his way, so the sheriff has decided that would be enough motive for me to kill him. After all, I'm a chemist, aren't I? And I'm a woman. What more proof does he need?" She turned to walk away.

Poor Clara. But she was so bitter, I could barely feel sorry for her. She had insisted on announcing her liaison with Bickford in this bold-faced way. She was giving Alden a shove over the brink.

But Alden wasn't finished. "What are you talking about? Why would you kill some man you didn't know because Bickford wouldn't vote his way? It doesn't make any sense." He reached out to grab her arm. "Clara, tell me. I want to know."

I thought he was being purposely obtuse. He didn't want to know, and he wouldn't believe what she was saying.

She shook off his hand. "Because he sees me as a woman scorned. You know how a woman scorned is expected to react. You know how jealousy and hatred can make a woman do anything?"

Alden was becoming furious in his frustration. "What are you talking about? What man would ever scorn you? He would be mad, it wouldn't happen."

She stared at him and I saw a tear start to roll down her cheek. Then she turned and walked away. I felt a huge wave of regret. They had cared for each other. I had never encouraged the attachment, but I could feel the strength of their attraction. If only she hadn't thrown everything away on her infatuation with Sinclair Bickford.

"Wait," Alden demanded, running after her. He jumped in

front of her. "You didn't kill him. Certainly not for Bickford. Look, Clara, I know you admire these eggheads..." He gulped. "...you like these academics. I can't be like that. I tried to go back to the bank, but I couldn't do it. It's not me. I know you think I'm shiftless, but I am what I am. You couldn't look up to me like you do to these professor types." He waved his hand. "But if you wanted a man, even one of them, how could he deny you? How could he turn you down? Look, you're beautiful, rich, intelligent. I don't believe that Bickford," he spat the word out, "or any other man would turn you down. It's not possible."

"You don't believe it?" she chanted in his face. "But it's true. He's engaged to Louisa Reynolds."

"He was engaged before they came here this summer." I couldn't help interrupting. I hated it that Clara had gotten involved with a man who was already committed to our friend. Much as I wanted to sympathize, I hated it, and she knew that disapproval was an obstacle between us.

She glared at me. "That's right. Sinclair Bickford was engaged to Louisa Reynolds when we arrived here and then he and I were together. We were caught in a compromising position in a boat shed by the man who is dead. And now Sinclair Bickford is still engaged and wants to remain so!"

Alden's chest was heaving. "Good. Good riddance to him. What would you want with such a deceiver, Clara?" She turned away from him, and he reached again to grab her arm, but this time she shrugged him off and spun around to face him.

She was bent forward, her arms locked close to her body and her face contorted with rage. Her voice was a rasp. "Don't touch me. Leave me alone. *Leave me alone.*" With that she spun around again and went running off. I grabbed Alden's arm to keep him from pursuing her, but he suddenly went cold and silent, and just stood there, watching her run away. I was appalled for my friend; her grief was so deep and feral. It made me wonder what she might have done and what she had discovered about herself and the man she thought she loved. It was more than disillusionment I saw in her, it was despair.

I felt some sympathy, too, for my brother, but also exasperation. If he felt so much for Clara, why had he turned away from her? Why had he let her leave him, only to stumble into this mess with Sinclair Bickford? I longed to turn my back on them and find Stephen.

$$\approx$$

We sat on a sand dune, silence hovering around us like the moment after a rifle shot. As if in answer to my prayer, Stephen had come out of the main building just as Clara ran away. I embraced him with abandon, and he led us away from the buildings, down to the beach overlooking the harbor. Alden followed like a disgraced puppy.

Eventually, Alden broke the silence and asked us straight out about the dead man and whether the sheriff really considered Clara a suspect in his murder. Stephen would have hidden the facts, but I told him that Clara had revealed her liaison with Sinclair already, and we recounted everything that we knew.

Alden's face was turned away, but I thought there must be regret in it. He made only a few comments, merely taking it all in. He seemed drained of emotion after the argument with Clara. I clung to Stephen's arm, grateful for the warmth of it, and of him.

Finally, we all returned to the Mess for dinner. There was no sign of Clara, but Cornelia joined us at one of the long tables. Alden was very quiet. We were halfway through the meal when people began clinking silverware against their glasses to get our attention. Professor Whitman, looking older than the last time I had seen him, was standing at the front of the room with Frank Lillie beside him. Sheriff Redding was in the doorway watching, Nellie Bly beside him, a look of expectation on her face. Something was wrong.

Whitman cleared his throat and, when he began speaking, an eerie quiet descended on the room. "I have something I need to tell all of you. I cannot say how much it pains me to have to tell you this, but it is necessary." He looked across to where Redding was glowering at the room. "As you know, there was an unfortunate accident a few weeks ago, a burst pipe, as the result of which Frank Lillie, here, lost much of the work he had already done this summer. We were all disappointed by the loss of such valuable research materials, but we pitched in to assist him in regaining lost ground by redoing his experiments. As you know, he and his investigators have been working day and night to reproduce his earlier results and I know many of you have lent a hand when you could, to help him. I am very, very sorry to say that today all of that work has once again been lost. Unfortunately, this time it cannot be put down to an accident or mistake. I am sorry to report that it was most definitely the result of sabotage."

The room, which had been petrified in an unnatural silence, suddenly came to life with rustles and murmurs of disbelief. Sabotage!

"Yes. It's true. Dye was purposely and maliciously spilled onto the specimens, destroying all of the work." I heard Cornelia Clapp opposite me gasp. She picked up a spoon, but her hand shook. I looked at her curiously. Meanwhile, Professor Whitman continued. "I must ask you all to cooperate with Sheriff Redding, who is here to ask you some questions, in case this act may have something to do with the death of Mr. McElroy. I am devastated by this turn of events. I can only admonish each and every one of you to do your duty and cooperate fully with the authorities as they attempt to find the misguided person who has done these very terrible things." He seemed overcome, and Frank Lillie helped him to a chair.

The crowd erupted with noise as the sheriff strode to the front of the room. I looked around and saw Alden heading for the doorway to confer with Nellie Bly.

The sheriff announced that he would interview each and every person and proceeded to go around the room asking where people had been during the afternoon. It was another public interrogation. It did seem that his tactic must discourage lies. Everyone heard everyone else's testimony and if someone lied about his whereabouts, someone else might well have seen him and would speak up to refute the lie. The sheriff was very clever in conducting his inquiry this way.

When he got to me, I said I'd been helping at the inn and then had come to the Mess with Cornelia and the others to hear him question the men from the *Sterling*.

"Were you here the whole time?"

"Yes."

"And the others—Miss Clapp, Miss Shea, Miss Reynolds?"

"Miss Reynolds stayed at the inn, she didn't come with us. I believe Miss Clapp was here for most of the questioning. I believe Miss Shea left at some point."

"Miss Shea? And where is Miss Shea now?"

"I don't know. She didn't come with us to dinner." I really dreaded his next question.

"Was that the last you saw of Miss Shea? Did you see her again during the rest of the day?"

"Yes."

"Well, where did you see her last?"

I gulped. "My brother and I met her coming out of the main building. We talked and then she left us."

He frowned. "That's enough. Where is Miss Shea now, does anyone know?"

No one in the room knew and he sent all of us off to find her. Stephen came with me as I ran to his room, but her things were still there. We went to the Snow Goose Inn, then back to the laboratory building. The others searched the remainder of the grounds. But, in the end, no one could find her. She was gone.

EIGHTEEN

I blame myself, it's all my fault." We found Sinclair Bickford
alone in his room at the laboratory. It was on the ground
floor of the new wing, like Cornelia's, but it was much
bigger. Four long tables were covered with microscopes and
glass bottles. He sat slumped in a low chair by a wooden desk,
an electric lamp throwing a pool of harsh white light over him.

I glanced at Stephen. I did not have a lot of sympathy for
Sinclair. I did not approve of the fact that he had seduced my
friend while he was betrothed to another. I wanted to leave, but
we were trapped, having already stepped inside the room.

"Clara would never have sabotaged someone's work. Never,"
I declared. "We must find her. Did you see her today?"

"That's just it. She told me she was going to do it. I didn't
believe her."

I felt my heart stop. This could not be. "What are you saying?"

He looked up at me, reaching a finger under his glasses to rub
his eye. He was a good-looking young man, but at the moment
he looked tired and disheveled, with his sleeves rolled up and
his suspenders creasing his white shirt. There was strength in
him, and longing. There was no pretense in the tears that were
gathering in his eyes, although he attempted to blink them away.
"She wouldn't give it up. She said she would fix it all, with Professor
Whitman. She said she knew it had damaged my reputation to
have to admit to things before the sheriff, there in Whitman's
office. I tried to tell her it didn't matter. It was over for me. Not
just the affair—the laboratory, the university, everything."

Despair seemed to emanate from him. It made me feel empty in the pit of my stomach. He was ruined by his actions—and Clara's—that was clear. All his dreams were in tatters. If he was like this with Clara, it would have spurred her to some action. But sabotage?

"Exactly when did you see her?" I asked. Clara had been with us cleaning at the inn most of the day.

"This morning, in Dr. Chapman's rooms. I went to look for her before she could talk to Louisa. There's no reason to tell Louisa, it would hurt her dreadfully. I needed to make Clara promise she would say nothing to Louisa, nothing of what you heard her tell the sheriff." He looked down, embarrassed.

I snorted. I couldn't help myself. It made me angry that the two of them had been so careless of themselves and others.

"I know. I'm sorry, but you must understand." He looked up suddenly and reached across to grab my hand. "Emily, you know Clara. She is beautiful, passionate, overwhelming. She came at me like a storm this summer. How could I resist her? But it was wrong for both of us. I was already promised to Louisa. Clara knew that. We never meant to hurt her. And I realized, as soon as Louisa came from Newport, that I had missed her dreadfully. She was always the one I loved, and that's still the case."

I pulled my hand away. I didn't want to hear this. Neither did Stephen, but he stood quietly in the doorway. Sinclair used his hands to rub his face, pushing his spectacles up onto his forehead. "I tried to explain that to Clara. She's so intelligent, of course she knew it. But she said she couldn't let the situation stand. She said she would, she'd make it right, that I couldn't lose it all because of her. Don't you see? She went to the laboratory this afternoon to sabotage Frank Lillie because she thought that would reinstate me as Professor Whitman's potential successor. I can't tell you how sorry I am."

I stood there thinking of how Clara had left the room while Sheriff Redding was interrogating the sailors. I thought she'd followed Sinclair, to stop him from seeing Louisa or to insist on confronting Louisa about the attachment. It never occurred to me that she'd gone to the laboratory, yet that was where Alden and I had seen her—coming out of the laboratory, very upset about something. It felt like a stream of icy water was running down my backbone. It couldn't be! But she had been so impassioned and so unreasonable in her defense of her actions. I felt like I was staring over the edge of a cliff, dizzy with the view.

"Emily, it's not her fault," Sinclair told me. "We must find her and help her. It's not her fault."

At that moment, Professor Whitman came into the room, making his way past Stephen in the doorway. "Sinclair," he addressed the young man, who hastily rose and attempted to make himself presentable.

"Professor Whitman," he said, interrupting the older man. "Before you say anything, I must tell you it wasn't Clara Shea who sabotaged Frank Lillie's experiment." He gulped. "It was me. I did it. It was all my fault."

Whitman started, as if he'd been burned by a fire. "What are you saying, Sinclair?"

"No," I protested. I could see he was just saying this for Clara's sake.

"Yes, Miss Cabot, please refrain from interrupting. I put the dye in Frank's experiments. It was dishonest and I fully understand the consequences. I will withdraw from the laboratory and the university."

Professor Whitman was aghast. "But why, my dear boy, why?"

"He's lying." I stamped my foot. I couldn't help it. Things were bad, but nowhere near as bad as he was assuming. He was throwing his whole life away at that moment. Little as I liked what he'd done, I couldn't stand by and let him do it. "He's just trying to protect Clara. He thinks she did it."

Whitman slowly turned, glaring at me from under his bushy white eyebrows. "Would you explain? Miss Cabot, is it?"

"Yes, sir." I motioned sharply to Sinclair Bickford to be quiet, and he sank into his chair, putting his face in his hands. "Mr. Bickford has just admitted that my friend, Clara Shea, told him she was going to sabotage Frank Lillie's experiment. She wanted to make up to him for the stain on his reputation caused by her admission to the sheriff yesterday—she admitted that she and Mr. Bickford had a romantic attachment and that Mr. McElroy knew of it and threatened to make it public. Clara was with me at the inn today, but when we went to hear the sheriff interrogate the two sailors, she slipped off. Mr. Bickford was back at the inn with his fiancée. My brother and I found Clara coming out of the laboratory, but then she ran away. Clara must have come here and done the damage to Frank Lillie's specimens. She intended to help Mr. Bickford succeed over him."

There was a sour taste of bile in my mouth after this speech. My friend Clara had disappointed me so deeply. But at least I couldn't let all her plans come to naught. If she was intent on destroying herself, at least her actions should damage others as little as possible. It was impossible to believe that the Clara I knew could act as she was. I finally realized how little I really knew her.

"But it *is* my fault," Sinclair insisted. "It *is* all my doing."

"This is thoroughly regrettable," the white-haired professor sighed. But he patted Sinclair on the shoulder. "Very regrettable. But we cannot succumb to mutual suspicion. That would destroy this place and everything we have done to establish it. We cannot let that happen. If Miss Shea has suffered a breakdown of some sort, we must strive to understand and forgive her. But at least we can know the integrity of the work has not been breached."

Integrity of the work! What of Clara's work? I thought. It seemed that Whitman saw only Sinclair Bickford as one of his researchers. Yet it was Clara's discovery that had been crucial to Bickford's work that summer. To Whitman, Clara Shea was little more than an appendage, an instrument that had broken or gotten out of alignment. The work he so prized could go on with the help of the other men. As long as that was true, Whitman would be satisfied.

"Is anything wrong?" It was Cornelia Clapp sticking her head into the room.

"Nothing of significance," Professor Whitman answered. "What are you doing here?"

She frowned. "I brought over Mr. Dunbar, the boat builder. I asked him to look at the pipe fittings—the ones that went and ruined Frank's experiments the last time. You remember that?" She seemed testy. "Wouldn't want a repeat, after all that's happened."

"Certainly not, certainly not." Whitman waved her on. Meanwhile, Sinclair kept his head down. When Cornelia left there was an uncomfortable silence. *Oh, Clara, what have you done?* I asked myself. *How could you do it?* I couldn't hate Sinclair—he was, after all, a sincere young man and I knew that Clara could be overwhelming. But what a mistake. To think in the end he would prefer her to the sweet and pliable Louisa. What a mistake for Clara.

Professor Whitman murmured something and followed Cornelia out, checking on the integrity of the pipes, no doubt. I felt weak in the aftermath of what I'd said. I'd betrayed my friend and, despite my anger at her, I felt awful about it. Sinclair Bickford sat despondent with his head in his hands. I felt Stephen come up behind me, putting his hands on my waist, but I pulled away, turning to face him. He beckoned me out into the darkening hallway.

"She's gone, Emily. She's not here. Do you want me to take you back to the inn?"

"Or what? There is something else you want to do?"

He looked beyond me at Sinclair Bickford. "There's something I thought of, something I'd like to check on."

He wasn't going to explain, that was clear. In any case, I wanted to be alone. I felt empty inside after what I'd said about Clara. I didn't want to discuss it further. "It's all right, I'll go back. I want to see that everything is ready for the funeral tomorrow. Poor Mrs. Gibbs still needs help."

NINETEEN

"ell, I don't care what he says. I don't believe she did it." Jane Topham was busy slicing a cake and laying the pieces out on a plate. It was the day of the funeral and I'd stayed behind with her to prepare for the mourners to return. Many of the local women brought food and we were laying it out buffet style in the dining room, preparing for an influx after the service. It brought back fresh memories of my mother's passing. It had been only the previous spring that we'd lost her forever, and I was sad to be reminded of it. But Jane was her normal cheery self, even making excuses for Clara. "About the dye in the experiments, of course I don't know about that. I have nothing to do with the laboratory and all of that, but for the fire here, why should they believe Clara set that? Why, perhaps it was that little Miss Reynolds herself. Could be she wanted the attention. You see how all the men want to protect her, poor little thing." She wagged a finger at me over the crumb cake she was slicing. "I've seen that type before. They seem so helpless, but somehow they get things to happen. Why did she come? Because her fiancé wasn't making time for her, isn't that so? She comes, she sees that he has an assistant who's a striking beauty, what can she do? How can she draw all the attention away to herself? Well, what about a little fire? Hmm? I'm telling you, I've seen that kind of woman before. I wouldn't be surprised if she set the fire herself just to get all that attention." She stopped her work and looked me in the eye. "You'd be amazed what you see as a nurse. Some of the families I've attended. You see all sorts of things about human nature and a lot of it is not pretty."

She returned to her work and I continued sorting through some laundered napkins, rolling them and placing them into round holders. I wanted to believe Clara was innocent. I still felt awful about telling Professor Whitman it was Clara—not Sinclair—who had ruined Frank Lillie's experiment. But I couldn't stand there and let him lie about it, when he had just told me he was with Louisa while Clara was at the laboratory. I shook myself. "But what about the other fires? Louisa wasn't here for those."

She snorted. "Children. Just like everyone thought. In fact, I wouldn't be at all surprised if it wasn't that Billy Gordon who set them. You know bad blood shows in the end. And there's a history there, in the Davis family—the grandfather, you know." She shook her head. "There's something very queer there. They keep the child away from his grandfather, have you noticed that? Don't you forget he's the one who thought it was all right for Freeman to stab his little daughter to death. Oh, yes, they keep the young ones away from the old man. They don't say it, but all the time they're afraid he'll snap like Freeman did. Ah, here they come. It must have been a short service." She wiped her hands on her apron and I took the plate out to fill the last spot on the buffet. Buggies were pulling up to the front and we opened the door to let the mourners in.

It was another warm day, but the salt breezes flowed through the old house as we had opened all of the windows. Everyone had done a good job the day before, so all was clean and even the upstairs bedrooms were usable, except for the one Louisa Reynolds had abandoned. Mr. Elliott and Mr. Dunbar had finished making the repairs, but the furniture for that room was ruined. The first floor was fine, with the newly washed lace curtains swaying in the breeze.

Soon the downstairs rooms were full of people. Minnie Gibbs and her father were settled on the sofa in the main room and people murmured their condolences as they stopped to talk to them. Jane whispered that the man standing behind Minnie was Henry Gordon, the dead woman's husband, come from Chicago. Billy was placed on a stool at his aunt's feet. It made me uneasy to see how close he was to the old man. There was something disturbing about Alfred Davis. Jane filled a plate with sweets and placed it in the little boy's hands. That seemed to occupy him. The two of us retreated to the kitchen as the rooms began to fill up.

I was replenishing a pitcher of lemonade when Mr. Gordon came back to the kitchen. He was a tall man, with straggly dark hair, and a full beard and moustache. I thought he must be about forty years of age. He frowned at Jane Topham and nodded to the doorway as if he wanted a word with her. I left with the pitcher, wanting to give them some privacy. When I came back, they had retreated to the entryway, but I could still hear their raised voices. I couldn't tell what they were saying and I didn't want to eavesdrop, so I turned to leave. Just at that moment they returned to the kitchen, and Mr. Gordon stalked by me rudely, heading for the front room. Meanwhile, Jane was red-faced and upset. She poured herself a glass of water.

Just as I was going to ask if she needed anything, Cornelia Clapp came down the back staircase, in an old skirt and a ratty straw hat. I wondered if she'd heard the disturbance. She, too, seemed to be in a bad mood.

"I'm going out hunting with Frank," she told us. "He needs fresh specimens if he's to redo his experiments. Please give my regards to Mrs. Gibbs. I'm sorry not to stay for the meal, but this is really quite important."

"Oh dear, let me pack a lunch for you to take along," Jane Topham fussed. "There is so much food—everyone brought something, you know. I'm sure Minnie would want you to have some."

Cornelia glared at her. "No, thank you. We'll be fine. We're taking one of the dinghies. We won't be out late." She left the house, slamming the back door behind her.

"Well, so much for that. Excuse me for offering!" Jane said, wiping sweat from her face. "She really can be very rude sometimes, but that's true of so many of the laboratory people. Perhaps I shouldn't say that to you, but it is true."

"I think she's just distracted." I didn't know why I needed to make excuses for Cornelia Clapp—perhaps because I fell into the category of bug hunters with her.

"Everyone's on edge. This weather's very hot. Almost like the calm before a storm. I'm certain you must think Mr. Gordon very strange as well." Her slightly protruding eyes stared at me.

"I'm sure he must be very upset by the death of his wife...it was so sudden."

"That's true. I nursed her, you know. You'd think he'd be grateful for that, but he has gotten it into his head that somehow his father-in-law was responsible."

"Mr. Davis?"

"Yes. Of course the old man's not right in the head. We all know that, but it's always been the case. I don't know if you've heard the story? I can see you've heard something. Old Mr. Davis was very friendly with that dreadful man, Freeman. That man was a preacher, would you believe it? And Davis was one of his most faithful followers. Freeman killed his little four-year-old daughter, Edith. Well, they locked him up in an asylum, you know. And Mr. Alfred Davis—he proclaimed to everybody that it was the will of God and Freeman was God's prophet and everything he did was right and just. Well, after that, they locked Alfred Davis up, too.

"As it happened, I was working at that asylum at the time. It was many years ago, but that's how I got to know them. Well, Mr. Davis was released with a severe admonition—I helped to get him out. He was just a follower, don't you know. He wouldn't hurt a fly. And the one who did it—that man Freeman—some five years later they proclaimed him cured and released him. It was all very tragic. That poor little girl. So you can see there's a bad history there. That's why they don't like to leave him alone with the children, don't you know.

"But Mr. Gordon, he wants me to say that Mr. Davis harmed his own daughter, Gordon's wife that is." She looked so distressed I went to her and made her sit down. "Of course, it's nothing like that. I mean, I wondered if perhaps she had developed the same thing that killed her mother, something contagious. That's always a possibility, some germ that was passed on. I was very careful when I nursed her, because I was afraid of that, don't you know. That's one reason I wanted to keep the boy away from her. Just in case. So I thought it was a natural death—tragic, but natural—and that's what I told him. I often think if I had only seen the mother when she was in Boston, I might have been able to nurse her back to health." She shook her head. "But Mr. Gordon wouldn't hear of contagion as a cause of it all—that she might have gotten something from her mother. He got quite angry. I'm afraid he'll blame the old man. He thinks the old man caused her death, but I was with her the whole time. She was ill. It's as if he believes the man had some special powers, to be able to call down a plague on her or something. He's wild not to have the old man touch his son. I'm not saying there isn't any reason for that, with the story from the past and all. But people can be so superstitious. It's hard to believe. There now, thanks for that." I'd made a cup of tea and set it down on a small table beside her. She sipped it and nibbled on a piece of cake.

"They certainly do seem to be having a very hard time in that family, with Mrs. Davis passing away, and then the fire and Mrs. Gordon," I said. "There's been so much going on at the laboratory, we perhaps don't realize the tragedy of it for them." I was thinking of my own preoccupation with Clara's fate.

She rocked a little in the chair. "Yes, not being a part of it, I see most of that drama from the outside. There was something going on about your friend, Miss Shea, and that Mr. Bickford, wasn't there? And then, of course, his fiancée showing up like that. And did I hear they found more ruined experiments and are calling it sabotage?" She seemed to have recovered from her exchange with Mr. Gordon, and was once again trolling for gossip. I didn't want to encourage her in that. "You don't want to talk about it, I can see that. But, of course, even *I* know about the expectation that someone will succeed Professor Whitman as head of the laboratory, and that Mr. Lillie and Mr. Bickford are the obvious choices. But you have to wonder about that Miss Clapp. I mean, after all the years she's spent here and all her effort, to be passed over for a couple of younger ones just because they're men. It must be galling and then of course there is her attachment to Mr. Bickford. She must be sorry to see him slip away."

"*Her* attachment?" I couldn't help myself. Even if I didn't want to encourage Jane's gossip, this was new and I wanted to know what she meant.

"Oh, well, in former years, don't you know. She took him under her wing, really got him started. Oh, yes, they used to go around together quite a lot last year and the year before. But this year he has his own laboratory, so I heard, and it's bigger than hers. And he has Miss Shea going around collecting specimens, or whatever it is they do when they go off wading. And Miss Clapp was left on her own. And then he and Mr. Lillie being in line to succeed Professor Whitman. It must be disappointing for her, don't you think? I should think having the very elegant Miss Reynolds show up must have been just the last straw, as far as Cornelia was concerned."

She stopped rocking and leaned forward, making sure she had captured my attention. "That's another type you see, don't you know. The aging spinster, being passed over as it were. They can be very vindictive in a sly way. Tenderness turned to spite. I've seen it happen. There was one woman, sister to one of my patients. He was not getting better and, do you know, I finally discovered she'd been watering down his medicine, purposely. Well, I had a word with the family physician and he sent her away and the man was finally able to recover, but you see what I mean. When I heard of this sabotage business, I couldn't help thinking of that. I'm not saying it was Miss Clapp, but I did wonder." She nodded to herself and began rocking again, back and forth.

She nearly had me convinced, but I remembered how we'd found Clara coming out of the Main, hanging on to the railing and trying to fight back tears. I doubted it was Cornelia Clapp who had damaged Lillie's experiment. As much as I didn't want to believe it, I knew it was Clara. But that was not something I wanted to share with Jane Topham. Discretion was not in her nature. I excused myself, saying I would check the buffet table to see if anything needed replenishing.

The rooms were filled with people wearing the dark clothes of mourning, everyone speaking in hushed voices. When I looked across to where the family sat, I was a little shocked to see that Nellie Bly had settled herself beside Mr. Davis on the sofa. She was offering him a plate of sweets while attentively listening to him. There was a strange glistening in his eyes. I wondered if she had discovered a sweet tooth in the old man, and I wondered even more why she was paying him such attention.

I consolidated some of the cakes onto a single platter and returned to the kitchen with two plates that needed refilling. There was certainly plenty of the food left, since so many people had brought contributions. I found myself followed by Miss Edna Thurston. The woman who had worried so much about getting Mr. McElroy's body shipped to his mother in Boston was attending yet another funeral.

"Pardon me," she said. "I just wanted a word with you, Miss Cabot."

"Certainly, and this is Miss Topham, Miss Thurston. Are you acquainted?" I asked, making the required introductions.

Jane started to say no, but Miss Thurston got ahead of her. "Not directly, but I believe you knew Mr. Lincoln McElroy. I remember him saying he saw you in Boston last June. He knew you from summers down here, of course. Poor Lincoln." She sniffed into a lavender-scented handkerchief.

"Why, now that you mention it, of course I knew Mr. McElroy. We were all so sorry to hear of his passing."

"I just wanted to tell Miss Cabot," Miss Thurston turned to me, "how grateful we are for the help of Dr. Chapman. Cornelia was able to tell me when his mother could have his body." She sniffed again. "I'll go up tomorrow, on the train. And he, Lincoln, will go with me. His mother will be able to have the service. We're very grateful."

"Oh, certainly. Dr. Chapman will be glad to know it's all worked out," I said. She looked like she was ready to break down. Jane came to the rescue.

"Now, here you go, Miss Thurston. You just sit down here and have a cup of tea. It's a hard time for all of us. I'm used to it, don't you know. Being a nurse you see a lot of death, but for you it's a shock. Here you go."

I was able to drift into my own thoughts as Jane once again took on her role as nurse and coaxed Edna Thurston to have a cup of tea and a slice of cake, talking all the while. Eventually the Boston woman hauled herself up and left us. Jane turned to me. "We forget. That's another death. It's not just the Davis family, is it? Now, I just wonder if he had somehow gotten the same sickness. Do you think that's possible?"

I vaguely recalled Miss Thurston mentioning that Lincoln McElroy had also seen Mrs. Davis in Boston in June, or perhaps it was Jane herself who'd said that. I had not really been paying much attention to that part of their conversation. Jane seemed to think that Mrs. Davis, Mrs. Gordon, and Mr. McElroy had all fallen to illness. It would be so much better if some mysterious disease was found to be the cause of the tragedies, but I already knew it wasn't so. Perhaps I should have been more discreet, but she was a nurse—I felt she should know. So I told her they'd discovered arsenic in Mr. McElroy.

"Oh dear," Jane Topham said. "That's certainly something very different. My goodness gracious, what can we think of that?" She put her hand to her mouth and I saw her looking over my shoulder.

When I turned, I found myself facing Louisa Reynolds. She said in her soft voice, "Emily, I wonder, could I talk to you privately? Could we go for a walk?"

TWENTY

I followed Louisa Reynolds out the back door. I wasn't sure what she wished to discuss, but I was instinctively uncomfortable. What did she have to say to me that required privacy? I was afraid it must concern Clara.

"We could go down to the water," she murmured, striding ahead of me down the street towards the docks in front of the U.S. Fisheries building. I followed more slowly, sensing that neither of us was looking forward to the conversation. She moved awkwardly in the black serge dress I had lent her for the funeral. Seeing how the big puffy sleeves and broad shoulders overwhelmed her small body, I felt a little guilty. When she asked for my help in finding something appropriate to wear, I chose my least favorite dress to lend her. But she took it with thanks, and cinched in the waist with a broad piece of black taffeta. She looked swallowed up in the oversized dress and it dragged on the ground, even as she tried to hold it up. I could have offered something less cumbersome.

When we reached a wooden bench overlooking the harbor, she paused but then paced back and forth again before speaking. I remained standing, as if to preserve the option of walking away if necessary.

Finally she stopped pacing and faced me, rolling up the veiling that covered her face. "It's about Clara. Sinclair told me some things this morning. Some very hurtful things."

I shifted uncomfortably. She should be having this conversation with Clara, not me. I was not in a position to defend my friend. Not from Louisa. I believed Clara had wronged her. I avoided her eyes, looking out at the placid water.

"Emily, I know that I am no beauty, especially not compared to Clara Shea. She has always been so vibrant, so brilliant, really. I've always admired her. She's so intelligent and so beautiful." There was nothing to say to that, it was true. "But how could she do this to me? I would never have believed it of her." Her voice rasped with anger and she paced back and forth a few times to quell her emotions before she spoke again.

"Sinclair and I became acquainted because he is a friend of my brother's. I have always admired him. He is so devoted to his work. But I don't understand it, not the way you and Clara do." I shook my head. I was no more a scientist than she was, but she needed to continue. "I do so value him and his friends and what they are doing. So does my brother. Like Mr. Elliott says, this is a time of great invention and discovery. The world is opening up to men like Sinclair, and Frank Lillie, and Professor Whitman. We're on the threshold of so much that is new and it is terribly, terribly important. Sinclair knows how much I admire his work, and we have been so happy planning our future together."

She stopped to take a breath, turning a little to look out at the water. The sunlight reflected fiercely off the surface, forcing her to squint. "Sinclair told me that he and Clara worked together this summer, and that they became close." She blushed. "He says they were carried away by their feelings, that they regretted it immediately—it was a madness, a form of summer madness." She paced away again like a caged lioness. "Oh, why did I stay in Newport when he didn't come? I should have known."

It took her a moment to compose herself. "He told me how sorry he is, how much he regrets it. How he knows it hurt me. He was wild. He didn't want me to hear about it from anyone else." She heaved a big sigh. "It's such a shame." She hiccupped, obviously gulping back a sob. Her gloveless hands were clasped together so tightly the knuckles were white.

I looked away. I would have given anything to be somewhere else. I could see that she was deeply hurt by this betrayal and, once again, I couldn't stop myself from blaming my very dear friend Clara. How could she do it? She'd known they were engaged.

"I'm so sorry, Louisa. I wish it wasn't so. It was very wrong of them."

She glanced at me with tears in her eyes. "Perhaps it was not so wrong. Perhaps after all they would be right together. I don't have Clara's dedication, you know. I cannot work in the laboratories with him. I cannot do that. And, Lord knows I can do nothing about her beauty," she said bitterly. "But, Emily, is it true that, for his sake, Clara destroyed Frank Lillie's work? That's what I need to know. It must be madness indeed for her to do such a thing. Did she really do that?" Now she was facing me, scanning my face relentlessly. I felt so ashamed for my friend. "And you told Professor Whitman of this, is that true?"

"Sinclair told you all this? Was that what he went to tell you yesterday afternoon?"

"Yesterday? No, not then. This morning. Before the funeral. He took me aside. He wanted to tell me before someone else did. I think he was afraid you might speak to me about it."

"No. I never would do that. I'm so sorry, Louisa. I don't know how Clara could do such a thing, but it *is* true. She admitted the attachment."

"Before Professor Whitman? Why would she do that, Emily?"

"Because Sinclair might have been accused of harming Mr. McElroy, Louisa. That's why she told the sheriff about their liaison. Sinclair would not admit it himself, so Clara felt obliged to tell the sheriff, so he would not believe something worse. Mr. McElroy had seen them together and threatened to reveal it." It was all so very dreary and petty. But not so petty to Louisa Reynolds, who'd planned to marry Bickford. What a mess.

"But Emily, did Clara really destroy Frank's work? Why would she do that?"

"Oh, Louisa. I'm very afraid that she did. Apparently she wanted to make up to Sinclair for having revealed their attachment to Professor Whitman. She told him she would. She wanted to make up for the damage to his career, because he's considered to be in contention with Mr. Lillie for the directorship."

"But how could she do that to Frank? He'd done nothing to her."

"I know. As you said, it is madness. But my brother and I saw her coming out of the laboratory building right before they discovered the sabotage, Louisa. And she was very upset. I can only think that she did it and then she left. I'm sure it was her way of trying to repair the damage to Sinclair's career. You see, he did not want to give you up, Louisa." I felt the admission being wrung from me. I hated to say these things about Clara, but Louisa needed to know that even if she was betrayed, they had not purposely hurt her. "He had no intention of giving you up for Clara. He told her so."

"Oh, Emily. That's what he told me." She sat down on the bench, leaning forward to put her face in her hands. "What am I to do? Should I forgive him? I think, perhaps, if I were to forgive him, the professor and the university might overlook such a transgression. He believes that. But what if he truly loves Clara? He tells me it's not so, that it was a temporary madness. What am I to believe? I do love him. I gave him my whole heart. He says if I *don't* forgive him, his career must be over for sure. Everyone will know that something happened. And surely it would do harm to Clara as well. Must they suffer for the rest of their lives for a weakness of a single summer, Emily? Must I? I had so many plans. What will I tell my brother? He'll be so disappointed. That's the dilemma. Should I forgive them? Must I be the one to sacrifice my pride by overlooking their frailty? And if I don't, what will people think of me? What will I think of myself? I will have destroyed their lives, I suppose. I don't know what to do."

At that moment I wished that Clara had remained in Chicago

for the summer and never come to the laboratory. What a dreadful end to her studies, to all her dreams—and for what? I had no advice for Louisa Reynolds.

"But there is something I truly cannot understand in all of this." She looked up at me. "That Clara might have thought she could somehow repair Sinclair's career by sabotaging Frank Lillie's work I find hard to believe. But now she's run away, and that seems to confirm it. Even if she did that, surely Clara Shea wouldn't poison a man? She would never actually kill a man, no matter how much in love she believed herself, would she?" She stared at me.

"Who suggested that—Sinclair?"

"No, it was Mr. Elliott. He said the sheriff has men hunting for Clara in Chicago and Kentucky, everywhere. He said it wasn't for damaging Frank Lillie's experiment, it was for poisoning the man they found in the tank. He told me that at the inn after the funeral. That was when I knew I had to speak to you. Clara wouldn't do that, would she, Emily?"

I looked at her and realized the enormity of what she was saying. Could Clara have poisoned Lincoln McElroy? I could see her, even picture her, pouring dye on Lillie's experiments in a burst of passionate feeling. But to poison the stuffy little friend of Edna Thurston? "Of course not," I said. "Never. She would never do that. They're all wrong about that. That's not why she left. Never."

TWENTY-ONE

This Sinclair Bickford seems to be very adept at handling you women!" Alden said, as he kicked at the sand and glared at me. It was late in the day. He'd delivered a message from Stephen, who wanted to meet us at the small beach where we'd been the evening before. While we waited I caught Alden up on events. He appeared to want to blame Sinclair for Clara's disappearance. "First, he gets you to tell Whitman that Clara sabotaged Lillie's experiment, then he gets his fiancée—who he's cheated on—to feel guilty that she'll ruin his career if she breaks off the engagement. Pretty slick, that."

"What did you want me to do, let him take the blame for Lillie's experiment, when he'd just told me she planned to do it? Besides, you saw Clara when she came out of the building—you saw how upset she was, and then she disappeared. What do you think happened? It's just the sort of thing she would do. It ruins her own life, but does something towards helping him. Just knowing she would be wild enough to do such a thing is enough to gain him sympathy from others."

"Right, poor guy is the victim of a hysterical woman. He's a cheat and a liar, Emily. And just because she left doesn't mean she did the deed."

"Oh, Alden, I know you don't want to believe it. I wish Clara had never come here. I wish she'd stayed in Chicago. I wish we all had."

"I'm telling you, Emily, don't assume just because she ran away it's an admission of anything. Why, she *had* to get out of here. That sheriff has it in for her. You don't really think she had anything to do with McElroy's death, do you?"

"No, of course not. I realized that when I was talking to Louisa. I *could* believe she would put dye in Lillie's experiments, even if you don't. But to poison a man. No, she would *not* do that."

"But Redding thinks she did it. He's got men out looking for her in Chicago and Kentucky. He's convinced she did it to protect that idiot Bickford. That's why Bickford had to tell his fiancée about it. He knew it could be made public at any moment because Redding wants to arrest her for murder. Do you hear me, Emily? *Murder.*"

Stephen joined us and I ran to embrace him. Alden stood with his arms crossed waiting impatiently for our greeting to end. Stephen had news.

"Mrs. Gordon was also poisoned."

"What? How can you know that?" I was shocked, to say the least.

He motioned to us to sit on the sand beside him. "When I left you last night, I went to the funeral home. I had no right, but I've been working with the local medical examiner and the sheriff. I made an excuse, saying it was a test for public health reasons. I took samples. I've sent some of them to Harvard for analysis, but I did my own tests last night." He looked like he'd had little sleep. I longed to find some peaceful place where we could be together. "I was looking for arsenic and I found it."

"We need to tell the sheriff," I exclaimed.

"No. I can't do that," he said. "What I did was not legal. We need to find out who is doing this. If we found evidence, we could have the body exhumed and we would still find the same thing but, until we know, we'd better proceed with caution. At this point Sheriff Redding is convinced the arsenic came from the laboratory here. In fact, he's sure Clara poisoned McElroy. He'll find a reason for her to have poisoned Mrs. Gordon as well, unless we can find out who really did it. To tell him now would only get me into trouble, and not help Clara." I felt fear at that. It was bad enough to have the sheriff after Clara, but I needed to be sure Stephen was safe.

"Who would want Mrs. Gordon dead? Who was she, anyhow?" Alden asked.

I remembered Jane Topham's argument with Mr. Gordon and told them about how the dead woman's husband suspected his father-in-law.

"He's a strange one," Alden said. "Nellie's interested in his story. He's been in the loony bin. You know she spent time in an insane asylum, investigating conditions. She says the kind of strength some of these loonies have is unbelievable. She thinks he might have a connection to the men who stole the gold and silver from the *Missouri*."

"But even if there was some reason for this man, Alfred Davis, to poison his own married daughter, what connection is there to Lincoln McElroy?" Stephen protested. "He had nothing to do with that family, did he?"

"Wait, Jane said something else. She said she saw McElroy with *Mrs.* Davis in Boston. She was Alfred Davis's wife and Mrs. Gordon's mother." I hadn't been paying close attention when Jane was talking to Edna Thurston, but I knew there had been a mention of some chance meeting. "Mrs. Davis also died earlier this summer. Maybe he's eliminating his own family."

"Why?" Alden asked.

"He's mad," I pointed out. "He was connected to a case a long time ago when a man named Freeman killed his own four-year-old daughter because he heard the voice of God telling him to do it. Maybe Alfred Davis thinks he's doing God's will. He defended Freeman back then. Jane Topham told me they're afraid to let him near the children."

My brother snorted. "Voices from God. I bet it has more to do with money from heaven. Maybe he thinks he had a divine mission to find that treasure that was pilfered from that sinking boat. I'll bet it comes down to that."

"I wish Clara hadn't run away," I confessed, and Stephen put an arm around my shoulders.

Alden grunted. "Why? If she'd stayed, Redding would've arrested her and stopped looking for the real killer."

"You don't know that."

"Yes, I do. He has a warrant. I saw it."

At that moment I heard a fall of pebbles and turned to see a figure picking her way across the stones to the sand where we sat. "Alden," I said in warning.

"It's Nellie. She must have seen us leave."

Sure enough, it was the newspaper reporter. She was dressed in a black suit for the funeral, accented with a creamy white cravat. Perched on the side of her head was a flat straw hat adorned with ·a fantastic bouquet of black and white satin roses. The suit was pinched in at the waist to show her stylish hourglass figure. As she searched around for a dry stretch of sand on which to sit, it occurred to me that she wore her fashions like someone who had worked hard to afford them, in contrast to the academic women of the laboratory, who mostly came from wealthy homes, but wore their oldest and least fashionable clothes at the summer sessions. They did it in the most offhand manner, while Nellie Bly's trim figure looked like it was the result of a concentrated effort to impress. From what I'd heard of her past, she worked hard to afford to dress fashionably while she supported not only herself, but her family.

"There we are," she said as she sat down, carefully gathering her skirts about her. "I've come to report and find out what you've learned, Mr. Cabot."

"The sheriff is looking all over for Clara Shea. That's what we've just been saying."

"True. But that's not his only interest. He's also gathered all the local men and sent them out looking for the missing treasure. But say, I've found out something interesting. Did you know," she paused as she pulled a small notebook from the string bag in her lap, "a Mr. Clifford Dunham is originally from Falmouth? That's one of the men who came in off the boat with the money. He's not the one who's brother to the captain on trial in Boston, it's the other one. He's from here. The locals know him. In fact, he's known to the Davises at the Snow Goose Inn. Now I find that interesting, don't you?" She beamed at us. "You don't understand, do you? Well now, I heard some stories about Mr. Alfred Davis."

"I saw you talking to him after the funeral," I said.

"That's right. They say he's not right in the head. And I heard the story about that man Freeman who stabbed his own little daughter to death, and then how this Alfred Davis proclaimed him right to do it. That's one dramatic scene when you think of it. They say Alfred Davis was put in the asylum along with the man who did the deed. They got him out soon enough, got him to take back what he said. But did you know they even let that Freeman go? Of course it was years later, but they proclaimed him cured and let him out. He's dead now, but you have to wonder, when bodies start appearing and there's that kind of history. You know what I mean."

"You mean you think Alfred Davis is responsible for the death of McElroy, the man they found in the tank of water?" Alden asked.

"But he was poisoned," I pointed out. Stephen squeezed my shoulder.

"True," Nellie said, looking at us with speculation. It made me aware of Stephen's arm around my shoulder, but it was too late, and besides, I was pretty sure Alden had already shared our secret with the reporter. "But still, you have to wonder. There's a dead man, and then there's a missing treasure, and there's a man who everybody assumes is deranged. That's why I wanted to talk to him. I spent time in an asylum once, did you know that? I was investigating conditions. I got to talk to quite a few women who really were out of their minds."

"So what did you find out? Is he crazy?" Alden demanded.

"Hard to say. Spent most of the time quoting from his Bible. Had to read from it, though. Not like he had it memorized. I'd say it's possible. I tried to ask him about the man Dunham. But he wouldn't admit he knew him. Kept pretending like he didn't understand the question. Still, I have it from a few of the men in town that they knew each other. So maybe he knew about the treasure, maybe that's why they came to the inn to try to get a room. Maybe they were really looking for the old man. Doesn't make any connection with the man who died at the laboratory, though. Seems like his death had something to do with a controversy about a vote on who would run the place. No connection to Davis. Still, it's pretty strange. Did you know the old man's wife died in June and now the daughter! She came from Chicago for her mother's funeral and stayed on. *And then she dies.* If it weren't some kind of disease they died from, we could ask if he was getting the kind of messages from above that his friend Freeman claimed when he killed his little girl. That would make quite a story."

I exchanged a look with my brother. I couldn't help wishing Nellie could get the sheriff to look beyond Clara, and at the Davises, for a murderer. I could see that Alden was having the same thought.

"You know, you may have something there," he said. "My sister was just telling us that the dead man, McElroy, was seen in Boston with the mother, Mrs. Davis, before she died. So maybe there *is* a connection we don't know about."

Nellie looked happy at the thought. "Now, that would be something, wouldn't it? A madman, a hidden treasure, and the gruesome death of a man in a tank of fish!"

TWENTY-TWO

ellie and Alden insisted that I take them back to the inn so they could interrogate Jane Topham about her sighting of Mr. McElroy with Mrs. Davis in Boston. She looked confused by the sudden interest, and when she caught on to the fact that they might be thinking Alfred Davis was somehow involved with the men from the boat, she scoffed at the idea.

"Nonsense. That old man is just senile. And it's the children they want to keep from him, not a man in the prime of life like Mr. McElroy. The person you should really talk to is Cornelia Clapp. If anyone saw that McElroy man away from Woods Hole, it would be her. Why, I believe I heard them arguing about that vote they were going to take. He sounded mad."

Nellie was unimpressed. She seemed much less interested in a story based on the politics of the laboratory than in a more lurid tale that could include a reference to Alfred Davis's past. She soon dragged Alden off to Falmouth to find out whether the missing treasure had been located. I stayed behind to help Jane finish cleaning up after the funeral buffet.

I was grateful to have the newspaper reporters deflected away from Clara as a topic. I knew Alden could go a long way towards making sure Nellie and others were following local tales of treasure and scandal. But, the fact that the sheriff had issued a warrant for Clara's arrest weighed on my mind. Alden knew that, but apparently he'd kept it from Nellie. It was enough to worry me.

And then there was the attitude of the other researchers. I didn't know most of them, as I had come so late in the season and only a few were from Chicago. But the warmth they had formerly shown me had turned very chilly since news of Clara's guilt in sabotaging Frank Lillie's experiments had leaked out. They weren't rude by any measure, but they tended to scatter at my approach like minnows.

Only Cornelia Clapp made a point of seeking me out when I went to breakfast at the Mess the next morning. Amazingly enough, right after she sat down next to me at the round table with the oilcloth cover, she was joined by none other than Frank Lillie. He nodded briefly in my direction and then monopolized her. Apparently, he needed her assistance in gathering more specimens in the afternoon. They agreed on a time to meet and he left as abruptly as he'd arrived.

Cornelia shook her head. "More *Unio*. They're the freshwater mussel that's Frank's beastie of choice. You'd think at a marine laboratory he might have chosen a saltwater animal, but Whitman set him on the *Unio* a couple of years ago and he's got cumulative data to deal with."

I couldn't help feeling uncomfortable at the thought of his ruined work. I wanted to offer to help, but surely my affiliation with Clara would make that awkward. "Now that we're finished helping Mrs. Gibbs with the inn, I suppose I should go back to gathering specimens for Captain Veeder," I told her.

"I'm sure that would be appreciated."

"I wish I could do something about this mess," I confessed. The topic of Clara and her transgression was there but unspoken. I changed the subject. "Cornelia, someone said they heard you arguing with Mr. McElroy before he died. Is that true?"

She considered me over her plate of food. "Nosey Jane, no doubt. Yes, certainly he argued with me. Like Edna Thurston, he wanted me to vote with them and against Whitman and the rest. I told him—as I told Edna—that I did not agree with them."

Suddenly, the atmosphere in the room changed; there was a silence and then a rustle. Glancing up, I saw people looking at me and I realized that Sinclair Bickford and Louisa Reynolds had come in. With an obvious cringe, I watched him lead her to a table as far from us as possible. Once they sat down, the murmur of conversation resumed. I thought Cornelia would politely ignore the pause, but she didn't.

"You know, I think Miss Reynolds is quite right in her choices." She sensed my confusion. "She doesn't try to become a scientist, it is not her realm. She wants to be a wife and mother."

I could see Louisa across the room, Sinclair solicitously helping her, introducing her, going to get her a cup of coffee.

"She'll make a good home for him and keep to it. She won't insert herself into his laboratory. She'll only visit his office to make sure it's clean and comfortable. She may take some courses at the university where he teaches, but only as an additional ornament. She'll never compete with him. And it will be no sacrifice for her, she wouldn't want to. She'll have children to fill her time and require all of her attention. Not like you, and Clara Shea, or myself. I understand from Miss Talbot that Clara was quite impressive as a student of chemistry at the university."

"You know Miss Talbot?" Marion Talbot, Dean of Women at the University of Chicago, had come from Wellesley College outside of Boston. She was my own best mentor and had helped me to achieve a lectureship for the coming session.

"Certainly. There's a strong network of women academics, you know. We keep each other apprised of advances for all of us. I have been corresponding with Marion for my own part. Professor Whitman has offered me the opportunity to work on a doctorate at the University of Chicago."

"That would be wonderful. But don't you...I thought you already had a doctorate?"

"From Syracuse University, yes. It's from several years ago, though, and the field has changed. Also, I've heard that the facilities at the University of Chicago are greatly advanced and, of course, there's the opportunity to work with Professor Whitman."

It was true. Many of the businessmen of Chicago were funding buildings and facilities that were the envy of older institutions. That was what had drawn Stephen, and many others, to the new university. But Cornelia was older than most of us. I couldn't help asking her how she felt about that. "It doesn't seem fair, though. You've already studied so much and done so much. You shouldn't have to prove yourself yet again, should you?"

She raised her eyebrows at that. "You think it a punishment?" she asked. "Oh, no. It's an opportunity that I will relish. For one thing, it will provide connections and opportunities for me to use for my own students at Mount Holyoke once I return there. My own success at such an endeavor will make their future successes more likely, believe me. It is a cumulative process to prove definitively that we women are capable of doing the work, you know. Each generation will make it more obvious. But you must not think it is in any way a trial. Not at all. You have no idea how much I'll enjoy it.

"Why, I even enjoy going out tramping through the marshes looking for *Unio*. But that can wait until this afternoon." Finished with her meal, she folded up her napkin and rolled it to fit back into the round wooden holder with her initials. We each had one to identify our napkins. They were kept in a box with pigeonholes and laundered twice a week. She stood up. "I believe you planned to collect specimens for Captain Veeder? I have time this morning. Have you tried the outside of the neck? I thought not. Come along. I'll show you my special place. We all started off specimen hunting, you know, and we all have our favorite places."

Grateful for any help, I followed her out of the Mess.

TWENTY-THREE

We went back to the inn for pails, short handled shovels, and specimen nets. Soon we were tramping over the bridge to the arm of land that curved around to make the bay. She led me to an inlet on the outside edge.

With no one to watch us, we took off our shoes and stockings and tucked our skirts up to our waists. Cornelia pursued urchins and small fish with gusto, slapping through the ankle-deep water with great enjoyment, and wading out deeper as needed. When she had caught an especially slippery little specimen and dropped him in her pail, she stood up, stretching, with a smile on her face.

"Let me tell you a secret, Miss Cabot. Women like me, who have chosen to live the academic life, do not do so as a sacrifice. On the contrary—it is a release. I know the conventional wisdom is that a woman should do as Miss Reynolds seems to be doing—locate a man who can support her comfortably, so she's able to bear him children and make him a home. And don't think I believe those are not laudatory goals, I do indeed. Women such as Miss Reynolds and her like bear great responsibilities and care for entire families, while those such as myself and Miss Talbot do not. True, we must find ways to provide for ourselves but, by so doing, we leave behind the unending tasks and duties of always sacrificing and nurturing others, for the freedom to be able to enter the realm of knowledge. We are able to spend all of our time and care on the exploration of those questions of universal interest and importance, and even on the enjoyment of chasing down specimens on a fine summer day like today." She laughed.

"Sometimes I feel quite selfish. By not having a family to take care of, I have saved all my energies to do the work I love." She looked around and let out a sigh of pure contentment.

"You don't really comprehend the pursuits here, do you?" She squinted at me in the bright sunlight. "You see the microscopes and the chemicals, and you collect the marine life for specimens, but you don't know what it's all about, do you? This difference between the work of Mr. Bickford and Mr. Lillie, for instance, do you understand that? It's about what actually determines life."

Putting her hands on her hips she began to lecture. "You see, Mr. Bickford is elaborating on the work of some of the Germans who believe entirely in the impact of environment on growth. For them, any specimen put into the pail will react to the outside forces of heat, light, and cold. But Frank and I are working to show that there are predetermined structures that will grow, *despite* changes in energy, saturation, gravity, or any other forces. We believe each creature has a pattern, a map of instructions, hidden within them which guides their growth. The vital question is what causes life to grow as it does? That's what we're looking for in those tiny worlds expanded for our viewing by our microscopes.

"I cannot tell you how important I believe it is to search for those causes. We don't agree here, you know." She gestured back towards the laboratory buildings in the distance. "On the one hand, Jacques Loeb, who your Dr. Chapman is working with, believes chemical energy can cause the actual changes we witness through the lenses, while others, like me, don't believe that at all, and will search until they find the keys to what determines the final shape that grows from those tiny cells that split and differentiate until we have the life form we know. Only by sharing what we find by looking at so many different species, in so many different ways, can we eventually unlock these secrets that make us what we are and the world we live in."

She smiled, looking around again. "I know not everyone would care to spend their time sloshing through marshes to net small shellfish, and then spend hours and hours watching their cells under a microscope but, for those of us who do, it is wondrous." She raised her hands in an expansive gesture. She was quite a strange figure—knee deep in water, her skirts tucked up, and a ratty straw hat on her head—but she appeared eminently satisfied with her life. "That I cannot be kept from this world, merely because I am a woman, is marvelous to me and not a burden by any means. So, when I tell you I am glad that Miss Reynolds is content to stay in the parlor and not open the door to academia, it is because it leaves some of us—like you, and me, and Miss Clara Shea—free to do so. You must not expect me to sympathize if Miss Shea has lost Sinclair Bickford. I only mourn the fact that, in so doing, she has sacrificed her academic career, especially since Marion indicated it might have been an illustrious one. That I do regret. And I hope the accusations against her will be disproved."

I may have left my mouth gaping open at this eloquent defense of her choices, I cannot say. I do know that it made me realize there was a whole level of experience at the Marine Biological Laboratory that was beyond my understanding. Cornelia was not the only one so passionately involved in the proof or disproof of their beliefs. It occurred to me that it was a good thing Sheriff Redding was unlikely to comprehend the intensity of these researchers. The fact that he did not realize how passionate they were about their work didn't help Clara, but it didn't hurt the laboratory and the community they all valued so much.

Glancing at a small watch pinned to her blouse, Cornelia grunted and said she had to leave to meet Lillie. She left me her pail of specimens to deliver to Captain Veeder and waved goodbye. I was content to continue on alone but decided to move to an inlet on the other side where I had found success the previous week.

I had much to think about and the solitude of my task helped me. I thought a lot about what had happened since I'd come to Woods Hole, and I saw some patterns emerging. I was so intent on my own cogitations that I failed to actually collect any shellfish as I walked, and I nearly tripped in ankle-deep water on a pole half buried in the sand. I was going to ignore it, but something made me dig it out. On the end was a handkerchief, soggy and collapsed. A few feet away, a small rake was washing back and forth in the surf. I came out of my fog enough to realize what it meant. I had found the treasure. It was a small inlet, far from the sandbar where the sunken dinghy had been found. The men must have gotten very turned around in the night to have ended up here.

I crouched in the lapping waves and pondered what to do. I had an idea how I could use my discovery. I had to get Clara to return to clear her name, and I had a very good idea who would know where to find her.

TWENTY-FOUR

I found Sheriff Redding at the Mess the next morning, and he gestured at me with a fork over his plate of bacon, eggs, and hash browns. "What makes you think you can come in here and try to pull my leg like this, eh? If you know where that stash is, you're going to tell me and no tomfoolery, you understand?"

"It's just that she might not remember so well," said Alden, who'd come with me. Or, you could say, who I'd dragged along, unwillingly.

"Oh, I remember very well where it is, but I want your word that you'll allow Clara Shea to return without arresting her."

"Now see here, missy, you're not going to tell me what to do. If you know where your friend Miss Shea is you're obstructing justice and I'll have you in jail this very minute."

The conversation was not going as I intended, but I was determined. "Fine. Arrest me and I'll tell my brother here—who is a newspaper reporter, by the way—where that treasure is. How much of it do you think you'll recover once that gets out? How would you like that? I'll tell you, I'll tell everybody." I raised my voice and the room went quiet while everyone else listened.

That brought the angry little man to his feet. He came around the table and took me by the elbow—not very gently—and he led me out the door to the porch. "Now, you listen to me. If you do that I'll have you arrested and your brother, too. You know what a panic that would cause." He looked behind, glaring at people who tried to follow us out. "You all get back there. Get back inside."

There was a buggy in the road. The driver was holding the

reins and looking off towards the harbor. I'd made Alden rent the same one he'd used to take Clara away. It required much yelling and many threats, but I finally got him to admit he'd been the one to spirit her away. "Sheriff, it's my brother's fault that Clara went away. He convinced her to leave."

"I was only trying to help. You were going to arrest her. You're wrong. She would never poison that man. I don't believe she did anything to Lillie's experiments either."

"I'll have you both in jail." He jammed the wool cap on his head and started stomping towards the road. "Well, what are you waiting for? Where is she?"

"I'm afraid you'll have to come with us to bring her back," I said. The truth was, I was not sure I could convince her to return on my own and if I did convince her, I didn't trust the sheriff not to arrest her as soon as she stepped foot in Woods Hole. I reasoned he would have to make the promise not to arrest her to her face. "I'm not sure she will come back unless you come with us."

"Now you look here. I have police all over the country looking for that young woman. She'll be found. It's only a matter of time. It'll go better for her if she turns herself in."

"I know, but if it is important enough for you to have police in Chicago and Kentucky looking for her, surely you can come yourself to get her? Please, sheriff, if you come she'll have to return with us."

"Doggone it." He took off his hat and slapped it against his thigh. "I've got a hunt for missing gold going on here, and people from Boston wanting to know who killed this McElroy fella. I don't have time for this." He looked at my face and shook his head. "All right, all right. If it's the only way to do it, come on. You take me to Miss Shea. Now." He began stomping towards the waiting carriage.

I ran ahead of him and turned to face him. "You won't arrest her?"

"She'll come back here until we finish this investigation, then we'll arrest her when we have a full case. But she will come back here. Now, where's that stash?" He glared at me. I hesitated. "All right, now *you'll* go to jail instead of your friend." He started waving over a couple of his men who'd followed us and were lingering on the porch. "Get down here, you. Arrest these two."

"No, wait. Do you promise to not arrest her if we go and get her and bring her back?"

"I'm not promising anything. You tell me where that stash is. Get that map," he snapped at a deputy. The man unfolded a stained map of the area. I looked at Alden, but he didn't seem to have any great ideas.

"It's here, I think, let me see." I took the map away from the deputy and looked closely. "Yes, here. It's on the other side, away from the harbor. I was out looking for specimens yesterday, and I found it. There's a pole in the ground with a handkerchief tied to it."

Redding berated his men for having missed the spot and directed them to take a wagon and go dig up the treasure, in order to protect it from anyone else. Alden helped me into the buggy, but he hesitated, not wanting to go get Clara. I protested that she had to come back or her name would never be cleared. While we argued, Sheriff Redding suddenly jumped in opposite me. "Well, come on then, what are you waiting for? If you think I'm going to let you out of my sight until I have Miss Shea in custody, you are wrong. We're going to get Miss Shea. And we are going right now. Both of you. In the buggy. Now. Let's go."

Alden climbed up and sat beside me and we started out. It was only when we'd gone a few miles that he revealed to the sheriff where Clara was. It was going to be a long ride and it only seemed fair and wise to warn him.

"Newport, Rhode Island? You took her all the way to Newport, Rhode Island? Do you know how long it's gonna take to get there and back?"

Of course Alden did, since he'd done the trip a few days before, but that only made the sheriff more furious. He hunched down in the swaying carriage, mumbling dire things into his moustache. His wiry eyebrows quivered with indignation. Alden offered to go and retrieve Clara without the sheriff but he did not trust us and I was not at all sure we could make her return without the sheriff. Fuming at the prospect of an overnight trip, he merely growled at us. We rode in uncomfortable silence for several hours, then stopped at a road house for a rest and change of horses. When we remounted, the sheriff had taken the forward facing seat and Alden and I were forced to ride backwards. Redding reminded me of a kettle, roiling and roiling and getting ready to let off a head of steam in a shrieking whistle. I just hoped he would stay on a simmer until our trip was over.

It didn't help that we rode in a blaze of sunshine. Alden and I had both provided ourselves with straw hats. Redding must have been hot under his wool tweed cap, but he just frowned and sweated. When we finally came to the resort town of Newport, Alden guided our driver to our destination, throwing in facts about the town as we passed along.

"We're almost there," he began nervously. He, too, was aware that the sheriff looked ready to blow his top. "Now, that's the Jewish cemetery. There've always been Jews here, beginning with the first settlers. Escaped from Spain or Portugal, it seems. Those are boarding houses, before you get to the real houses, and that's the Redwood Library—it has a select membership." The sheriff rolled his eyes at that, but Alden went on. "Most everything here does now…have a limited membership. Some of the wealthiest people from New York come here, you know." We passed a row of shops and he pointed out the road to the beach that turned off to the left. "That's the Casino. It's not for gambling, they have lawn tennis and golf, and in the evenings they have concerts and balls there. It's another place where you have to be a member."

As Redding cursed and wiped sweat from his forehead, Alden hurried on. "And that's the Ocean House. Not really on the ocean, but it's one of the few remaining hotels. In recent years, the hotels have closed down and the land's been bought and people build 'cottages'—at least that's what they call them. Mansions, more like it." Alden was always talkative, but I thought his nattering on in this way showed he was nervous about the coming confrontation with Clara.

We got to a stretch where there were acres of well-tended lawns off to the east, rolling down to the sea and providing a green setting for several large, new houses. Each was far apart from its neighbor. Alden consulted with the driver and we turned into a paved drive. Through the iron gates we could see a huge white building. As we came up to it, it was like a Greek temple that I had seen in prints, with four fluted Corinthian columns framing the front door. White marble wings were topped with a balustrade, and another curved balustrade at the ground level led to the door.

"It's called Marble House," Alden told us. "They say Alva Vanderbilt copied it from the Petit Trianon. A marble home for a marble heart, that's what they say about it." Sheriff Redding glowered as we came up the drive and stopped under the shadow of the columns.

My black dress seemed dusty and unfashionable as I stepped down from the carriage and mounted the stairs. A pair of tall, blond young men in maroon livery met us at the door. One went to deal with the carriage, while the other led us into an immense foyer. There was yellow marble everywhere, and a carved staircase wound up the wall on the left. Behind us, grill work let in sun from beyond the Corinthian columns. Everything was oversized. I had been in Prairie Avenue mansions of the wealthy in Chicago but nothing that matched this. I had never been to Europe but I had heard that the millionaires of Newport had bought up or copied the old aristocratic decorations and transported them here. Sheriff Redding grumbled to himself in an even more disgruntled manner that did not bode well for the meeting. At that moment, I sympathized with him.

Alden informed the very tall, very English butler that we had come to visit Mrs. and Miss Shea. With a flick of the hand, the man sent a lackey off, presumably to find them, while he led us into an immense sitting room to the right of the foyer. We waited, stranded in the huge echoing space. The woodwork was painted gold, and there were murals of gods and goddesses on all of the walls, replete with winged figures reclining on puffy clouds. The chandeliers looked like gilded vines that had sprung from the ceiling. A huge fireplace of black-veined marble monopolized one side of the room, and heavy maroon velvet drapes hung from the windows. I sat down on a delicate-looking couch, but Redding took one look at the fragile furniture and began stalking back and forth. It did not bode well for the interview to come.

Finally, Clara's grandmother sailed into the room wearing a pale lavender dress, with a silk shawl draped over her shoulders. She was small but vibrant, and wore a large diamond pendant at her neck and a brilliant sapphire surrounded by diamond chips on her hand. Behind her, I could see a shamefaced Clara dressed in a blue and white striped dress and, lurking beyond her, the black-coated figure of the butler.

It was all too much for Sheriff Redding. At the sight of them his protests burst from his mouth like seeds from an overripe melon. "That is enough. That is quite enough. I have come here to arrest Miss Clara Shea and I do not care how big your house is, or how many rich people from New York you know. A man has been poisoned. This may be Rhode Island, but if you think you can intimidate me, or hinder my investigation, I must warn you, you are in for a shock. I know a thing or two, and I know people in the statehouse in Massachusetts and you will not get away with it. You can bet your diamond ring on that, lady, no matter what you may think. I don't care how big your house is, you can't get away with murder."

Mrs. Shea was brought to a halt by this onslaught and the butler drifted forward, but she noticed and stopped him with a slight wave of her hand. "And you are?" she asked.

Redding's red face turned apoplectic. "I am Sheriff Seth Redding of the town of Falmouth, Massachusetts, and I have come to take this young woman back to face the consequences of her actions. And, as I said, I am not intimidated by these surroundings, or how much money or influence you may think you have. I've come to take Miss Clara Shea back to Woods Hole with me."

Clara's grandmother eyed him as she let him have his say. "I see. You are wrong, Sheriff Redding, if you think I will do anything to stop you. On the contrary, I quite agree with you and I applaud your diligence. My granddaughter should never have run away and she must return immediately." This unexpected pronouncement took the wind from the sheriff's sails, and she took advantage of his surprise to continue. "Meanwhile, I see you are as unimpressed by the rather gaudy display of the current mode of decoration here as I am. I suggest we adjourn to the terrace. Milton," she addressed the butler, "could we have some lemonade and those sandwiches they provide for tea, and perhaps some sweets? Thank you. This way."

It was as if a cloud burst had suddenly passed through, leaving everything dripping, yet peaceful. We all took a big breath and followed her to a stone terrace overlooking a lawn that sloped down to the sea. She maneuvered Sheriff Redding to a seat which faced the calming waters from under a red and white striped canvas awning. The rest of us also took seats around the iron-topped table and savored the cool breeze, while she went on talking. Her southern drawl was soothing.

"Oh no, this is not my idea of a 'cottage'—cottage indeed. It's more like the palaces torn down by revolutionaries in the Old World. No, I'm afraid that what you see here is nothing more than the excrescence of a very unhappy marriage. This belongs to the Vanderbilts. Alva Vanderbilt is my goddaughter, you see. Her mother and I were at school together. Her father lost much of his money, you know. Alva made what was supposed to be a very good match. In fact, her father died knowing she could take care of the rest of the family, but at what price, I ask you? It would seem this," she waved a hand towards the house, "was a birthday present from her husband, but it must have been penance for some peccadillo." She seemed to be contemplating the marble glory we had escaped. "Imagine the peccadillo that would require this much recompense—it doesn't bear thinking about. No, this is not my place and not my taste. My hosts are not at home. Willie is on his steam yacht, called the *Alva*, while Alva is out at a lawn tennis tournament with Oliver Belmont, a bachelor neighbor." She shook her head.

Servants arrived and spread a white linen tablecloth over the table, which they then loaded with glasses of cold lemonade, flowered china plates holding dainty egg and chicken salad sandwiches, and trays of small frosted cakes. The tart flavor of the drink was reviving. Along with the breeze and the view, it all went far towards rescuing the afternoon.

Redding hesitated, but eventually took a couple of sandwiches after a hearty drink from his glass. "Thank you for the refreshments, Mrs. Shea. I take it you are Miss Shea's grandmother? But I will still need to take your granddaughter back with me." It seemed he wanted to make his position clear before he bit into his sandwich, but having spoken, he took a big bite.

"I quite understand, Sheriff. My granddaughter's actions have been reckless. It is my understanding that—having chosen to go to the laboratory at Woods Hole this summer instead of pursuing her studies—she became entangled in a romantic liaison which has gone astray."

Redding gulped a bite. We were all silent. How much did Mrs. Shea know about Clara's involvement with Sinclair Bickford? I couldn't look at my friend. Redding cleared his throat. "It's the death of a Mr. Lincoln McElroy that's brought your granddaughter under suspicion."

"Yes, I understand that you believe that his death was due

to this affair—with the man she was supposed to be working with. From what she's told me—under duress, you understand—the dead man found the two of them together in an entirely compromising position. Isn't that true?" He nodded. "And because of that, you believe the dead man tried to blackmail my granddaughter, threatening to ruin her reputation, so she poisoned him to prevent that. That is the theory, am I correct?"

Clara moved as if she wanted to say something, but she was quenched by a fierce look from her grandmother. She pursed her lips and rolled her eyes, but did not interrupt.

"He was heard threatening Mr. Sinclair Bickford, and your granddaughter admitted that he'd also threatened her. Seems the consequences would have been more severe for Miss Shea than Mr. Bickford." Redding looked uncomfortable. That we were discussing this topic so openly with Clara's grandmother was unthinkable, but it was happening.

"Because he is a man, you mean? His reputation would recover, while hers would be ruined forever? I'm sure you are correct in that, Sheriff Redding. However, I would dispute the absolute importance of the consequences. You may not know that my granddaughter is already a very wealthy young woman. I have settled a rather large estate on her. In view of her actions, I may regret that. She was to have been committed to her studies. That inheritance was intended to make her forever free to indulge in her education. However she may have failed to live up to my expectations, the money is hers, irrevocably. So, while it may be true that there are many admirable young men who would rightly spurn her, I'm sorry to say there is an equal number who would be quite happy to overlook this stain on her reputation, in view of that fortune. Yes, she has only to come to a place like this and she would have a line of suitors, no matter if her reputation was besmirched. It is amazing what a large fortune may overcome."

Redding had his mouth full, but he was frowning. Clara closed her eyes as if determined to suffer in silence. Alden,

meanwhile, gasped at this plain-talking speech and looked ready
to interrupt. Mrs. Shea glared at him and continued. "Not that I
wish to hinder you in taking my granddaughter back to Woods
Hole, Sheriff. I do not. I will warn you, however, that she does
have resources, and we have already alerted a firm of lawyers from
Boston. They will be on hand to protect her interests—within
the parameters of the law. I would ask you to consider whether
it would be necessary to actually arrest her at this point." Alden
shifted in his chair, but he received another glare. "My concern is
not for my granddaughter's reputation, you understand, but rather
for the health of this young man with whom she has become
involved. Thus far, I have managed to keep this situation from
the ears of her father and brothers, but I very much fear what
will happen if they become informed. I am a lot more worried
that they will end up incarcerated, after taking a bullwhip to
the unfortunate suitor, than I am that Clara will ever be found
guilty of poisoning the man who died.

"And as for you, Mr. Cabot," she said, turning a steely glance
on Alden, "I would thank you not to be the cause of any more
unfortunate behavior on the part of my granddaughter. I don't
know what you were thinking, convincing her to run to me in
this instance. What did you expect I would do?"

"But he has a warrant to arrest her," Alden protested. "He was
going to arrest her! She didn't do it. She would never poison that
man, or anyone. And she didn't ruin Frank Lillie's experiment. I
don't care if she said she did it, she didn't. I don't care what she
told Emily and me, she didn't do it."

Mrs. Shea turned her gaze on Clara, who was shaking her
head. "No, Gram…don't."

"How very foolish." She turned from us and back to address
Sheriff Redding. "Sheriff, apparently my granddaughter's friend
here was convinced that she ruined some experiments?" she
asked, nodding in my direction.

I spoke up. "We saw her come out of the laboratory just

before they found that dye had been spilled on Frank Lillie's experiment."

"And you assumed she had done it? Clara, you did not tell them the truth? She did not ruin the man's experiment. The reason she was so upset—the reason she ran away—was that she saw that man, that Bickford man. He did it."

TWENTY-FIVE

I was shocked. Sinclair Bickford had tricked me. Of course, that explained how upset Clara was when we saw her leaving the Main that day. Bickford, the man she believed loved her, was a cheat. She saw him ruin Frank Lillie's work and, all the time, I believed he was with Louisa at the inn. I just assumed it. But *he* was the one who went to the laboratories, and Clara slipped out to follow him. She saw what he did. Bickford must have wanted to win Whitman's praise and support so badly that he was willing to destroy his rival's work. And I was stupid enough to let him convince me that Clara would stoop to such a terrible act, while all along he was the guilty one. Clara was my best friend, but I let that man deceive me. I was livid with fury thinking about it.

By the time I came to myself Sheriff Redding had put an end to the discussion. He announced that Clara would need to return to Woods Hole. No matter who was guilty in the matter of the destruction of Lillie's research, the sheriff was concerned with the murder of McElroy. When Alden reminded him of his promise not to arrest Clara, Redding snapped that he would delay that action until all the evidence was in, but he dismissed the suggestion that Bickford should be arrested instead. He stood up and warned Clara that she'd better be ready when he came for her at dawn, vowing to arrest whomever he saw fit in his own territory back at Woods Hole.

It was arranged that he and Alden would spend the night in the town while I remained at Marble House with Clara. Redding glowered as Mrs. Shea assured him we would be confined to the premises but he allowed it. We were escorted to the room Clara occupied, with the information that our dinner would be sent up on trays, like children banished to the nursery for bad behavior.

I was still engulfed in a fog of anger and hurt as I followed Clara up the massive marble staircase. We passed a landing, off of which the owners had mismatched personal rooms on opposite sides. His study was all wood and checked wool with paintings of yachts and horses, while hers was a dainty parlor of needlepoint, silk, and gilt-edged mirrors.

At the top, Clara led me to a wing where we entered a room with two wooden-framed single beds.

"It's the bedroom of their sons," she told me. "They've left for boarding school already. For such an imposing house, they have only a single guest room, where Gram is staying. Mrs. Vanderbilt is known for lavish entertainments, but she likes her guests to go home when they're done."

I collapsed gratefully on the nearest bed, while Clara opened the tall windows to let in a sea breeze. I quickly removed my boots and stockings, relishing the release as I drew my legs up under me on the bed. I sighed with relief but, before I could unburden myself to Clara about what had happened, there was a soft knock on the door.

Clara settled herself on the other bed and called out. A head peeped around the door. "Connie, come in. This is my friend, Emily Cabot. Emily, this is Consuelo Vanderbilt...Connie."

She was younger than us, perhaps seventeen or eighteen. She had a willowy figure and was quite tall, with a long neck and dark hair piled high on her head. She wore a blue silk kimono patterned with birds and flowers over her shift. "I'm not disturbing you?"

"No, you can come in."

"I have to dress for dinner at the Astors, but I heard you."

Clara beckoned and she came in and perched on my friend's bed.

"Are you doing research at Woods Hole, too?" she asked me.

"You're at the university with Clara, aren't you?"

"I'm not a scientist, like Clara. I study sociology in Chicago." I guessed she was unaware of the situation that had brought Clara to Newport. "I just came to visit at the end of the summer. I've done some collecting of specimens while I'm there. But I'm not a researcher."

"Oh, you get to go out hunting for them?" She seemed to envy us. "It sounds so interesting."

"Connie's been in Newport for the summer," Clara explained. "In fact, she's just gotten engaged." I sensed she wanted to avoid talking about Woods Hole at the moment. She took the girl's hands.

"Congratulations, you must be very happy," I said, startled by the announcement. I was not much in the mood to listen to news about the happy couple. I thought it must hurt Clara to be presented with such a contrast to her own love story. But somehow the girl didn't seem very happy about it.

"Thank you. My mother is very happy. My fiancé is the Duke of Marlborough, you see."

"My goodness, that's very impressive," I said, trying to sound enthusiastic. The truth was, I had never met anyone who frequented such exalted circles of society. It seemed unreal to find myself sitting in a bedroom with a future duchess. And she was so very shy, biting her lips and bowing her head after making her announcement.

She sighed. "Yes, it *is* very impressive." Suddenly she looked up at me with large brown eyes. "But I do envy you and Clara. To be free to go where you want, to walk in the surf. When I was younger we used to go to my father's place on Long Island. When we were there we would go crabbing and fishing. I learned to sail with my brothers. How I wish I could still do that."

I looked at Clara. "Well, perhaps you could come and visit Woods Hole. It's considerably less formal than here in Newport." Considering the state of affairs back at the laboratory, I was not at all sure it was a reasonable suggestion, yet I felt an impulse to make it. She really ought to get away from Newport society if it was that oppressive.

But she stiffened at the suggestion. "Oh, no. My mother would never allow it. We have many engagements here, especially now." She put a slender hand to her face. "Sometimes I think I am my mother's greatest creation, like a sculpture she's molded from clay. She is very, very happy about my betrothal. I believe I've finally fulfilled her wishes for me."

I thought of my own mother and how happy she would have been to attend my quiet wedding. But she had not lived to see it. "I hope you will be very happy," I told her.

"Thank you. I am sure I will." When she heard that we were to leave in the morning she hugged Clara goodbye and wished us both well before she drifted out, anxious to dress in time for her dinner appointment.

After she left, Clara shook her head. "Every day she's dressed up in whalebone collars and laced into a corset so that she can wear an enormous hat stuck to her head with long steel pins and take her gloves and parasol to be driven to Bailey's Beach. There she has to wear a wool bathing outfit and hat to stand in the waves before being driven back to prepare to show herself in a different outfit at the Casino. Her mother keeps her a prisoner here. It's true she molded her. Even the poor girl's bedroom was completely designed by her mother. You should see it. It looks like something in a Renaissance painting, with a bed on a platform, covered by a canopy they call a 'baldaquin.'"

"Perhaps she'll have more control of her life after she marries," I suggested. There was something disturbing about that willowy figure.

"She confided in me, Emily. She doesn't know the circumstances of my visit, of course. That was kept from her. Even her mother wasn't informed, or I'm sure she would have me removed, so as not to contaminate her daughter. But I think Connie sensed something was wrong. She told me how her mother kept her from the man she wanted to marry and, when she rebelled, her mother had a heart attack. Can you imagine how that made her feel? The woman kept to her bed until Connie finally wrote to the man to break off their secret engagement. Her mother planned for years to marry her to a duke and now she's succeeded."

"How awful. Can't she run away?"

"To do what? She has a fortune but it's only available to the man she marries. Not to her. I'm afraid she tried to stand up to her mother and, having failed, her spirit is completely broken." Clara looked around the room. "All this show of power and money and within it all is a girl as powerless as a penniless beggar. Perhaps less than that, considering she can't even leave the house without her mother's permission."

"And yet she'll marry a duke," I said wondering what could make the young woman refuse her heart like that.

"It's a fairy tale that's nothing but a nightmare. Yet who's to say, if she *had* prevailed and married the man she thought she loved, it would not have been as bad? She's very young. I couldn't help but suspect her failed lover was as much enamored of her dowry as the duke is. How stupid we women can be. Look at me. Look at what I've done, squandering my independence on such a dreary, pitiful person. What a fool I've been!"

"You mean Sinclair?" She covered her face with her hands. "Oh, Clara, I'm so sorry. I have to tell you he tricked me. He made me believe *you* had ruined Frank Lillie's experiment." I gulped. "I don't know how he made me believe him. He said you were so passionate about him that you insisted on doing it for *him*. He even claimed you'd told him you would do it."

She moaned. "Such a desperate little man. But he was right to think I would do anything for him, Emily. I was so sure of his love for me. I refused to believe he would give me up for Louisa. How could I be such a fool? All along, it was Whitman he wanted to impress, not either of us. Fool, fool, fool."

"Oh, Clara, I'm so sorry. You don't know what I've done.

I made them all believe that *you* were the one who sabotaged Frank's work. We must tell them the truth. You *must* tell Louisa. She didn't believe you'd do such a thing. She told me. She was wondering whether she should stay engaged to Sinclair Bickford or call it off. You must tell her what he did."

We were interrupted by another knock on the door. This time it was the butler, followed by two maids with trays of food and a pitcher of cold water. They set us up at a round table by a window and, when they left, we pulled up chairs and found strong appetites for the cold meat, cheese, and pickles. I was more hungry than I could have imagined and Clara, too, dug into the meal with relish. It was comfortable. Once again we were two naughty children confined to the nursery for bad behavior.

As I looked across at Clara I felt a wave of relief. She was my best friend, my second self. She was closer to me than my sister since she loved and longed for the same things that I did, things my sister Rosie would never understand. Clara shared my passion for the work at the university. We had started our studies together as a great adventure. Somehow this summer we had drifted apart so much I feared that I'd lost her forever. It occurred to me that it was the men in the lives of my women friends that so often created those gulfs too great to bridge. Stephen and I had finally recognized our love and come together that summer, and Clara had not been a part of that. Meanwhile, she'd fallen in love with Sinclair, only to find him unfaithful. I despised him and knew him unworthy of my friend, but it didn't matter. Their feelings were completely beyond my reach and influence. Clara had needed to find out the truth about the man herself, and it was a wrenching experience. There was nothing I could do to help her come to terms with that. But at least, now, I felt that the breach we'd experienced might heal with time.

"Clara, you must tell Louisa," I said, wiping my crumbs from my mouth.

"How can I tell her after what I've done?" She shook her head.

"It is so much my own fault. I was so determined that he should be what I wanted him to be…what I needed. I never questioned why he could so easily set aside his feelings for his fiancée in favor of me. Foolish me. I believed it was only because he felt so deeply for me that he could forget Louisa so easily." She gave a bitter laugh. "How vain of me. The night that McElroy died Sinclair told me he had to give me up. He was frightened of what the exposure of our liaison would do to his position at the university, and McElroy threatened to go to Whitman. But, even then, I refused to believe what was before my eyes. I told myself he feared hurting Louisa, but that was not it at all. Not at all. He was grateful to me for the help I gave him with his work over the summer, but he *never* planned to give up Louisa."

"Clara, did he kill McElroy?"

She looked at me, her eyes foggy with memories. "I don't believe he would have the courage to do such a thing," she said finally.

"You must tell Louisa. She should know he was the one who ruined Lillie's work." I thought of my talk with Louisa Reynolds and how she had not believed in Clara's guilt. "She should know."

Clara gave a big sigh. "Emily, what good would it do? I'd only appear to be a jealous lover. Why would she believe me?"

"I think she might. I think she's no longer so enamored of Mr. Sinclair Bickford," I said, spitting out his name. "He's preying on her sympathy to make her forgive him, so he won't lose his place at the university. You must warn her about him."

"There is no reason for her to believe me, Emily. I'm ashamed of my actions."

"Try to talk to her, Clara, please."

TWENTY-SIX

Sheriff Redding was true to his word, and we were ready for him when he arrived with Alden soon after daybreak. The servants scurried to load Clara's bag and we all climbed into the carriage. By the time we departed the sky had clouded over and there was a scent of rain in the air. At least it would be a cooler ride back, but we would be lucky if we could reach our destination before there was a downpour.

Mrs. Shea came out with us and reached in to pat Clara's hand, but her voice dripped with sarcasm. "Don't worry, my dear. Once the sheriff finds the real culprit, you can return here and I will undertake to provide you with a batch of eligible bachelors who are none too fussy about morals. And if that should fail, we can always follow the season here with a grand tour. I have no doubt we could find you an impecunious count whose lack of language skills will prevent him from understanding any slurs on your reputation. You know the type, I'm sure." Clara pulled her hand away. "At the very least we can find someone who will be an improvement upon your more recent choices." Mrs. Shea cocked an eyebrow in Alden's direction and stepped back. Before he could protest, Sheriff Redding banged on the driver's seat and barked, "Go!"

Clara blushed to the roots of her hair and looked away. I remembered how she'd ridiculed a young woman from her hometown who did just what her grandmother described, returning from Europe with a sleazy Italian count for a husband. Her own scorn for the woman was thrown back at her now.

Clara had confided everything to her grandmother and she now had to endure that lady's ridicule. Her grandmother's disappointment cut my friend deeply. It was Mrs. Shea who had seen to it that Clara was not in the position of poor Connie Vanderbilt. She had made my friend financially independent so that she would not have to marry unless she wished. But it had left Clara free to make mistakes as well.

Alden avoided looking at Clara, but launched into a diatribe about how Sinclair Bickford was a villain and how he was the one Redding ought to be pursuing. We had barely reached the main road when the sheriff told the driver to stop and ordered Alden out of the carriage. It was only after I pleaded that he allowed my brother to climb up with the driver and continue with us.

After that, there was silence. The sheriff slumped in a corner with his hat covering his face and his feet stretched out on the seat, while Clara and I sat opposite. Eventually I heard his snores and I gritted my teeth to endure the ride. We hit a bump in the road and raindrops began to splash down with some regularity.

Soon the rain was coming down steadily, so we stopped to raise the buggy top. When we continued on, the noise of the downpour drowned out any attempt at conversation. Alden found an expanse of oilcloth to cover himself and the two of us were left to our individual thoughts as Sheriff Redding snored away the time. I sank down to think about what we had learned. It was a long ride back.

By the time we reached the Snow Goose Inn that afternoon, the steady rain had stopped. But raindrops were still spitting and the wind had whipped up. There were whitecaps on the harbor. Clara jumped down first, but I was stopped by the sheriff.

"No, you don't. Miss Shea, you can stay at the inn. Don't you dare try to leave town again, young woman. As for you, Miss Cabot, you're coming with me to make sure that treasure was where you said it was. You, too." He frowned at my brother.

"Clara," I pleaded. "You must find Louisa and talk to her. Promise me."

She shrugged and took the bag of clothes her grandmother had provided. As we drove away Alden watched her walk slowly up the steps to the porch.

At the Mess, Alden and I followed the sheriff into the dining room where several men were drinking coffee, including his deputy.

"Did they get it?" the sheriff asked.

The man stood up and looked uncomfortable. "Well, they had to wait for the digging tools to come from Falmouth. And then they had lunch. Then Murray sent them to the wrong side and he sent Cliff back and I had to straighten him out, so I sent him back with a map. But by then it was night, so we had to wait till today, and for the men to come back again from Falmouth. But the storm came..."

Redding slapped his hat on the table. "You mean to tell me I've been gone a whole day and night and most of today and they still haven't dug it up?"

A gust of wind blew over a couple of chairs near the window. Captain Veeder got up from the table to right them. "The water's rising fast, Sheriff. If they don't get that gold dug up, it's likely to be washed away."

Redding frowned at him.

"There's a big storm coming in," Veeder continued. "The surf's already lapping at the road in the harbor. The laboratory folks are worried the Main will flood. They're over there now moving things to higher floors. Your boys are liable to get cut off. The neck may be impassable already and if not, it will be in a couple of hours."

"They'll be stuck over there," the deputy observed.

This didn't make Redding happy. "Incompetents. I'm surrounded by incompetents. We're not having that gold wash away. Let's get out there."

"They took the buggies and the wagon," the deputy said.

"Besides, if you try to go now, you'll probably get stuck over there with them," Captain Veeder pointed out. "It'll take you at least an hour to get there by land."

Redding cursed. "By land...what about by sea? Can you get us over there in a boat?"

Veeder looked out the window. There were whitecaps and surf scudding across the normally calm harbor. Waves occasionally broke over the wall and onto the road. "It's pretty rough. I was just going to go out and put down some extra anchors." He contemplated the view for a few minutes. "I was going to move the *Sagitta*, anyhow." He mentioned the steam-powered boat used to harvest specimens. "It's not far by water. We might be able to just about make it over there and back, put out the dinghy for them."

Soon they were on their way, gathering a few others to help them. Redding released me and my brother with the warning that he wanted to see us again when he returned.

"But what about Sinclair Bickford?" I yelled, as Redding followed Captain Veeder out of the Mess and down to the docks. I had to run to catch up with them. When I grabbed the sheriff's arm, he turned towards me. It was starting to rain in big drops that splashed on my nose. I blinked.

"Now, you just let go." He pried my fingers from his arm. "I have to go get those fools before they're washed away with sixteen thousand dollars of treasure."

"But he did it. He's the one who ruined Frank Lillie's experiment...he was so desperate to beat him. He's the one who killed Mr. McElroy, not Clara. You have to question him. You have to make him admit it."

"Says you. Far as I can see, Clara Shea never actually said he done it. And even if he did put dye in that other fella's experiment, it doesn't prove she didn't poison McElroy. In any case, we've got an emergency here and that'll have to wait." He waved me off and turned to run down the hill to the dock.

"But—" It was too late. With the wind whipping waves that sloshed onto the road, he couldn't hear me. The steam-powered launch was rising on the waves and knocking against the dock in an alarming manner. Veeder and his mate were already aboard and they yelled at the sheriff to release the dock lines and jump on. He hunched over and waited for the boat to go down in a trough, then jumped aboard. They steamed away, fighting the waves.

Exasperated, I looked around and saw no trace of Alden. Sheriff Redding might not think that talking to Sinclair Bickford was urgent, but I suspected Alden did.

By the time I reached the Main I was damp all over, but I jumped inside just as it began to pour. I heard a bump and crash from Sinclair's laboratory. Other people put down boxes they were carrying and hurried in after me.

Alden was hunched over, preparing to lunge at Sinclair, who scooted behind a long lab table just in time. Alden hit the edge of the table instead.

"You frog-faced, lily-livered coward!" Alden screamed. "Come out and fight. What's the matter? You can only hide behind skirts, is that it?"

Sinclair looked up at the crowd slipping through the open door. "Somebody stop him. Look what he's done." He pointed at the broken glassware. "Stop him."

Stephen pushed his way in. "Alden, what are you doing?"

"He's the one who sabotaged Lillie's work—not Clara," he said, not taking his eyes from Sinclair's face. "He's a liar. He tried to make everyone believe it was Clara—but it was him all the time."

I heard a gasp beside me and I saw Cornelia Clapp standing there. She grabbed my arm. "Is it true?" she asked quietly. I nodded.

"That's not true. Clara Shea did it and then she ran away," Bickford insisted.

"Liar, you did it. She saw you. That's why she ran away. She couldn't believe you could be such a hypocrite."

Sinclair glanced around at the people drifting into the room.

They were quiet, as if not wanting to provoke Alden, but they were watching intently. I saw Professor Whitman pushing his way through the crowd.

Sinclair saw him too and it made him even more insistent. "I'm sorry. It was Clara Shea. She wanted to help me. It was misguided. The truth is she was jealous. Once Miss Reynolds arrived, she saw how much Louisa meant to me and she was jealous. You don't understand. She thought if she did it, that it would bind me to her. It's my fault, in the end, yes. But I didn't do it, Clara did."

It was quite a performance and it turned my stomach to realize that the people in the room believed him. They believed poor Clara was a woman so infatuated and jealous she would do anything to get this man back, even if it ruined him. At that moment I saw what a worm the man really was.

Alden screamed, "Liar!" But, when he began to climb across the glassware on the table to get to Sinclair, there was a struggle and Stephen and Frank Lillie restrained him.

"Alden, stop it. This won't help Clara," Stephen told him.

"He's a liar!"

"Alden's right," I yelled. Everyone turned towards me and I felt Cornelia's hand tighten on my arm. "We thought Clara ran away because she did it. But she didn't. She saw you putting the dye in Mr. Lillie's experiment. She was so shocked and so ashamed for you, she wouldn't even admit it."

Professor Whitman stepped forward. "I don't understand, Miss Cabot. You were the one who told me Miss Shea was responsible."

I was staring at Sinclair. His facial muscles didn't move an inch but I could see a slight gleam in his eye. Of course. He had planned it this way. He had gotten me to accuse my friend. He was a very clever man and I burned with hatred for him.

"He tricked me. He made me believe Clara had done it. I thought he went to see Louisa, but he went to the laboratory while the sheriff was questioning those men. Clara followed him.

She saw him do it. That's why she was so upset."

"That's not true, Miss Cabot," Sinclair insisted. "I never went to the laboratory, Clara Shea did it."

"Oh, yes you did," Cornelia Clapp spoke up. "I saw you and I said nothing. Clara ran away, so I believed it was a sign of guilt like everyone else. But what about the other time?"

"I don't know what you mean."

"I mean when Frank's experiments were ruined the first time. By the flood. That was supposed to be an accident. But just in case, I had Dunbar take a look the other day. It was not an accident. That was sabotage, too. The valve was broken off on purpose."

There was a stir in the room. Sinclair looked around, his gaze coming to rest on Professor Whitman. He looked like he was imploring him for help.

"I know nothing about that," he said helplessly.

"I saw you in the laboratory that time, too. I was wondering what you were doing in the basement," Cornelia said.

"She's lying. She and that Thurston woman were trying to sabotage Frank and me. They wanted Miss Clapp to head the laboratory. They're the ones who did it."

Professor Whitman looked like he was in pain. He stooped and picked up a broken flask that was leaking on the floor and took it over to the sink. People were talking amongst themselves and Alden was practically growling with rage as Stephen held on firmly and whispered in his ear.

Finally the professor spoke. "This is all very distressing, but at the moment I believe we must concentrate on moving as much as we can to the upper floors. There is a very good chance that the water will rise far enough to flood the basement and perhaps the first floor." The window panes rattled with a blast of wind and rain as if to emphasize his words. "Miss Cabot, Mr. Cabot, I promise you there will be a very careful investigation of your claims as soon as this storm is over. But you must forgive us if we have to put it aside at this time and tend to laboratory business."

He turned to the crowd. "All of you, please continue to pack up everything you can and move it to the upper floors. Frank? You agree?"

Frank Lillie had been listening to the accusations with a look of stupefaction on his face. He came to life now and, shaking his head, let go of Alden and followed Professor Whitman as he led the others out. Sinclair Bickford skittered ahead of the stragglers, losing himself in the crowd, in order to escape Alden, who was still being held by Stephen.

"Where is Clara?" Cornelia Clapp asked when they were gone.

"We left her at the inn."

"We should get her and bring her here."

"But what about your laboratory?"

"Perhaps Dr. Chapman and Mr. Cabot could see that my things are moved." Before Alden could argue, she added, "It might be a good idea for someone to keep an eye on Mr. Bickford to make sure he doesn't sabotage my work, or leave altogether while no one is looking."

That appealed to Alden, and Stephen also agreed. He thought it would be wise to bring all of the people at the inn back. If the water rose enough to flood the inn, people would be safer on the upper floors of the Main.

Cornelia and I were drenched by the time we fought our way back to the inn. I saw with alarm that the road in front of the Fisheries building was already awash and, down the road, Eel Pond was also overflowing its boundaries. In the front hallway we shook ourselves, and wiped our faces. My hat was ruined, crushed in my hands when I grabbed it before the wind could take it away. We yelled, and Jane Topham came bustling out of the kitchen with towels for us to use to mop ourselves off.

"Where is everyone?" I asked. "Where are Miss Shea and Miss Reynolds?"

Jane was tottering around trying to wipe up the pools of water we were shedding. "They're gone. Everyone's gone," she said. "They went to find out what Alfred Davis has done with his grandson."

TWENTY-SEVEN

Jane insisted we come into the kitchen and warm ourselves by the stove. She'd been busy stuffing sheets and towels under the back doorway where water was already trying to seep in. A bucket with a mop was set out in the corner but, as time went on, the water kept seeping in, as the wind and rain battered at the door.

"How long have they been gone?" I asked, as I attempted to pin back wet strands of hair.

"It was just after Miss Shea arrived back. You see, she came right into the kitchen, looking for Miss Reynolds, who was in here with Edna Thurston trying to decide what to do about Billy Gordon."

"What was wrong with the Gordon child?" Cornelia demanded.

"He's missing. Well, Edna saw him go into the woods with..." she paused, "Alfred Davis."

Cornelia was impatient with the dramatic airs Jane had taken on. "Oh, for heaven's sake, the old man is his grandfather. What's it to Edna Thurston? Where were Minnie, and the boy's father?"

"But that's just it. They're gone. No note, just gone." She waved toward the front rooms. "They're all gone, all of them. That's what made it so strange. And everyone knows they wanted to keep the old man away from the children."

It did seem strange when she said it. Here we were, three women in an old house that was creaking with strain as the rain and wind furiously buffeted the outside. I was so used to the inn as a busy, even noisy place. It was strange to learn that it was empty. The glass panes rattled in the windows and more water came in under the door.

"We didn't know what to do. Then, the young ladies, they said they'd go looking for him, and Miss Thurston, she knows the neck better than them newcomers, so she said she'd go show them where she'd seen the old man and the boy go into the woods."

"Where exactly did Clara, Louisa, and Edna go?" Cornelia asked.

"They decided to follow to see where Alfred Davis had taken the boy. I thought it might be to the old fishing shack out on the neck. Miss Thurston saw them heading in that direction, don't you know. The old man used to go out there, but Minnie forbid the boy to go with him. She was afraid of what the old man might do, don't you think?" She looked out the window with consternation in her face. "Of course it was nowhere near as bad out when they left. Miss Thurston knows the way to that shack. That's why they went with her. She didn't want to go alone and they didn't want to wait to get any of the men. The sheriff has all the men off digging for gold anyhow, like I told them. So they told me to stay here, in case Mr. Gordon came back, from wherever he went, and was looking for Billy. We thought he had to be back soon for his son, don't you think?"

"They went to the neck?" I asked. "Captain Veeder said it'll be cut off by the rising water. We'd better go after them."

"No, that's the absolute worst place to go if the water is rising. Anyone here would know it. We need to go back to the laboratory," Cornelia insisted. "There's no sense getting lost in the storm with them."

"But…"

"From the top floors of the Main we might be able to see where they went. And we can get more help." Of course she was right. She turned to Jane. "Get a coat or something. You need to come with us. No use taking an umbrella, the wind will just turn it inside out."

Jane looked crestfallen. "Oh no," she said, glancing at the window. "I couldn't go out in that." She was afraid. The way the wind was howling and rattling the door, like a sinister stranger trying to force his way in, I could understand her concerns.

"Don't be a fool," Cornelia snapped. "Look at that water coming in under the door. Pretty soon you'll be up to your waist in it. No telling how long a clapboard structure will hold up. No. We need to get back to the Main. It's solid brick and, even if the bottom floors are flooded, it'll stay put. This house is liable to float away."

"Float away?" Jane looked shocked, her face white and her eyes wide. "No, surely."

"Yes, surely. Come on, Emily, you might want to get a coat if one's available, and Minnie probably has some boots around here somewhere."

It took a great deal of arguing on my part to finally convince Jane to accompany us back to the laboratory building. I'm certain Cornelia would have left her behind rather than stooping to entreaties. But, while she rummaged around finding us oiled jackets, hats, and boots usually used for fishing, I warned Jane not to stay alone. I think when she realized we really meant to go back out into the driving rain she gave in. But she insisted on wearing a walking jacket and even a black straw hat. There was no way that would stay on her head, but she was horrified when she saw Cornelia and myself hitching up our skirts as we did when we went wading for specimens.

"It's all right, Jane," I told her. "There won't be any men around to see us."

Cornelia grunted. "As if it would matter if they were. Come on, now. It'll only get worse."

We struggled out the front door and down the steps, hurrying through puddles and rushing streams of water on the road. When we got near the Main, we had to wade through a low area that had turned to calf-deep marsh. I took Jane's elbow as she struggled with her heavy sopping skirts.

When we made it inside there was already an inch of water on the first floor. Stephen and Alden had been preparing to go after us, but we told them that Clara, Louisa, and Edna were missing. Cornelia led us up the four flights to the roof.

The wind roared and the rain fell in sheets. I thought Alden would be blown away, but he doubled over and crept his way to the edge. Stephen held me around the waist with his good arm and covered us with an oilcloth from one of the laboratory tables. We followed Cornelia to the tall brick chimney where we sheltered, peering through the torrents, trying to see the women. The sheer angry power of the natural elements was overwhelming, the sky a dirty green with great piles of gray and black clouds. I clutched the brick and through the curtain of rain I could see the water of the harbor churning and roiling like a pot coming to a boil.

"Look." Stephen pointed. It was the steam-powered launch.

"It's Captain Veeder and Sheriff Redding," I yelled against the scream of the wind. "They went to rescue the men who were getting the treasure."

I hoped they would make it back. There was steam coming out of their smokestack, so they were under power, but the boat alternately popped up on the top of a breaking wave or slid down into a trough as if it were a cork bouncing on the water.

Alden stood up, waving. We followed his gestures and saw three figures on a strand of beach beside the channel that separated the neck of land from us. "It's them," I yelled into Stephen's dripping face, while I clutched his shirt. "It's Clara and Louisa. They're with Edna." I was overjoyed. They were far away, but no doubt three women, two tall and one short, were out there.

"They must not have found Billy and Mr. Davis," I yelled at Cornelia. She didn't try to reply, but shielded her face from the rain as she stared grimly out and assessed the situation. When I followed her gaze, I realized it was not good.

For one thing, I could see that the fishing shack they were looking for was in waist-deep water with waves crashing around it. I wondered if Billy and his grandfather were in it. I watched as it broke away from its foundations and began floating out into deeper water. I could see no movement from inside.

The women had retreated from the shack, if they ever had gotten that far. They were on a small beach besieged by a rising tide of surf. Behind them was a sand dune covered in tufts of beach grass. I saw them struggling to climb the dune, continually causing the sand to collapse, which sent them sliding back towards the surf as they grasped at grass that came out in clumps in their hands.

But the real problem was that, from our vantage point, we could see what lay beyond the hill they were trying to climb. There was no salvation there. The other side of the dune was already inundated with water. To the right was a deep channel to the harbor and eventually out to sea where the shack seemed to be heading. To the left, the normally shallow pond had already risen in height to completely cover the causeway they would have used to walk out to the neck. They were trapped; there was no way out.

Alden scrambled across the roof. "We've got to get them. The water is rising. They'll drown," he yelled. I grabbed him and we all retreated to the stairwell so we could hear each other. We descended to the first landing.

"There's no way to get to them," Cornelia observed.

"But they'll drown," Alden yelled.

"Dr. Chapman, can you find Mr. Elliott? He may know what to do."

"I'm going," Alden proclaimed.

I grabbed his arm as Stephen hurried away, calling for Elliott. "No, wait. You want to save them. So do I. But you can't do it alone. At least listen to what Mr. Elliott has to say."

At that moment Elliott came up the steps, followed by several other people. I didn't see Jane among them, but I knew she was safe enough. After our trudge she was no doubt cowering somewhere trying to dry off. I had no worries about her. It was Clara and the others who were in desperate straits.

Mr. Elliott's grave expression did not bode well. "Miss Reynolds and Miss Shea are trapped on the neck?"

"And Miss Thurston," I told him. "They went looking for Billy Gordon and Alfred Davis at a fishing shack over there. There's no sign of the boy *or* his grandfather and we saw the shack swept out to sea."

"Show me," he said.

Alden led the way up the stairs. As Cornelia pointed out, there was no sense in the rest of us following, so we waited for them to return. They came back dripping wet. Elliott was shaking his head.

"It's very bad. There's no way to get out there."

"We have to help them," Alden insisted.

"I know, Mr. Cabot. But there is no way on earth to cross that channel on foot. There's an outside chance we could do something. I saw the *Sagitta*." He mentioned the steam-powered launch I had seen. "It looks like it's going to try to dock."

I explained that the sheriff and Captain Veeder had gone after the sheriff's men.

"I don't know if he can do it. But if Veeder thinks it's possible, we might pick them up the same way they're getting Redding's men. We've got to get down to the dock."

"Excuse me, excuse me, pardon me." At that moment we heard Nellie Bly's voice as she pushed her way up the stairs.

"Nellie, where did you come from?" Alden yelled.

"Boston, of course. I'm sorry. Is Dr. Chapman up there?" People leaned aside and helped her through. She was a little breathless.

"I'm here," Stephen called, releasing his grasp from around my waist. "Are you hurt?"

"Not me. It's my driver. We had an awful time getting here from the station. I would've turned back, but he insisted we'd be safer here as it's the highest building in the town. But the horse panicked at one point and he got kicked." She held her side and gasped for air. "He's downstairs on the third floor."

"I'll go." Stephen began sliding through people to get down the stairs.

"Everybody go down. We need to get to the docks," Mr. Elliott called and the crowd began an orderly descent.

"The docks? What for?" Nellie asked. Alden explained to her what the problem was as he shuffled impatiently down the stairs.

"Miss Shea and Miss Reynolds and even Miss Thurston are trapped over there? Why, whatever possessed them to go out in the storm?"

I tried to explain how they'd been following Billy Gordon and his grandfather because they feared for the boy's safety.

"Billy? You mean Minnie Gibbs's nephew? And her father, Alfred Davis? But that's impossible. I saw them earlier today—all of them, Mr. Gordon and his son, and Minnie and her father— they were in the train station in Boston. They came up from the Cape and were fine."

TWENTY-EIGHT

I stopped dead on the staircase. Billy and his grandfather were safe with the rest of the family in Boston? The picture of that shack floating away in the surf suddenly became innocuous. There was no one in it. They hadn't drowned after all.

"Emily, get out of the way. Clara and the others are still out there." Alden pushed past me and joined Mr. Elliott on his flight down the stairs. I followed close behind.

"Why did they think Alfred Davis was there?" Nellie asked, hurrying to keep up.

Why did they? Because Edna told them she saw him take his grandson to the fishing shack. But why would she lie about such a thing? Suddenly, I understood and I was afraid for Clara and Louisa. The boy and his grandfather had never been out at that fishing shack. They had been in Boston all along. Everyone here knew the neck would be cut off by rising waters. Everyone from here knew the awful danger, but Clara and Louisa were not from here and they had been led into danger, thinking they were needed to help the little boy. The only reason could be to cause their deaths. And how easy that would be, in a storm like this, was now clear to me.

Mr. Elliott held a hand up when we reached the bottom floor. "Wait!" The water was ankle deep as he sloshed to the nearest door. "Mr. Bickford, Miss Reynolds and Miss Shea are trapped on the neck!" he announced, as he entered Bickford's room.

Alden went to follow, his face flushed and his teeth gritted. I grabbed his arm. "No, Alden, go down to the dock. Tell Captain

Veeder we need the boat. Quick. Don't let him get away."

Alden's blue eyes stared at me, but he wrenched himself away and ran for the doors. Nellie and I followed Mr. Elliott into Sinclair Bickford's room. I worried what would happen when my brother and Sinclair were on the same boat going to rescue the women.

I needn't have worried. Sinclair Bickford had no intention of assisting with the rescue. He was packing glass bottles into a carton as Elliott watched him with his mouth hanging open. "But they're trapped! The only hope is to convince Veeder to rescue them with the steam launch."

Sinclair looked grim. "I'm sorry. I must get this moved. I'll lose everything—all my work—if I don't get it moved." He looked up at the amazed stares of Elliott and Cornelia Clapp. "I wouldn't be any help. You and Veeder must get them."

"Bickford," Cornelia snapped. "It's Louisa Reynolds, your fiancée, and Clara Shea, your assistant, out there with Edna Thurston. If we don't do something, they'll all drown!"

He glared at her. "And if I don't save my research I'll be ruined. But that's what you want, isn't it? If Frank and I both lose our work, there'll be nobody left but you for Whitman to fall back on. That's what you want, isn't it? You and the Woman's Education Association. That Thurston woman wants you to prevail. That's what this is about, isn't it?" His eyes shone behind the rimless spectacles. I thought he was mad.

"Sir," Mr. Elliott said in his deep resounding voice. "I don't know what you're talking about, but if anything happens to those women, I wouldn't be able to live with myself if I hadn't tried to save them while there was still a chance."

Sinclair pulled his gaze away from Cornelia and tried to focus on the broad-shouldered Elliott. "You do that. Yes, you do that. I'm sorry I can't help. I need to attend to this." He went back to his packing as Elliott rushed from the room and Cornelia followed. I hurried behind them with a sinking feeling in my heart. This was the man that Clara had loved? He was so very petty.

I saw Nellie staring at him wide-eyed as I left, but she quickly caught up with me and we ran down the hill together to the dock. It was still pouring.

The *Sagitta* was attempting to dock. There were several of Redding's men on the dock with Alden, and now Mr. Elliott and Cornelia. One of the men was dripping wet, as if he had fallen in the water and been pulled out. They were all yelling at the men still on the steam-powered launch. Captain Veeder was operating the boat, conducting a kind of dance—he would approach the dock, then they would be lifted in the air by a large wave. As the wave broke over the dock, the boat was maneuvered in reverse enough to stay clear of a collision.

I could see a red-faced Sheriff Redding, yelling imprecations at his men from the boat. As Nellie and I stepped onto the dock, Captain Veeder came out of the enclosed wheelhouse to listen to Mr. Elliott. We rushed up to Cornelia and grabbed her arms to steady ourselves. The dock creaked and moved beneath us.

"Redding still wants to get the gold and silver unloaded, but they're saying it's impossible," she yelled against the screeching wind. "Elliott's trying to get Veeder to agree to go rescue the women." We were too far away to interfere. I shuddered as I saw Alden jumping to catch a heavy bow line from the boat. Veeder yelled to him to leave it loose, not tight, as Alden wound it around a bollard. I could see why, as the boat rose on a wave that broke over the dock, the distance straining the line and snapping the bow towards the dock as it tightened. But it was still ten or fifteen feet away and they managed to keep the boat from smashing into the wooden pilings.

Elliott beckoned to us and we rushed forward.

"Veeder will try," he shouted. "Redding will stay aboard, as he won't leave the treasure. Mr. Cabot and I will attempt to board." Another wave smashed against the dock, hitting us with a huge spray of water. I cringed. "One of Redding's men is hurt," he continued. "They'll take him up to the Main."

Three of the men carried another away, slipping as they went. Another caught a stern line from the boat. Elliott watched. "I believe we'll be sufficient in number." He did not seem certain.

"I can come," Cornelia said.

"It's too dangerous." He turned away to follow Veeder's instructions, waiting for the boat to dip down again in a wave, and then jumped aboard. Veeder and Redding caught his arms.

"I could never do that," Nellie yelled to me. "I suffer terribly from sea sickness. Found that out on my trip around the world, believe me. Look, Alden is calling."

We rushed to the end of the dock where he was. He ignored my warnings and helped Cornelia to time her jump. Suddenly she was aboard. The man with the stern line unleashed it without warning, letting it sail through the air to land in Mr. Elliott's hands just in time to prevent the boat from hitting the dock. The stern swung out and Alden grabbed my arms. "Emily, as soon as I'm on, throw the line to me." He handed me a coil of rope he'd removed from the bollard after giving a final tug. The bow of the boat tipped away from us, then back. Redding was yelling something. Suddenly Alden was gone. I clutched the rope until I saw he had made it safely aboard. The bow tipped away and was pulling on the heavy line. I leaned forward to throw the coil of line to him, when suddenly I felt a push. A wave broke on the dock, sweeping me up into the air over the roiling water. Oh, no! I was going in! As I dropped, the deck of the boat suddenly shifted and rose toward me. I fell onto it, collapsing with a mighty slap. I, too, was aboard.

TWENTY-NINE

The world was turned upside down. I was on the deck of the *Sagitta* and the dock loomed above us. I landed so heavily it took my breath away and I couldn't move. My jaw hit the deck, sending my teeth into my lip so I tasted blood. The deck tilted and I slid, but Alden and Mr. Elliott caught me and suddenly I was in Elliott's arms as he staggered into the covered wheelhouse. Captain Veeder was struggling to keep the boat from colliding with the dock.

"We have to take her back," Elliott told him. "She shouldn't be here."

Veeder concentrated on the controls, turning the wooden spokes of the wheel with one hand as he moved a lever for the power with the other. "We none of us should be here. We can't try to go back. That dock is breaking up. It would be more dangerous to try to get her off."

"It's all right," I said, feeling silly but safe in Mr. Elliott's strong arms. "I'm all right. Please put me down."

Elliott staggered as the boat lurched through a wave. Then he let my feet down to the floor and Alden took my arm.

"Come here, Em. Sit down on the floor over here."

He led me to a corner away from the controls. He was right about staying on the floor. The boat tipped and lurched as Veeder maneuvered through the waves. Great sprays of water sprang up from the bow and then landed with a loud splatter on the roof of the wheelhouse. We all huddled there under cover. The rear part of the launch was covered, but open on the sides. Only the wheelhouse in the middle was comparatively dry. Cornelia and I were almost as well dressed as Veeder and his first mate, Luther, in our oilskins. Elliott, Alden, and the sheriff were less well protected.

Mr. Elliott was describing to Veeder the location where the women were stranded, while Sheriff Redding fussed about the treasure. He was furious to know he'd recovered it but was unable to get it ashore. Veeder told him there was no chance to unload it until the storm had passed through.

It was hard to believe the storm would ever be over even though, rationally, I knew it would. The wind howled, the rain battered the windows, and Veeder gripped the wheel with white knuckles, only occasionally trading a grunted observation with the first mate. I felt a bit frightened in the moments when I wasn't concentrating on remaining in one spot and not rolling around the floor with the motion of the boat. I had never been seasick before, but I was beginning to feel a bit queasy when Elliott yelled something and Alden followed him out to the deck.

I struggled up and followed Cornelia as she carefully clung to the door frame, waiting for a shift of the boat, before she grabbed something else to cling to and made her way out. Staying close to the wall of the wheelhouse, I saw Alden pointing to the shore. Between curtains of rain I could make out three figures on the land. But as the boat tilted and rose on a wave, only to dive again into a trough, I held on for dear life. I began to doubt there was any way we could ever get to them. They'd made it to the top of the dune, where they huddled together, but the water was still rising and beginning to lap at them. How could we ever reach them in time? If they saw us, how could they get to us through the roiling water and crashing waves that divided us? It was hopeless.

Alden felt his way past me and climbed to the roof of the wheelhouse. My heart stopped as the boat plunged down into a trough, smashed into a wave, and shuddered from the impact.

But Alden hung on and I realized he was untying a dinghy from the roof and lifting it down. With the sheriff's help he got it onto the deck, but it looked puny compared to the force of the waves sloshing under our feet and breaking all around us.

They were yelling in argument while the first mate brought a huge coil of rope. He tied one end to the dinghy and another to a large winch on the bow.

Cornelia tapped my back and motioned. She led me back into the wheelhouse where we could hear ourselves enough to speak. Captain Veeder was still operating the controls, balancing the forward and reverse power as he swung the wheel to compensate for waves. He was trying to keep the boat in about the same place. He did not seem happy.

"Mr. Elliott will row ashore," Cornelia told me. "They'll let out the line attached to the dinghy in case he can't row against the waves. They can pull him back if necessary."

I looked out, clutching the door as the boat shook. "Can he really row there and back?"

"He's going to try." Cornelia looked grim.

Fascinated, we watched from cover as the boat bobbed up on the crests of the waves and then was lost from view. As he got nearer to shore the figures rose and waved as best they could. They were watching with as much suspense as we were. The little boat swamped a couple of times, but Elliott clutched the gunwales and kept it upright, stooping to bail water twice.

Near the shore the waves would suddenly converge and rush forward as a solid mass of water, building and building. Swimming in smaller waves, we used to ride surf like that into the shore when I was a child. But these monsters grew to a head of surf and broke with a pounding force of hundreds of gallons of water. They were deadly.

We saw Elliott, facing us, his oars out of the water, being carried along on a wave. It was too far to see the expression on his face, but I imagined it was one of resignation. The dinghy flew up, over the top of the wave, and then the water collapsed and the dinghy was gone. And so was Mr. Elliott. I shivered.

We saw the boat pop back up. It was broken in half with only the front part still waving at the end of the line. Elliott was gone. Then I saw the figures on the shore wading into the water, and through the downpour we could see them dragging something to shore.

"They got him," Cornelia yelled.

"But the boat's gone."

Alden pushed his way into the wheelhouse, followed by Redding and Luther, the first mate. "I can do it."

"It's suicide," Redding told him.

Luther went to a locker and pulled out another huge coil of line.

"I can do it. I have to do it."

Veeder listened as Alden and Redding yelled at each other. Alden wanted to swim ashore with a line. Using the rope, he would tie himself to the women, and Elliott, and they would swim or be pulled back.

"You can't swim in that. It's not a picnic, you dimwit," Redding argued. "What do you think—you're a swim champ?"

"No, but no matter what I do, I'll be pushed ashore," Alden told him. "I just have to keep my head above water enough to keep breathing. I'll be thrown ashore."

I saw Veeder and Luther exchange a glance. At least Alden was right about that part of the plan.

"We can't necessarily swim against that to get back, but that's what the rope's for. You'll have to pull us." He sensed the gloom. "We have to do something. At least it's a chance. At least some of us might make it back alive. Captain Veeder, it's the only chance. Let me do this. Please!"

The captain looked at Alden, sizing him up, and finally he nodded to the first mate. They headed out to the deck and we followed. I was afraid. I pushed forward and gave Alden a hug.

He grinned, hugged back, then pushed me away as Luther wound coils of rope around his middle.

Cornelia held on to me as Alden jumped overboard. Luther paid out the line. Soon we couldn't see Alden. I stared hard, trying to pick out his dark head, but between the wind, rain, and spray it was impossible. I said prayers privately, but I wouldn't allow Cornelia to pull me back inside. I had to stay where I could see Luther still paying out the rope.

As the boat deck continued to slope down and then rise up under our feet, it was impossible to see what was happening. Suddenly Sheriff Redding yelled, "He got there. He's ashore."

Luther didn't respond, but wrapped the rope around a cleat and took off his wool cap, squeezing out the water with his gnarled hands. Cornelia pulled me inside to watch through the window.

The group on shore tied themselves together at the waist like a string of unlikely pearls. It looked like Elliott first, then the women, with Alden last. They began to wade into the water. Luther and Redding took up the line, leaving the end wrapped around the cleat for purchase. How would they know when to pull on it?

We couldn't see the swimmers as the waves rushed forward, climbing high before they broke with a terrible pounding. How could they ever survive and get through the spot where the waves broke? I dug my fingernails into my hands as I watched.

Then I saw the men start to pull on the rope. Cornelia and I ducked outside. We could see some dark dots on the water. I couldn't count. The men grunted as they pulled in a few yards, then let the boat ride up and down before pulling a few more.

As I strained to see the figures in the water, I saw the broken dinghy off to the left. It floated like a cork. I worried it would smash into one of the swimmers. How could they swim in that? Especially the women in their long dresses.

The men pulled. Cornelia joined them. She seemed to know when to apply pressure to help them. I would only have been a hindrance. We rose high up on a wave and then suddenly—as we sank way, way down—I saw Elliott two waves over. I yelled. They pulled harder and soon he was hanging off the side. We all helped to pull him in. As he lay on the deck, they heaved a few more times until Edna Thurston was flopping around the side of the boat. They were having a terrible time getting her aboard as she was practically unconscious. I watched impatiently, staring out, trying to see the others. Louisa Reynolds was next, trying her best to swim towards the boat, but she floundered. She was pulled back by the rope still attached to Clara and Alden, who were some yards behind her, struggling to keep their heads above water. But they were alive.

A huge wave broke and I heard a scream. Straining, I saw it was Alden being carried away. The rope had broken.

The release of tension allowed them to pull Edna aboard and Mr. Elliott helped to grab at Louisa next. I could see Clara now, looking back, searching for Alden. Suddenly Louisa was thrown into the boat and Clara was pulled close. "Alden," she yelled.

They pulled her aboard. "No," she yelled.

"Wait," I shouted, pointing.

"The dinghy—he's on the dinghy rope," Cornelia yelled. She and Luther jumped to the line on the bow that was still attached to the dinghy. I wanted to see what was happening, but Elliott was stumbling across the deck. I helped him carry Edna into the wheelhouse, then he staggered back out for Louisa. She was coughing up water, so Elliott dragged her inside. Meanwhile, Clara had been helped aboard as well. She was with Luther, Cornelia, and Redding. They were struggling to reel in the dinghy, but the line had no purchase and kept slipping.

"Get the captain!" Cornelia yelled at me. "Alden's hanging onto the dinghy. We've got to pull him in."

I rushed to the wheelhouse.

"You'll have to keep the boat steaming," the captain yelled.

"But I can't."

"Just move this forward or back to compensate for the waves." He put my hands on the lever. "Move the wheel if we get pushed off. Look up there." He pointed ahead. "Stay forty-five degrees to the waves."

"I can't. Wait—Mr. Elliott." I looked around, but he and Louisa had both gone back out onto the deck.

"Just do it."

"But what if I do it wrong?"

"You've been watching me. If you don't do it, your brother won't make it. See…how much worse can you make it?" He put my other hand on the wheel. He stayed long enough to do several corrections with his hand over mine. "That's it. 'Til we get him in." And he was gone.

The boat shuddered after hitting a wave and I felt the bow fall off. I swung the wheel to correct for the shift. Too far. I brought it back, moved the lever forward, then back. Felt a wave, swung the wheel over again, then back.

I had no time to see how the rescue was proceeding. I concentrated completely on the task, convinced the boat would capsize if I failed. There was a particularly sickening roll, but the boat righted.

"Ouch."

I jumped at the voice, taking my eyes from the bow long enough to see that it was Edna Thurston who had rolled into a metal locker and was waking up. She wailed and wept for a while, but I paid no attention. When she quieted down I looked over and saw her take a sip from a flask she pulled from her pocket. I saw a soggy sandwich, or some part of it, spill from a checked napkin. She was still weeping as she sipped, hiccupping now and then.

I stole a look at her, propped against the wall, and wondered if I was alone with a murderer. She purposely led Clara and Louisa to the neck, where she must have known they'd be cut off. If not for our desperate efforts, she would have led them to their deaths. Why had she done it? Sinclair Bickford claimed that she'd ruined the experiments of the men to further Cornelia's career, but that seemed ludicrous.

Was it madness? Passion? Could she and McElroy have been lovers? Surely she was not so devoted to the cause of her society that she would kill, especially if it meant risking her own life. Why, then? Ever since I'd learned that Mr. Gordon and his family were safe in Boston, I'd known it was treachery that led the women out into the storm.

Suddenly there was a strange sound. After an adjustment of the wheel I looked over and saw that Edna was having a fit. She was shaking and frothing at the mouth. She vomited and went into a series of spasms. I yelled for help, but the wind was too loud. I couldn't leave the wheel. I looked again and screamed. I screamed and screamed, clutching the controls as if glued to them, but by the time they heard me she was dead.

THIRTY

They retrieved Alden successfully. Mr. Elliott and Captain Veeder dragged his sodden body into the wheelhouse, one on each side. They laid him on the floor, where Clara fell down beside him. He was coughing, alive.

Unable to release my hands from the controls, I stopped screaming and babbled, "Edna, Edna." Elliott, Louisa, and Cornelia surrounded the woman while Captain Veeder tried to take over the wheel and engine lever from me. But my hands were frozen to the controls. I had gripped them convulsively, convinced that, if I let go, the boat would plunge into the sea. Veeder pried my fingers away and gently pushed me towards the others. The boat heaved on a wave and I dropped down beside Clara and Alden.

The boat lurched as Veeder attempted to head back to the shore. "She's gone. There's nothing we can do," Elliott told him, rising from the floor, grasping a railing to steady himself. Cornelia and Louisa stayed beside Edna Thurston's body, wedging it against the wall as the boat rocked violently.

"We've got to get back while there's still light," Veeder said, peering through the glass in front of him. We all grabbed on to whatever we could, to keep from being thrown across the floor, and Clara and I managed to get Alden wedged into a corner away from the wheel. Looking up occasionally with the violent motion of the boat, I could see the sky was growing darker and darker.

Elliott put his head in the doorway and said, "It's no good. The dock's gone."

Gone? How could it be gone? I struggled up and followed

Cornelia, who stumbled across the floor and out the doorway. I was struck in the face by a blast of wind and rain and felt the deck beneath my feet rise, then drop away. I grabbed the door jamb. Clutching that and a fixture on the outside wall, I saw what Elliott and Luther had seen. Water was rushing all the way up to the Main. The dock, or what was left of it, was barely visible in the trough of a wave, then covered again. There was nothing to pull up to, no way to stop and get off. The only alternative was to swim, and even that was not a possibility. The waves would smash a body against the shore and crush it. I could see figures on the roof of the Main. Stephen was there, surely.

Suddenly there was a smack, then the boat stopped abruptly. The deck shivered, no longer moving up and down with the water. The men yelled, and Luther waved frantically. We were stuck on something. Water was cascading over the deck, into the wheelhouse, up to my knees. We were going to break apart, pounded into the shore. Then, just as all seemed lost, the boat rose on a swell and steered away from the shore towards the open water. I had to crane back towards the stern to see Stephen and the Main and safety disappearing in the falling darkness. This violent motion, rising and falling, wasn't going to end. It would never end.

We fought our way back into the wheelhouse where Veeder told us we would have to ride out the storm, and give up trying to return to shore, until it had passed. Redding was furious. Like me, he had no faith in our ability to stay afloat. Even if we crashed ashore, wouldn't there be a chance that we could reach the laboratory building? It was Elliott who explained that our only hope was to cling to the boat, and stay away from the shore where it could be washed up and broken apart.

Water streamed over the floor, where Louisa tried to keep Edna Thurston's body from rolling away. The men saw her predicament and stopped arguing. It was better for them to have something to do. It took them a while to find a tarp to roll her in and a line, and for Elliott and Redding to carry the body to the open part of the stern where they lashed the package to the wooden benches under the direction of Luther.

We hunkered down in the wheelhouse as night closed in. That left us with the truly horrible sensation of being tossed around in total darkness. I'd never been seasick before, but even the captain and his first mate suffered that night. We all heaved into buckets until sometime later, when the boat was swamped. Then Luther emptied the buckets and we were all impressed into bailing water. There was no past, no future, no tomorrow, only the impossible task of trying to stay ahead of the water, in darkness. The captain and first mate occasionally indulged in yelling matches as they attempted to steer the heavy boat away from the surf crashing on a beach that they could only hear, not see. More than once the little steam launch seemed to be set on its side, and I was sure it would flip in the wave and we would be thrown into the water with the boat landing on top of us. But each time it managed to right itself. Veeder clung to his wheel, peering blindly ahead, steering by feel and sound. Redding grumbled and grunted about how all that work to find the missing gold and silver was for naught if it just ended up at the bottom of the sea.

I have no idea how long the storm went on—it seemed interminable. Nor do I recall when it was that I succumbed to sleep. It seemed impossible that anyone could sleep while being tossed, and drenched, and in danger of final drowning. But we all did. I do remember waking and feeling wet and heavy. I lay looking at the wheelhouse from my place on the floor with my cheek pressed against the deck. Clara was wedged into a corner, curled around Alden, his head on her hip, his hands clutching her skirts. Mr. Elliott snored as he sat slumped against the wall, his arm around Louisa Reynolds, who leaned against his chest. Captain Veeder still clung to his wheel, barely standing, his face ashen and frozen, still counteracting the motion of the waves as if by rote. Luther was curled at his feet between the steering post and the doorway.

Sheriff Redding was beside me, all in a heap on the floor as if he had given up hope and surrendered to a childlike sleep of total exhaustion. As we jerked on a wave, I felt my stomach lurch, but I knew there was nothing to heave up. I felt terribly thirsty. Then I realized the real difference was the light—there was a gray light filtering in. I struggled to a sitting position, feeling terrible but able to see that dawn was coming. There were no longer several inches of water on the floor, but I felt stiff and sodden.

The others soon stirred. We'd made it through the night. The boat was still rocking through great waves, but they were more predictable and, as the light increased, Veeder headed us back to shore. We'd only stayed in the middle of the harbor, not gone out to sea as we'd feared. Soon we realized the important thing was that the tide was low. As we steamed back towards the laboratory buildings, we could see the water had pulled back and revealed the shore again.

Parts of the docks at the Fisheries building were damaged, but still visible and, after some discussion, we headed there. We could see figures on shore that followed us and were waiting with lines.

In some ways what came next was the most difficult part. We could see, and yell to, the people on shore, but Veeder struggled to keep us from being slammed into the dock. To come this far and still drown, or be crushed, would be so cruel. I could see Stephen on the dock—he was so near. Every bone in my body wanted to leap off the boat and into his arms. It was painful to restrain those instincts. So painful that I remember only the alternate feelings of fear and joy as Elliott and Redding barely made it onto the dock and then coached us women into jumping at the right moment. Finally it was my turn. I leapt with all the energy remaining in my body, was caught by numerous strong hands that pulled me and shoved me until suddenly I was in Stephen's arms and he was holding me so tightly I could barely breathe. I wept and let him carry me away.

I saw Alden and Clara being helped to land. I did not care

about the rest, but I heard Redding yell hoarsely, "Leave it, for crying out loud. Leave it." The precious treasure that he wanted so much to save was no longer important.

≈

A few days later I trudged across the still damp ground with Jane Topham at my side. She rattled on as we walked from the Snow Goose Inn to the Mess. All around us repairs were still being made. I had not seen Minnie Gibbs or her family since our adventure on the water. Jane said something about the train line being down because of the storm. But the upstairs of the inn was still inhabitable and we had tried to clean up the worst of the flood damage downstairs.

"I still can't get over it," Jane went on, as she huffed along. "That Miss Thurston did all that just to try to make Cornelia Clapp the head of the laboratory. She certainly was a fanatic." When I'd gone to summon Jane to a meeting called by Sheriff Redding in the Mess, she insisted on changing into a walking suit complete with bows and flounces and a matching hat. It was hardly necessary, considering the mud-caked appearance of the rest of us during the extended cleanup, but she was determined. I managed to refuse a cup of tea she tried to press on me and got her out and on the way to the proceedings. "So Sheriff Redding finally sees the light, is that it?"

"I think he wants to let everyone know what really happened." I shuddered as my memory summoned up the image of Edna Thurston convulsing in the wheelhouse. "He wants you to tell him about what Edna did that last day—when she got Clara and Louisa to go out to the neck. Here we are. They're all inside." We reached the Mess and I hurried up the steps. I had a very bad feeling about what Redding was doing.

Inside, Sheriff Redding stood at the front of the room talking to Clara and Louisa. The rest of the laboratory people were scattered around the room—Frank Lillie with Professor

Whitman, Sinclair Bickford at a different table. Only Cornelia
Clapp sat alone near the front of the room, looking perfectly calm
with her hands folded in front of her.

At the sight of us, Redding clapped his hands. "All right, here
they are. Quiet, everybody. We'll get this over with and you can
all go back to work. Now, Miss Topham, will you come up here
with Miss Shea and Miss Reynolds. They've been telling us about
the day of the storm and how you told them that Alfred Davis
had taken his grandson to the neck, and that the rest of the family
was missing. That's right isn't it?"

Jane let him usher her to a seat on a bench between Clara
and Louisa.

"It was Edna Thurston who came in and said she saw Alfred
Davis take his grandson to the neck. She got me to call down
Miss Shea and Miss Reynolds then, and she convinced them to
go with her."

Clara spoke up. "It seemed there was a chance he might harm
the boy. Miss Topham insisted he was in great danger. She was
repeating an old story about how Alfred Davis supported a man
who killed his own daughter. We were only to follow to try to see
where they went, until you, Sheriff, could catch up and take care
of matters. Miss Thurston was the one who knew the way to the
fishing shack, Louisa and I did not."

"I might have come, had I been told," he said. "I was on the
Sagitta retrieving my men and the treasure."

"She said she sent someone to get you," Jane contributed. "But
she must've wanted to do away with Miss Shea and Miss Reynolds.
That was her real plan. That's why she brought the poison, from
what I heard."

"Ah, yes, the poison. The flask. This flask." He took it from
his pocket and placed it on the table in front of Cornelia. "This
is the flask? You provided her with it, Miss Topham?"

"I provided them with some sandwiches and some brandy in
case of a medicinal need."

"I took it away from Edna," Clara interrupted. "She wanted to sip from it while we were trying to find the old man and his grandson, but I didn't want her getting tipsy. Then, when we saw we were trapped, she became hysterical. I was afraid she would lose control if I let her drink. It was only when we tied ourselves together with the rope to try to swim to the boat that she convinced me to give it back to her. It seemed too late to worry. There seemed no harm."

"But when she knew she was discovered, she added the poison and ended her life," Jane Topham added. "She asked me about poisons, you know. I never thought it would be for such a purpose, never." She shook her head. She seemed to like being the center of attention. "To think she did it all. And it was all just so Miss Clapp could win out over the men." Everyone looked at Cornelia, who did not flinch. "So sad, really. She did it all. She ruined the experiments and I suppose Mr. McElroy must have found out, so she poisoned him. All to promote her women's society. Tsk, tsk. Just to think."

There was a hush in the room. Redding's gruff voice tore through it. "Edna Thurston didn't ruin any experiments. Mr. Bickford did that. He's admitted it." This was not news to the laboratory people, who all looked away from Sinclair Bickford, but it was news to Jane.

"What? Really? I had no idea," she stuttered.

"And another thing. Why would Edna Thurston, or anyone else, believe Alfred Davis would harm his grandson? Why would they believe a story like that?"

"Because Mr. Gordon, the boy's father, was afraid of that very thing," I said, wanting to help clarify the situation. "He told Jane that—after his wife's funeral—he was afraid that Alfred Davis would harm Billy, isn't that so, Jane? He told you in the kitchen that day, remember?"

Jane pursed her lips and nodded her head.

"Well, that's very interesting. The day of the funeral, you say?

Mr. Gordon talked to Miss Topham to tell her he was afraid for his son? He feared his father-in-law? Do you want to explain that to us, Mr. Gordon?" He looked up towards the back of the room and we all turned around. There were Mr. Gordon, his son, Minnie Gibbs, and her father, Alfred Davis. Apparently the trains *were* running, after all. "Do you want to explain what you told Miss Topham that day?"

Gordon stepped forward, a frown on his face. "I told her we wanted her back rent. I told her to give us the rent owed to us or I would have the sheriff on her."

THIRTY-ONE

There was a murmur from the onlookers and Jane Topham stiffened. She turned back to face the front of the room as Gordon explained to us that she owed them her rent from the previous year. She'd been staying at the inn during the summer for the past six years but, in early June, Mrs. Davis realized that Jane had neglected to pay her bill for the previous year. So, while she was in Boston doing other business, she met with Jane to tell her in person to pay up or she would not be welcome again. Jane had no response to this revelation from Mr. Gordon.

"Dr. Chapman?" Redding called on Stephen to testify. "Tell us what you found out."

Stephen stood and cleared his throat. "After Mrs. Gordon died I had her remains tested. A pathologist at Harvard confirmed my suspicion that she was poisoned with arsenic." A collective gasp rose from the crowd. "With that I couldn't help but wonder about her mother's death. But it was not until after the death of Edna Thurston that the Davis family allowed the authorities to exhume Mrs. Davis. It was confirmed that she, too, died from arsenic poisoning. The same poison that they *also* determined killed Mr. McElroy." Another gasp.

"Thank you, Dr. Chapman. That is most interesting information," Sherriff Redding said, gesturing to Stephen that he could be seated.

I leapt to my feet, unable to restrain myself, and shook my finger at Jane. "You killed Mr. McElroy because he saw you with Mrs. Davis in Boston, didn't you? Mrs. Davis went to the city to force you to pay your back rent, and you gave her the poison. Did you tell her it was medicine? Did she believe you because you're such a well-known nurse?

"Mr. McElroy heard you telling Minnie Gibbs how you could have saved her mother if she'd only called on you. But he'd seen you with Mrs. Davis in Boston, so he knew that wasn't true. And he told Edna Thurston about it as well.

"But Edna didn't realize the significance of what she'd been told. I heard you talking about it with her in the kitchen, after the funeral. You insisted that you had never seen Mrs. Davis in Boston. You claimed, again, that you could have saved her if she'd called on you. But you were lying *again*. Was all of this really just because you didn't want to pay your rent?" I was incredulous.

"Oh, not just that, I think." It was Nellie Bly who stepped forward. Redding nodded. "At the request of Dr. Chapman, I went to Boston to do some more research. It seems that the state police were very interested to learn of Jane Topham's involvement in a poisoning. It seems they've had their eyes on her for a while. A number of her former patients in Boston and Cambridge died mysteriously. Finding out about the deaths in the Davis family led them to exhume other bodies. In the past week alone they've autopsied the bodies of six former patients of Nurse Jane Topham and found traces of arsenic." She looked satisfied with her scoop. "So what do you have to say about that, Miss Topham? Are you going to deny it? Do you want to try to blame those deaths on Miss Thurston as well?"

"Looks like it's not just arsenic." Alden pushed his way through a crowd at the door, carrying two bottles. "Take a look at these." He handed them to Stephen.

Stephen shook his head as he read the labels. "This one's Paris Green—it's an insecticide made of arsenic and copper. And here we have prussic acid, a form of cyanide. That's what was in the brandy. That's why Edna Thurston died so fast. The others died more slowly, from the arsenic. It made theirs seem like natural illnesses.

But she couldn't wait that long for Miss Thurston. Edna might have realized what she'd heard about in Boston, just as McElroy realized it. He must have confronted Miss Topham about having seen her with Mrs. Davis and that was enough for her to kill him."

"The bottles were in her closet at the inn," Alden told the room.

Sheriff Redding grunted. "So what do you have to say, woman? How do you explain this? Did you kill all those people? Why?"

Jane Topham sat hunched over on the bench. People near her had pulled away in alarm. She didn't look like a monster. She looked like a dumpy middle-aged woman in an overly frilly dress. But she rolled her eyes around the room while she held her head perfectly still and her little tongue flicked out to lick her lips. The room waited in silence.

"Well, I don't know," she said to the room at large. "You might have to consult an alienist." She pursed her lips and raised her eyebrows, waiting for a response to that.

She didn't have long to wait. "Alienist? *Alienist?*" Redding sputtered. "Consult an alienist? You will hang, woman, that's what you'll do, alienist or no alienist. I know what you're trying and you won't get away with it. It's that Freeman case all over. You've known the Davises since way back then. I know your tricks. I know what you're up to. You think if you convince these so-called doctors you're insane, you'll get away with it. You think, like that bloody Freeman, you can spend a few years in an asylum and then they'll let you out. You've got another think coming, lady." He was red in the face as he stopped and turned to her accusingly. "You're not denying you killed all those patients? You're not denying that? How many have you done in, anyhow? You want to prove you're insane. Tell us that, then." He was shouting at the end.

She closed her eyes as if in thought. "Let me see. You said six, is that right?" I saw her peeking at him from under her eyelashes, trying to measure the effect. "My memory is not very good, I forget things. But I think it's…thirty-one. Yes, thirty-one. I think." She opened her eyes and smiled at him.

Redding turned away. The expression on his face was the one I had seen on the boat just before he heaved into a bucket. She was defeating him. He was overcome by the horror of it.

At that point it was Clara who resumed the interrogation. The room sat shocked into silence, and Clara's voice was low and husky with the gentle lilting drawl of her Kentucky accent. She leaned forward on the bench and turned her head towards Jane. It occurred to me that Jane envied Clara. Clara was young, beautiful, rich. She was attractive to men and her clothes were of a style far beyond the taste or means of the middle-aged nurse.

"But why did you do it?" Clara asked softly. "Was it really because of the rent?"

Jane sat back and wriggled in her chair. "They didn't know who they were dealing with." Her eyes glittered. "Mary Davis met me at a tea shop...we were having tea, like ladies. But she had to bring up the rent from last year. It was so rude. Her daughter Genevieve was sitting there like a dressmaker's dummy. They wouldn't even drink their tea and eat their cakes, even when I told them to. And that McElroy man saw us there. He stopped to greet us. They were rude to him too. But I said, 'Oh, what a mistake. You are right. I have it, of course, at my flat.'

"When they heard that they relaxed, and they drank their tea then, those two. They liked their sweetening. They put teaspoon after teaspoon into their cups, not knowing I'd added a little something to the sugar bowl." She chuckled. "They even ordered another pot of tea. So greedy of them, since I was paying the bill. But that stopped them from coming back the next day for the rent. By then Mary was gone. It just took a bit longer for the daughter. She never suspected, not a bit. All they ever worried about was the rent money." She smiled with contentment. There was a rustle in the room, but people kept quiet, seeming to hold their breath in order to hear the rest.

"You also set the fires, didn't you? Now, why did you do that? Did you like to see the flames? Did you like to see all of Miss

Reynolds's pretty lacy things consumed by them? You weren't trying to hurt her, were you? You just wanted to see the flames. Am I right about that?"

Jane was still staring at Redding, trying to provoke him. Her eyes flicked sideways to glimpse Clara, and she licked her lips again. She took a moment to consider her answer, perhaps judging how it might add to her plea of insanity. She must have decided it would contribute. She released the sheriff from her stare and turned to Clara with a wide smile. "It's just a feeling it gives me. It's so, so thrilling. You can't understand." She giggled. "Well, maybe you can. You did things with Mr. Bickford. We all know that. Well, I did things with the flames. That thrill you got, I like to feel it, too." There was a widespread gasp in the room at this pronouncement. She was repulsive.

"And poisoning those people, that gave you satisfaction, did it?" Clara enquired mildly. "There you were, *making* them sick, and they depended on you to nurse them back to health. How did that make you feel? Was that thrilling?"

Jane laughed. "You have no idea." She gave a little shiver of pleasure at the memory. "Once you've felt it, there's nothing like it. That Edna, she thought she got a thrill by making difficulties for these men taking over that laboratory she was so worried about, and Cornelia there thinks she can get a thrill from acting like one of the men and doing what they do. They don't know a real thrill, though. Not like you and me. You got yourself into all kinds of trouble getting a thrill with a man, one man. I had thirty-one, and I can relive those thrills, I can still remember them, I can see them in my mind."

"Enough!" Sherriff Redding exploded. "That's enough. You're under arrest. You want a thrill? I'll give you a thrill. It'll be a thrill for me when I see you hang from a rope until you die."

THIRTY-TWO

S he probably won't hang, though," Stephen said, as we sat on a hill having a picnic a week later. We were in Falmouth Heights, looking at land on which Mr. Elliott planned to build a house. It was a sparkling day and children flew kites from the bottom of the hill in a pleasant breeze. Stephen, Clara, Alden, Louisa, and I sat on blankets and watched Mr. Elliott pace out where he wanted the rooms to be.

"She's already got an alienist lined up," Alden told us. He was reclining with his head in Clara's lap. They'd been inseparable since the storm and did not try to hide their attachment from anyone. Proven innocent of all charges and free to leave now, Clara had no intention of re-joining her grandmother in Newport. She planned to return to Chicago with Alden where they would marry. Unlike me, she would not keep her marriage a secret. She planned to continue her studies, but she would have to fight the restrictions against married women to do so. She didn't care. And Alden had given up resisting the attachment due to his lack of fortune. It no longer mattered to them.

"With so many dead, how will she not hang?" I asked.

"That's just it," Alden told me. "To kill that many people she *must* be insane. Nellie plans to stay and cover the trial."

"What she's wrong about is thinking they'll let her out of the asylum, though," Clara said. "They won't. And Nellie knows what it's really like in those places. She'll be alive, but she won't be able to kill, and she'll just barely survive."

Louisa Reynolds was paying no attention to us. All her

attention was on Mr. Elliott. I was glad she no longer felt compelled to support Sinclair Bickford.

"Did you hear? Cornelia's coming to Chicago," I told them. Professor Whitman had offered her a fellowship to do a doctorate after all.

"We'll all be back in Chicago soon," Stephen said, rubbing his hand along my arm.

"And perhaps I'll never convince you to come back here again after all this," I told him, looking into his brown eyes. But they crinkled at the edge with laughter.

"I do recall you telling me how peaceful it would be at the seashore. I can't say I agree with your idea of peace and quiet."

So much had happened—the death and tragedy at Pullman, and then the events here at Woods Hole. In the city we were at the mercy of the actions of men, greedy competitive men, who fought with each other tooth and nail. But here we were at the mercy of Nature in a way I'd never experienced before. That night on the *Sagitta* I believed I would never get back to Stephen's arms, I believed I would die and there was nothing I could do but try to endure.

Much like a terrible storm, the insanity of Jane Topham had swept through the community of scientists and local people, devastating them all. There could be no reason behind her actions. There was nothing to do except stop her.

Yet, the scientists at the laboratory were not content to simply endure the vicissitudes of Nature, they wanted to understand it. Perhaps someday they could control it, or at least predict and influence it. The world they (and my husband Stephen with them) explored was a dangerous world, yet I felt they were on the threshold of great discoveries and changes in the coming century. And one thing they had managed to do after all the events of the summer was to keep the laboratory as a separate, independent entity controlled and administered by the researchers. How long that would last in a world rocked by economic and natural disasters,

I could not see, but the people involved were determined. They planned to return the following summer, and the summers after that, to pursue their investigations and argue their findings until they could answer the questions that were so important to them. I had a feeling those questions were actually of great import to those of us not directly involved, but I had no idea exactly how.

I squeezed Stephen's arm and grinned at him. There was something I suspected, although I still hadn't said anything to him. If my suspicions were correct, by this time the next year Stephen and I would have welcomed a son or daughter into the world. A child who we would protect and nurture, who would no doubt bring us all sorts of joys and sorrows, and who would grow up to cherish the scientific discoveries these brave men and women were only now uncovering.

AFTERWORD

Even today, when I mention to people that I have written a novel set at the Woods Hole Marine Biological Laboratory (MBL), it seems that almost everyone knows someone, or of someone, who spent time there. With the addition of an Oceanographic Institute, and other research institutions, it has remained an important place for American scientists to research and to share ideas with each other. Since scientific advances were so critical at the end of the nineteenth century, it seemed natural that my University of Chicago characters would be drawn to such a research center.

The Marine Biological Laboratory at Woods Hole was closely connected to the University of Chicago through its early directors, Charles Otis Whitman and Frank Lillie, who feature in this novel. Lillie's history of the MBL, *The Woods Hole Marine Biological Laboratory* (1944), was a useful source. Also helpful were Jane Maienschein's two books, *100 Years Exploring Life, 1888-1988* (1989) and *Defining Biology: Lectures from the 1890s* (1986).

The controversy about governance that is part of my plot is fictional, as are the characters of the murdered man, McElroy, and Edna Thurston. However, somewhat later in the 1890s the MBL did reach a moment when funding was at issue. Several universities, including the University of Chicago, made proposals to take over sponsorship of the laboratories, but the researchers voted to keep it a separate, independent institution. It remains a private, non-profit corporation to this day.

Sinclair Bickford, E. C. Elliott, and Sheriff Redding are entirely fictional, but Captain Veeder was a real person, as was Cornelia

Clapp. As a matter of fact, Mount Holyoke College named one of the main buildings on its campus after her as an honored graduate. As a fellow alumna I was extremely interested to learn that she was a founding member of the MBL, and that she came to the University of Chicago to pursue a second PhD around the time this novel takes place. I thought that she was an excellent woman for Emily to meet, representing, as she did, women trying to develop academic careers in the 1890s. In addition to reading some of Miss Clapp's research on the toadfish, the volume *Women Scientists in America* by Margaret W. Rossiter (1984) was helpful.

For the true stories of Jane Topham and Charles Freeman, who murdered his little daughter, I am indebted to *Cape Cod Confidential* by Evan J. Albright (2004). I loosely based the Davis family on people mentioned by Albright, but they—and the Snow Goose Inn—are my inventions, although the inn's name was inspired by a charming little store in Sandwich on Cape Cod. I chose to present a fictionalized version of Jane Topham, and her Woods Hole victims are my inventions. I also have Albright to thank for the story of the *Sterling* and the treasure plundered from the *Missouri*.

For the anecdotes about the Vanderbilts, Marble House, and Newport I relied on the memoir of Consuelo Vanderbilt Balsan, *The Glitter and the Gold* (1953). She was married off to a European aristocrat and had the sort of unhappy marriage Clara's grandmother was threatening. Mrs. Shea is a fictional character who also appears in my earlier Emily Cabot novel, *Death at the Fair*, but Alva Vanderbilt was a real and very colorful character.

Visit the MBL website (http://hermes.mbl.edu/about/visit/visit_tours.html) for information on touring their facilities during the summer months. On my website (http://fmcnamara.wordpress.com/) you can see pictures from my tour there in the summer of 2011, along with pictures of Marble House in Newport, another place I highly recommend. As always, the resources of the University of Chicago Library have been extremely helpful to me in preparing this story. Any historical or scientific errors are all mine.

READ THE OTHER EMILY CABOT MYSTERIES

Death at the Fair

The 1893 World's Columbian Exposition provides a vibrant backdrop for the first book in the series. Emily Cabot, one of the first women graduate students at the University of Chicago, is eager to prove herself in the emerging field of sociology. While she is busy exploring the Exposition with her family and friends, her colleague, Dr. Stephen Chapman, is accused of murder. Emily sets out to search for the truth behind the crime, but is thwarted by the gamblers, thieves, and corrupt politicians who are ever-present in Chicago. A lynching that occurred in the dead man's past leads Emily to seek the assistance of the black activist Ida B. Wells.

ⓒ

Death at Hull House

After Emily Cabot is expelled from the University of Chicago, she finds work at Hull House, the famous settlement established by Jane Addams. There she quickly becomes involved in the political and social problems of the immigrant community. But when a man who works for a sweatshop owner is murdered in the Hull House parlor, Emily must determine whether one of her colleagues is responsible, or whether the real reason for the murder is revenge for a past tragedy in her own family. As a smallpox epidemic spreads through the impoverished west side of Chicago, the very existence of the settlement is threatened and Emily finds herself in jeopardy from both the deadly disease and a killer.

ⓒ

Death at Pullman

A model town at war with itself ... George Pullman created an ideal community for his railroad car workers, complete with every amenity they could want or need. But when hard economic times hit in 1894, lay-offs follow and the workers can no longer pay their rent or buy food at the company store. Starving and desperate, they turn against their once benevolent employer. Emily Cabot and her friend Dr. Stephen Chapman bring much needed food and medical supplies to the town, hoping they can meet the immediate needs of the workers and keep them from resorting to violence. But when one young worker—suspected of being a spy—is murdered, and a bomb plot comes to light, Emily must race to discover the truth behind a tangled web of family and company alliances.

ALSO PUBLISHED BY ALLIUM PRESS OF CHICAGO

Beautiful Dreamer
Joan Naper

Chicago in 1900 is bursting with opportunity, and Kitty Coakley is determined to make the most of it. The youngest of seven children born to Irish immigrants, she has little interest in becoming simply a housewife. Inspired by her entrepreneurial Aunt Mabel, who runs a millinery boutique at Marshall Field's, Kitty aspires to become an independent, modern woman. After her music teacher dashes her hopes of becoming a professional singer, she refuses to give up her dreams of a career. But when she is courted by not one, but two young men, her resolve is tested. Irish-Catholic Brian is familiar and has the approval of her traditional, working-class family. But wealthy, Protestant Henry, who is a young architect in Daniel Burnham's office, provides an entrée for Kitty into another, more exciting world. Will she sacrifice her ambitions and choose a life with one of these men?

‫ଔ‬

Set the Night on Fire
Libby Fischer Hellmann

Someone is trying to kill Lila Hilliard. During the Christmas holidays she returns from running errands to find her family home in flames, her father and brother trapped inside. Later, she is attacked by a mysterious man on a motorcycle. . . and the threats don't end there. As Lila desperately tries to piece together who is after her and why, she uncovers information about her father's past in Chicago during the volatile days of the late 1960s . . . information he never shared with her, but now threatens to destroy her. Part thriller, part historical novel, and part love story, *Set the Night on Fire* paints an unforgettable portrait of Chicago during a turbulent time: the riots at the Democratic Convention . . . the struggle for power between the Black Panthers and SDS . . . and a group of young idealists who tried to change the world.

A Bitter Veil
Libby Fischer Hellmann

It all began with a line of Persian poetry . . . Anna and Nouri, both studying in Chicago, fall in love despite their very different backgrounds. Anna, who has never been close to her parents, is more than happy to return with Nouri to his native Iran, to be embraced by his wealthy family. Beginning their married life together in 1978, their world is abruptly turned upside down by the overthrow of the Shah, and the rise of the Islamic Republic. Under the Ayatollah Khomeini and the Republican Guard, life becomes increasingly restricted and Anna must learn to exist in a transformed world, where none of the familiar Western rules apply. Random arrests and torture become the norm, women are required to wear hijab, and Anna discovers that she is no longer free to leave the country. As events reach a fevered pitch, Anna realizes that nothing is as she thought, and no one can be trusted...not even her husband.

ભ

Visit our website for more information:

www.alliumpress.com